BECAUSE
I'M
YOURS

A ROMANTIC SUSPENSE NOVEL

CLAIRE

NEW YORK TIMES BESTSELLING AUTHOR

CONTRERAS

ISBN: 978-0-9995844-9-1

Edited by: Gina Licciardi
Formatted by: Champagne Book Design
Cover Design: Hang Le

NOTE FROM THE AUTHOR:

Dear reader,

Thank you so much for picking up my book. It really means the world to me. While this book isn't as dark as the rest in the serious, there are some scenes with graphic content and gun violence. There is no rape or cheating.

Xo,
Claire
I hope you enjoy it as much as I did <3

To the good girls, and to the "good girls" ;)

BECAUSE
I'M
YOURS

A ROMANTIC SUSPENSE NOVEL

PROLOGUE

I DON'T KNOW WHY I THOUGHT SEEING HER IN A WEDDING DRESS would be easy. But as the bridal song began to play and everyone stood in unison, waiting for her to walk down the aisle, the knife in my chest twisted a little deeper. Somehow, I kept my eyes on the groom—a wealthy nobleman. I didn't care about his useless pretentious title or what his bank account looked like. I'd made it my business to find out everything about Adriano Salvati. He lived in his father's shadow. He didn't like getting his hands dirty, but they were filthy nonetheless. He threw orgies in Milan and New York when he was in town. He liked to dominate sex workers to make them bend to his will. The fact that he hurt people who were just trying to make a living pissed me the fuck off. Of course, none of them dared speak against him. Not publicly, anyway. His serious girlfriend, who would soon become his side piece, had penthouses that he paid for. He didn't physically hurt *her*, as far as I knew. She was seeing Adriano's cousin behind his back, though she seemed genuinely in love with the guy. *The devil works hard, but karma works harder.* Right now, both were working against me, and no doubt, making me pay for every fucking wrong I'd committed. I would get down on my knees this instant, if it meant she didn't have to go through with this.

The heavy wooden doors opened, and the mics the guys were wearing picked up a few gasps. I glanced at my watch and checked the time. Two minutes. We had a two-minute window to get this done. I looked for the others one last time—Petra standing outside on the roof and Michael wandering down the block, waiting for his cue to get any innocent bystanders out; Gil and Lorenzo pacing their marks in the pews; Rosalyn and Emma observing from the altar. . . across from two Salvati men. Dominic was sitting in the first pew. When I looked at the aisle again, my heart stopped beating.

She looked virginal, but I knew better; I had already defiled every hole in her body. I would have laughed if I could find it in me to be amused. Even if I were, the amusement would've died when I saw her face. Her dark eyes, bloodshot and pained, seared into me, despite their inability to meet mine. She wouldn't know where to look even if she wanted to. Her father looked around, though. Of course, he did; his paranoia had been heightened. I turned to her groom again, who was waiting for her with a stoic look, though his eyes gleamed with excitement. I couldn't be sure whether it was the idea of finally having her or whether it was the large chunk of De Luca empire he'd be inheriting.

She made it to the third pew and stopped walking. For a brief moment, she let go of her father and fixed the bottom of her gown, and her heel stuck at the edge. Her father gave her an impatient look and turned to smile at the audience. I could practically feel my mother's ghost judging me for what I was about to do. I closed my eyes for a split second, habitually asking God for forgiveness in silent prayer. I was one of those people. The ones who avoided church and talking about God but were willing to get on my knees when my life was falling apart. He was always my last resort. I tapped the side of my weapon once, twice—another habit. I took a breath, then another, and held it as I pulled the trigger.

CHAPTER ONE

Lenora

'D ALWAYS KNOWN I'D BE A YOUNG AND INEXPERIENCED BRIDE. IT WAS what I was bred for, like a prized horse whose only job is to win races. It was why I felt such kinship with my Clydesdale. With animals, in general, but Aanya was special. She had been through everything with me—fights with my parents, tears over fake friends, and boys who wouldn't give me the time of day because of who my father was. Saying goodbye to her was killing me.

"I'll never forget you." I grabbed the sides of her face and pressed my forehead against hers.

I didn't bother holding back tears. I didn't bother explaining that I wasn't sure when I'd see her again. She knew. Aanya always knew. She nudged my face with her muzzle and snapped me out of my sadness. I kissed her one last time, pulled away to dry my tears, and took a breath before walking away.

Walking away had never been difficult for me. I'd attended boarding schools and summer camps all over the world. My entire life consisted of walking away from people, but this was different. I couldn't just pick up the phone and FaceTime Aanya whenever I missed seeing her face the way I did with my friends. Not that I did that often. I had two friends, both a few years older than me. One was married and pregnant, and the other was making a name for herself in tech. Neither had much time to talk to me these days. To be fair, they thought I was busy as well. After all, I had a wedding to plan—an arranged marriage to a duke, no less. Adriano Salvati was my perfect match, according to my father, who didn't know a thing about me.

To think, I was once considered a daddy's girl. These days, I didn't speak to him at all. He saw it as a sign of rebellion. I saw it as an act of defiance. There was a slight difference.

Nevertheless, I ran out of time and had to devise a plan today. I'd met Adriano several times over the years, and even though he'd been nice, I felt no attraction to him. I said as much to my mother, but of course, she told me I was being ridiculous. "Attraction has very little to do with this arrangement, Lenora," she'd said. Of course, it was easy for her to say such things. Her marriage to my father wasn't arranged, per se, but it might as well have been. She caught my father's attention during a visit to the Dominican Republic, and my grandfather, being the businessman he was, insisted that it was a great match. After all, not many men had enough money to marry her, an heiress to a billion-dollar empire.

Even though we were extremely well off, Dad was nowhere near a billionaire. Knowing my mother would be one someday was the icing for him. So, yeah, I should be used to the idea that I would one day be sold off like cattle in the 1800s, but I wasn't. I've read too much, watched too many programs, and dreamt of a life free of all this. I took off my boots and walked into my parents' Connecticut home. Instead of going to the kitchen or to my room to pack for my trip to New York, I quietly walked toward my father's office. I needed something, anything, that I could use to delay this. The fact that I was resorting to blackmail proved that I was a De Luca. My last name had never bothered me. Most of the boys stayed away from me in school because of the stories they'd heard about my older brother, Dominic. They stayed away from me in Italy because of what they'd heard about my father. It annoyed me, but I knew nothing I could do about it, so I adjusted. I always focused on boys who didn't go to school with me. Once in college, where no one knew who I was, I was free to see whomever I wanted, even if it was in secret.

After an exhaustive search of the office, I seated myself in the chair behind the desk with a defeated sigh. I needed something more useful for me here. I scanned the room, and my eyes came to rest on the monitor. I clicked on the keyboard to power it up, but I couldn't access it without a password. I tried several times to no avail. As I let out an exasperated groan, I sunk further into the chair, giving into its embrace. I looked up and found myself staring directly at the security camera in the corner of the room.

I wanted him to know I'd been here without confronting him. I didn't have the courage for that. I lowered myself to the floor and scoured his desk for something that could give me an advantage. After a few minutes of searching, a small black box caught my eye. When I opened it, a tiny gold key fell out. Relief washed over me as I picked up the key, tried it in the lock, and finally pulled the drawer open.

I don't know what I expected to find inside, but there was a black notebook and a USB drive. I pulled out the notebook and skimmed through it. It was a ledger, like Dad's accountant Andrea always carried. On every page, names and dollar amounts were written on each line. The top of each page was dated. I went back to the beginning of the book. The logs started in 1980. The last page was dated just one month ago. Was this money he'd loaned people? What was on the USB drive? I picked it up and shut the drawer, locking it and setting the key back where I'd found it. I wasn't sure what I was looking at, and I knew I couldn't show it to my brothers. They weren't supportive of my impending nuptials, but they wouldn't do anything to go against my father. I'd figure it out alone like I always did.

CHAPTER TWO

Lenora

I HAD TO PLAY IT COOL. CALM, COOL, AND COLLECTED. THAT WAS ME. *Totally*. Champagne flute in hand and a smile plastered on my face, I walked around the ballroom my father had reserved for the night. I listened while people spoke to me, thanked them as they congratulated me on my engagement, and even made small talk with Adriano, who didn't seem perturbed by any of this. He stood next to me, speaking to anyone who spoke Italian while I half-listened and laughed at the appropriate times (when Adriano did). The only person I spoke the language to, these days, was my father. I sometimes spoke Spanish with my mother and English with everyone else. Immersing myself in these Italian-only conversations with Adriano was a good reminder that even though he spoke five languages, Italian would be the one we spoke at home. I wasn't sure how I felt about that.

On the one hand, I loved the language. On the other, it reminded me of my father, and being in a forced marriage with that reminder wasn't easy to withstand. A heavy arm draped over my shoulder, jolting me back to the present. I glanced up to see my brother Dominic smiling down at me and turned to give him a full hug. I'd always loved how my older brother's hugs felt like they engulfed and shielded me from everything around us. My other brother, his twin, gave great hugs too, but where Dom was all muscle, Gabe was lean.

"I'm surprised Dad let you wear that dress," Dom said as he pulled away.

"I thought the same," Adriano said behind me.

"What's wrong with my dress?" I looked down at my dress as if I didn't know what I was wearing.

It was a sheer sequin mock neck gown with a high neckline. It also had a high slit and was designed to look like I was naked underneath, even though it had a bodysuit. Adriano looked plain in a dark suit and tie. Honestly, I was making him look good, playing the part of the perfect trophy wife-to-be, so I didn't know why he would complain about my dress.

"You look naked," Adriano replied, making a face like I was beneath him.

"It's Oscar de la Renta." I smiled my perfectly fake smile at him.

Adriano shook his head. "Nice to see you, Dominic."

Dom nodded in greeting and did the same to the men in front of us. They nodded back, their eyes widening in fear. Whether fear or respect, I wasn't sure there was a difference between the two. For a long time, I didn't understand why the men in my family elicited such a response. Even Gabriel, who had nothing to do with the organized crime life, was feared by everyone. My best guess was that they knew that if they messed with him, Dominic would be the one to come knocking. As far as I was concerned, Dominic, Giovanni, and Lorenzo were big teddy bears. To everyone else, they were monsters. The only two I didn't know well enough were Dean and Rocco. Dean rarely traveled to Italy to meet with Dad. And Rocco? Well, I wasn't sure why he didn't come around. He used to when I was little. Back then, I had the biggest crush on him. How could I not? With his sharp jaw and piercing blue eyes, he looked like one of the G.I. Joe action figures my boy cousins used to own. The last time I saw Dean was a few years ago. The last time I saw Rocco was around my thirteenth birthday.

"I'm going to borrow her for a moment," Dom said to Adriano, who waved his acceptance and smiled as I walked away.

"Oh my God, thank you," I said as we left them behind. "I

was dying. I would have cried if I had to hear them discuss his dukedom and family history any longer."

"That's what they were talking about?" Dom chuckled, shaking his head. "I guess you better get used to it."

"Don't remind me," I muttered.

"I'm sorry, Norie." He set his hand over my shoulder and pulled me to his side as we walked. "I've spoken to Pop countless times, but he doesn't budge. Maybe he's right, though. You'd be a duchess, and that's much better than being a mafia wife."

"Is it, though?" I twisted my neck to meet his gaze and raise an eyebrow. "And he's old, Dom."

"He's not that old."

"He's thirty-five. I'm twenty-two. That's disgusting."

"Nora." Dom sighed, stopped walking a few steps away from Rosie, and made me face him. "We all have to do things we don't like."

"He's ugly, Dom." I shut my eyes, hating how I sounded like I was whining, but every time I thought about Adriano touching me, my stomach revolted.

He sighed heavily and gave me a sad look before we continued our walk to the cocktail tables, where Lorenzo, Catalina, Gio, and Isabel spoke to Rosie and Dean. Again, no Rocco Marchetti in sight.

"Nora!" Rosie smiled wide as she hugged me and kissed my cheek.

"You look beautiful," I said as we pulled away and did the same with the rest of them.

Rosie always looked beautiful. They all did. From what I could tell, despite their rocky beginnings, the three seem perfectly content being mafia wives. From my vantage point, it seemed much better than whatever awaited me with the Duke. Even Catalina seemed perfectly content as Lorenzo's wife, and she'd been completely against marrying into this life. She'd been raised in boarding schools like me. The difference was that Uncle Joe wasn't like my father. Cat and her sister Emma had always been free to choose their spouses. Dad said it was because Uncle Joe was more American than Italian. My father disapproved of this, yet he sent me to boarding school in the U.S., and in turn, I now felt like I related more to their rules than those of the old country. Unfortunately, I couldn't abide them.

"Have you gotten to know Adriano?" Isabel asked.

"I can't believe he's a duke," Rosie added with a raised eyebrow. "That sounds like the beginning of a fairytale."

"Fairytale," Dom said, grumbling as he put his arm around his wife and squeezed her into his side, biting her ear. "I'll give you a fairytale."

"Dominic." Rosie slapped his chest and pulled away with a laugh. "We're having a conversation."

"Well, I don't like it."

"I don't like it either," I said. "I don't want to marry a duke, prince, or anyone. It's not my choice."

"Arranged marriages aren't all bad," Isabel said, and Gio grinned.

"First off, Giovanni is hot, respectfully," I said, making them laugh. "Secondly, you two got very lucky."

"You're right. We did," Isabel agreed and gave me a small smile. "I'm sorry, Nora."

I shrugged. I didn't know how to respond to the apologies everyone was offering.

"To be fair, Nora," Cat said. "A guy hit on you the last time we went out, and you ignored him."

"He was hot," Isabel added.

"Who are you talking about?" Gio said. "Where was this?"

Isabel rolled her eyes. "We are allowed to look at other men, you know."

"And we're allowed to wipe them the fuck out," Dominic responded.

Everyone laughed, including me, though I'm not sure they

were joking. One could never be too sure with this bunch. Even their jealousy and possessiveness were something I longed for. Yes, they could be annoying and over the top, but at least they knew they were loved. Besides, it was a healthy possessiveness. It wasn't like they were locking up their wives at home. I looked over at Dean, who had been on his phone the entire time. He leaned in and said hello with a kiss on the cheek and a smile. Dean was also hot, and even though he was over thirty, I would gladly accept an arranged marriage to him. That thought made me hold back a laugh. I was such a hypocrite.

"What about you, Dean?" I asked. "No arranged marriage?"

"No marriage at all." His hazel eyes danced as he took a sip of his drink.

"Are you going to tell me you're not the marriage type?" I asked.

"I wouldn't say that. Unlike some people," he said, looking at the three men in front of us, "I have nothing against relationships or marriage. I haven't met anyone I didn't get sick of after 24 hours."

"You haven't met anyone you didn't get sick of after *two* hours," Loren laughed.

"I can't wait for you and Rocco to find a woman who will finally bring you to your knees," Rosie said. "Especially Roc, since he's sure it won't happen for him."

Dean opened his mouth to respond but was interrupted by a deep voice behind me.

"Highly unlikely," he said, making my skin prickle from head to toe.

I had never moved as slowly as I did at that moment when I turned around. My heart was pounding hard, knowing it was the man I had pined for my entire life. Everyone else was caught up in Rocco's words, but I couldn't dredge up anything to say. My words and logic had flown from my mind when our eyes met. I saw his expression change too. His eyes were also bluer than I remembered, darker like deep ocean waters. To say he was gorgeous was an understatement—he was breathtaking. I heard my brother say something behind me, and it snapped me out of my daze. Rocco seemed to, as well, his smile turning up again.

"The Principessa, as I live and breathe." He opened his arms and pulled me into a hug that felt electric.

I forced myself not to react to it by closing my eyes, but then his scent was all I could smell, and that, too, made me feel like I was losing my mind. To top it off, being in his arms like this felt right. His body was a wall of muscle, and I instantly wanted to be enclosed in its fortress and never leave. He dropped his arms but didn't pull away completely. I looked at his chest, afraid that he could read my thoughts. When we took a step away from each other, and I met his eyes again, my pulse was throbbing everywhere. He seemed to know it, too, as his expression shifted momentarily. I'd always been fascinated by how the people in my life, men and women alike, could mask their genuine emotions so well. I'd only mastered it in certain situations, like in front of teachers.

"That doesn't bother me anymore," I said. It used to drive me crazy when he called me Principessa.

"Ah, that's too bad. I'll have to think of another nickname for you then." His eyes danced when I pursed my lips.

"Just call me Nora," I said. "That's what my friends call me."

His eyes narrowed slightly. "Eh, I'll think about it."

"Where are you coming from, Roc?" Isabel looked at his cracked red knuckles.

"He's always on his vigilante shit." Loren smiled. "I'm surprised Dom wasn't out there with him."

"I wish I could've gone," Dominic said.

"I told you to take care of whatever you needed to take care of," Rosie said, looking up at her husband through narrowed eyes.

"And leave you wearing tights alone in a room full of men?" He raised an eyebrow. "I think not."

"They're dancers, Dominic. Jesus Christ." She sighed heavily.

"Every time you guys say vigilante shit, I just pretend you're Swifties," Rosie said, smiling. Cat and I laughed.

"A what?" Rocco's brows pulled together.

"Taylor Swift stans," I said. He nodded slowly like he was thinking about it, which made it even more amusing. After a moment, I winked and added, "Don't worry. We'll recruit you soon enough."

"I'm willing to be recruited." His eyes pierced mine when he said it. The way he said it made me feel he was talking about something else entirely.

He stared at me, making my heart skip more than a few beats. I could swear I saw a fire burning in those eyes. His gaze left mine and fell to my throat, chest, and back to my eyes before he finally tore his attention away completely. I took a breath and looked around the room, playing it off. I'd never looked at a man for that long. I'd never had a staredown in my life. If I could, I would have excused myself and left the room to throw water on my face. I needed to push this feeling away before it consumed me. There was nothing to do about it anyway. I was getting married, and I was still Dominic's little sister. Giuseppe's prized daughter. Just another woman who had to bear what it meant to be in La Cosa Nostra.

"We were talking about marriage," Cat said after eating her hors d'oeuvre.

"And how you're next in line," Rosie added, smiling at Rocco.

Something twisted in my stomach at the thought of him getting married. I pushed it aside.

"Highly doubtful," Rocco said, taking the drink the bartender brought him. "Maybe Russo will go next."

"Fuck off," Dean said, barely paying attention, his eyes on his phone.

"No more Crystal then?" Lorenzo asked. My ears perked up.

"Fuck that," Rocco said under his breath.

"Crystal is old news," Dom said, amused. "She finally stopped stalking him."

My eyes widened. *A stalker?* My brothers were big exaggerators, so maybe he was joking. I wanted to be part of the conversation with a thousand and one questions, but I bit my tongue. As it was, I felt like an intruder. Like the pesky little sister, I'd once been, following my older brothers around until they gave in to my pleas for tea and slumber parties. It was stupid since I was a grownup and knew they wanted me to feel welcome here, but it didn't feel right to jump into a conversation like this. I held my words back, waiting for someone else to ask more questions about this Crystal person. Someone asked, but I missed it while I was lost in thought.

"She's fucking one of Gabe's friends," Rocco said. "Good luck to him with that psychopath."

"A Wall Street guy?" Gio asked, raising an eyebrow. "That's a far cry from you."

"Is it, though?" Dean asked, pocketing his phone. "Wealthy, shady, cut-throat?"

Everyone laughed.

"The difference is that I don't need party favors to have fun." Rocco winked.

They all laughed again, and even though I laughed along, I couldn't keep my heart from skipping at the sight of a wink that wasn't even directed at me. Dear God, I needed help. I also couldn't stop looking at his eyes and lips or fantasizing about how they would feel against mine. I tried not to. I did. I looked around, drank some more champagne, and kept listening to the rest of the conversation. The way they communicated was fascinating. Some of their jokes were borderline offensive, and of course, those were the ones that made them laugh the hardest. I looked at the married couples and noticed how their husbands were always touching their wives—brushing hair out of their faces, dropping kisses onto their heads, and holding them by the waist. I would kill to have something like that.

My parents had always embodied the same rules as the British Royal Family, showing little affection in public. My attention turned back to Rocco, who was watching me intently. My heart skipped again. I wanted to drown in those blue eyes. His lips turned slightly. I was sure no one else noticed, but my entire body heated with that tiny smirk because it told me he somehow knew what I was thinking. Two months ago, that would have embarrassed me. I'd never been forward or obvious about checking out a man, but I was to be married in less than a month, and that alone was enough to throw myself at the first man who would take me. I decided that I wanted that man to be Rocco. He wasn't just some random man, though. Rocco Marchetti was *the* man. I knew it was dangerous and probably impossible, but I wanted him to be my first. I just needed to figure out how to make that happen.

CHAPTER THREE

Lenora

"T HERE WILL BE ANOTHER ONE OF THESE TOMORROW," MY FATHER said, tapping the tip of my nose.

I hated these parties, though *party* wasn't the word I'd use to describe this, since there was no dance music and the lights weren't dim enough even if there were. I never liked parties in the past, but they were far worse when centered around me. I'd never minded having people look at me. Watching my mother taught me to hold my head high in every room. I did it at boarding school, where everyone thought they were better than the next. They hadn't yet figured out that none of it mattered in the end. Then again, my father hadn't figured it out either, and he was much older and more experienced than the kids at boarding school. He'd been born a king and would die a king. No one ever questioned my father. Not his motives, not his actions, not his words.

"Why so many parties?" I asked. "It seems like overkill."

"Well." Dad moved his head from side to side, as he did when he was about to explain something he knew I wouldn't like. "It's like a kid's first birthday party. Is it for the kid or just an excuse for adults to get together?"

"So this is just an excuse for you to get every single person on the FBI's Most Wanted in one room?" I asked.

"Careful." He shot me a look. His eyes looked so much like my brothers' when he did that. It was the look most people feared, but I never cowered under that stare. It was a privilege very few had. "We're businessmen."

"Right." I snorted.

He smiled a little. "Your mother couldn't be here for this one, so we'll have another. You don't want your mother to miss out on all of this, do you?"

I sighed heavily. I had a million comebacks for that, but I didn't want to use them. Mom was visiting my ailing grandmother, and I was sure this was the last place she wanted to be. She didn't agree with this wedding either. The only ones who were okay with it were Papa and Adriano. They'd be the sole parties reaping the benefits from the shady business deal they had going.

"Maybe we should delay the wedding because of Grandma?" I said quickly.

"No." He took his phone out of his pocket. "So you know, I'm taking a quick trip to the farm in the morning. I'll be back in time for the party."

My heart stopped beating. "I thought you were going back to Palermo for business?"

"After the party." He took out his phone and checked his messages, scoffing at whatever he saw on the screen.

I looked, unable to help myself, and saw a half-dressed woman blowing a kiss at the camera. My face burned in shame, and I glanced away quickly, pretending not to have seen it. It was what Mom always did. It was what I'd have to do with Adriano. My mother had given me countless talks about marriage over the years, preparing me for what was to come. I'd only half-listened since their marriage was not the example I wanted to set for myself. It was the only one I'd ever known until Dominic married Rosie, which made me realize I wanted what they had. I knew I wouldn't get it, though. Not in this lifetime, which was why I was resorting to begging, and if that didn't work, I'd make sure these next two weeks would be the best of my life.

"What if we just wait another year?" I pleaded, setting a hand on his arm. He turned to me, eyes softening as much as they ever did, which wasn't much. "Please, Papa. Just one year. Let me have one year."

"Lenora. We talked about this."

"Six months then."

"No." He grabbed my hand and squeezed it. "You're always talking about how hard I work, how many sacrifices I make. This is your sacrifice. This is your job."

"You sent me to an incredible university to study business administration, yet you want me to call this my job." I shook my head. "I don't understand how marrying Adriano will help anyone."

"I've told you this."

"Tell me again," I said quietly, my voice breaking.

"He's a *duca. Tu saresti una duchessa,*" he said, smiling as he pinched my chin.

"Italia has no nobility, Papa."

"Lenora." He dropped his hand and shot me an impatient look.

"Papa." I mimicked him and crossed my arms.

His eyes lit up with amusement. "This marriage is not surprising news, Lenora. You've known about this your entire life. You've never complained before."

"Because it wasn't a reality before. It was like letting me wear an astronaut suit around the house and telling me that someday I'd go to the moon."

"Hm." His lips twisted. I stopped breathing, thinking I had him agreeing for a moment, until he said, "Well, they own Milano, and I want it, so this is what we need to do to get it."

"Why do you need to own Milano? You already own all of Sicily—Catania, Taormina, Palermo, Roma," I said, checking off just some places. "If you wanted to own all of Italia, you should have tried to become Il Papa."

At that, he laughed loudly. "It has crossed my mind."

I sighed. "I only want one more year."

"And then you will want another, and another, and another."

"Just one."

"No."

"Papa."

"No is *no*, Lenora. I've given you long enough."

"I'm twenty-two!"

"*Precisamente.*" He raised an eyebrow. "Maybe the noble title means nothing, but the man is set to inherit billions of dollars."

Ugh. As far as I was concerned, Adriano could take his billions and shove them up his ass. I wanted to scream that to the world. Instead, I turned around and started to walk away, grateful that he didn't say anything about it. My father wasn't someone you walked away from without being dismissed. He only let Mom and me get away with it. I let out a breath. I didn't know why I expected this plea to be any different than the rest. If Dominic and Gabe hadn't been able to get through to him, I stood no chance. I missed Aanya. I pulled out my phone and looked at my screensaver, a photo of her after we'd explored the one hundred acres of land my father owned. In the photo, she had mud on her face and looked at the camera like she's smiling. She probably was. Aanya was always smiling, which in turn, made me smile. Today, looking at her picture wasn't enough. I took a breath and texted my mother.

Me: I don't want this. AT ALL. I hate everything

Mami: I'm sorry

Me: I really really hate this

My phone rang with a call from her, and I answered quickly as I climbed into the backseat of the unmarked SUV that would drive me to my parents' penthouse.

"I hate this," I repeated into the phone.

"I'll be there early in the morning. Let's go to breakfast," she said. "No phones allowed."

I agreed, and we hung up. I tossed the phone into my purse

and looked out the window. New York was truly remarkable. It was the only city I'd ever been to that—despite the number of people that inhabited it—giving you a sense of belonging. Sometimes I liked to close my eyes and think about what I would do if I had the choice if I was free. If I were, I probably wouldn't live in the city long-term. There was no space for Aanya here. She was the only thing I needed to discuss with Adriano. If I was expected to marry him, a stranger, he needed to promise I could bring her with me.

CHAPTER FOUR

Lenora

I BURIED MY FACE INTO MY MOTHER'S HAIR AND RELISHED HER TIGHT hug. She smelled like my grandmother's soap, *jabon de cuaba*. It was the only one she ever used and kept in her household. Despite marrying into a wealthy family, my grandmother held onto little things like that. I'd never understood why until now. It was her way of keeping pieces of herself. It was the only way not to get lost in a powerful man's orbit. Mom pulled back and smiled at me, wiping tears from my face. Sofia De Luca always looked polished, like a president's wife, perfectly put together whenever she came and went from the house, even at seven in the morning. I got that from her. I had always tried to look flawless, though these days, I wore things my mother would never have worn. She hadn't said anything about it. It was almost like she knew it was my small way of rebelling against all of this bullshit.

We were standing underneath an arch of white flowers in front of Maman, a cute little cafe on Centre Street that she frequented. This should have made my public crying humiliating, but I couldn't bring myself to care. She turned to the bodyguards that flanked us and shot them each a pointed look. Their expressions didn't change, but I could see a million questions in their eyes.

"You checked inside?" She asked. When they nodded, she smiled. "Good. You can stay outside while I have breakfast with my daughter."

"Ma'am."

"Outside," she said, grabbing my hand and pulling me into the cafe.

The employees were already smiling, but their smiles grew bigger when they saw my mom.

"Your usual table is ready for you," a young blond behind the counter said as a tall woman started talking to Mom while leading us to our table.

As we followed, my mother asked her about her family, the new apartment she moved into, how she was settling in, and whether or not she'd been able to register for school again. By the time we reached our table, which took less than a minute, I knew half of Riley's story. My mouth dropped when I looked at the table. When the guy behind the counter said the table was ready, I figured he meant it had been cleaned. I didn't think he meant there would be a tower of different croissants. Before we sat down, the guy behind the counter brought over two cups of coffee.

"We didn't want it to get cold," he excused himself.

"Enjoy." Riley hugged Mom and followed behind him.

"Wow," I said, taking the seat closest to me. "Did you buy the place?"

"No. Would you like me to?" she asked, and even though she was smiling, I knew she wasn't kidding. Nothing sounded better.

"I wouldn't be able to run it," I said quietly, tears threatening again. "I'm getting married, remember?"

"Lenora." She sighed, reaching for my hand over the table. "Let's talk about this. Did you leave your cell phone in the car?"

"Yes. Always."

"Good." She took her hand back and sipped her coffee. Mom never spoke about anything important on the phone since we knew that the government or my father probably bugged them. Maybe both, but we were only apprehensive about Dad.

"Before we get to that, how's Wela doing?" I asked, setting my hand over hers and squeezing it as she'd done for me.

"She's. . .made peace with death." Mom swallowed.

"I'm so sorry, Mami." I sighed.

"It doesn't matter how old you are. Losing a parent sucks." The grief in her eyes broke my heart.

Growing up, I was never really close to my parents. At home, I had two nannies with me day and night since I was born. My mother still participated in things like picking out my clothes and food, and sometimes, though very rarely, she'd tuck me in. When I turned eight, I was sent away for school. There, I was free, or as free as you can be in a boarding school that felt like a prison at times, surrounded by guards.

I only saw Dad during the holidays. Mom tried, though. She visited me throughout the year. She convinced Dad to buy the property in Connecticut so she could be closer to me. Still, she was married to my father and seemed to tell him everything, which strained our relationship. Sometimes, that mother-daughter bond doesn't form because of things like that. Trust is important, so it's hard to get it back when someone breaks it.

"I can't even imagine." I took my hand back. "I won't see her before she goes, will I?"

"I doubt it, babe." She took a croissant and started tearing it apart on her plate. "I wanted to meet out of sight to tell you something."

"You're finally leaving Dad?" I asked, sitting up straight.

"What?" She laughed. "No. I don't think your dad would let me leave even if I wanted to. He's too dependent on me."

No truer words had been spoken. Giuseppe De Luca didn't let go of anything until he was ready, which was never since Dad was a hoarder—of people, land, and things in general.

"So, what is it? You're not sick, are you?"

"Will you let me talk?" She shot me a stern look, and I shut my mouth. "I want to give you a chance to get away."

I snorted. "As if I could ever get away from this life."

"You can take a break for a couple of days," she said. "I have a place no one knows about. Not even your father."

"That's impossible."

"Do you want to take a break from all of this and recharge for a few days?" she asked, ignoring my disbelief.

"Can I even leave? Won't Dad . . ." I was trying to wrap my head around it.

As far as I knew, my father was leaving for Connecticut today and Italy for a business trip soon after. My stomach clenched at the thought of my father realizing something was missing from his office. I wasn't stupid. Dad had cameras everywhere. I knew, at some point, he'd watch them as soon as he noticed. I placed my hands on my lap, twisting them together. Now that it seemed to be coming true, I felt the pressure to leave.

"I already told you not to worry about your father." She reached out and set her hand on the table, palm facing up.

I looked up at her as I slid mine onto hers. Her eyes held love and compassion. My mother had always been too kind. She lent a hand to anyone and everyone who needed it. I always thought it was her way of counteracting all the bad shit my father did. I never understood why she'd married him, to begin with. I'd heard how they met, but it was always told through my father's lens. He was in the Caribbean, meeting with some important people when my mother walked by, and sparks flew. I'd never heard the story from my mother's angle, though. I took my hand back and popped a piece of the croissant into my mouth.

"Oh, my God. This is so good."

My mother laughed. "I can buy it for you if you want."

"The cafe?"

"Yes." Her eyes twinkled. "You've always wanted your own coffee shop."

"Mom." I looked down at the croissant and indulged the idea for a moment. I could own and run this little cafe, ordering dough and everything else we might need. It would be a dream to do it, but how would I? I wasn't even going to live in this country. Still, out of curiosity, I asked, "Is it for sale?"

"No, but everything has a price."

Everything. Including her. Including me.

"Where will I go? If I want to get away?" I kept eating the things on my plate.

"I have a condo in Naples."

"Naples?" My brows shot up. "Mom, by the time I get to—"

"Florida," she said. "Naples, Florida."

"Oh." I felt my brows pull. "And you're sure he doesn't know about it?"

"He doesn't."

"He'll know about it if I go. He'll have me followed. He always does."

"I'll get you there without his knowledge."

"He has all the resources in the world."

"But I have more." She kept drinking her coffee, watching as I sat back in my chair. "How do you think your father and I ended up together?"

"I don't know." I shrugged. "Because your father wanted you to marry someone rich?"

"Oh, Nora." She laughed. "My father has more money than Giuseppe will ever have. I did not need to marry your father."

"So you love him?" I asked, frowning. "You guys don't act like. . .I don't know, like other couples I see."

She smiled softly. "Your father and I have . . . an interesting relationship, but yes, I loved him then, and I love him now."

"Why?" I asked.

I couldn't wrap my head around it. Dad had never been mean to my mom, not in front of me anyway. They didn't kiss in public. They didn't hold hands or do whatever else couples in love do. I would say it was because they'd been together for so long, but my mother's parents always showed affection.

"I can't explain why. Love is just a feeling," she said.

I tore into another croissant. Strawberry, this time. "The two of you don't even touch or kiss."

"In public? Not often, no."

"You don't look like you're in love."

She laughed. "Love changes."

"He has mistresses."

"He does," she said matter-of-factly. "I didn't expect him not to. After all, I was his mistress in the beginning."

"What?" I dropped my croissant.

"He was still married to the boys' mother."

I gasped. "And you knew that?"

"We became friends first. He told me his entire life story, including everything about his wife. They'd been living completely separate lives for a few years by then. He'd been in Italy and hadn't stepped foot in America, while his ex had fallen in love with another man. She'd been after your father for a divorce, but he wouldn't grant it."

"Because he doesn't like letting go of people," I said.

"And she was the mother of his children," she said. "It was hard for him to give up control, but then he met me and decided he wanted me more than he wanted to control her."

"Did she know about you?"

"Oh, yes. She was thankful I came along and finally granted her wishes. We got along great. Carmela was an incredible woman. She raised two great men. I was only there to help out."

"So technically, you weren't his mistress."

"If you take it at face value, I was."

"These women are just mistresses, though."

"Who's to say he won't leave me for one of them?" she asked, amused.

"Wouldn't he have done it by now?" I asked. "Besides, what's the point if you let him walk all over you?"

"Nora." She laughed. That melodic sound always made me

smile, but my head felt like it might explode, so I wasn't laughing now.

"I'm serious."

She shook her head, still smiling. "Maybe sending you off to boarding school your entire life wasn't the best thing."

"Then, why did you?"

"It was more stable than what was happening at home with the attacks at the time."

"You mean the one that killed Dom and Gabe's mom?"

"Yes," she said, her eyes glossy, her voice wavering. Anytime she talked about their mother, she cried. *For them*, she'd always say, *for the loss they had to bear.* "It got pretty bad in Italy as well."

"Oh." I didn't know that.

"But to answer your previous question, your father does not walk all over me. Maybe it seems that way, but it's not the case. He has other women because I allow it."

"And you have other men?"

She shrugged. "I know who I married. I knew it then, and I know it now. I love your father. Maybe it doesn't seem that way, but we have mutual respect and look out for each other. That's more than I can say about many couples who supposedly married for love."

"How do you think my marriage will be?" I asked quietly.

"It will be however you want it to be."

"I don't want it at all." I looked at my empty plate. "Adriano is old and I'm so not attracted to him."

"Older men are experienced."

"And they die faster," I mumbled, making Mom laugh loudly. I fought a smile as I looked at her. "I'm serious."

"I know you are." She returned my smile. "Let me know when you want to go to Naples for a couple of days and regroup. You'll have the beach, room service, massages, and whatever else you'd like. You just can't tell anyone about it, especially not the girls."

"I won't, but even if I did, they wouldn't say anything," I said. "Cat, Isabel, and Rosie are trustworthy and loyal. They can keep a secret."

"Absolutely, but they're loyal to their husbands first," Mom said, and then she paused to think about something. "I would say they're examples of great marriages, but they're all so obsessed with each other, and I don't think that's healthy."

"They're in love."

"Nora." Mom shot me a look. "These kinds of men don't fall in love. They become obsessed."

"Like Dad."

"Dad's a little different. Your dad may love and respect me, but I don't think he'd take a bullet for me." She paused, deep in thought for a moment. "Those boys would die for their wives. No questions asked. No hesitation."

"Would you take a bullet for Dad?" I asked.

"No." She scowled. "I'm not an idiot."

We laughed again.

"Listen, when you're ready to get away, text me the words 'Idk if I can do this.'" She looked me square in the eyes. "Do not text that to me unless you're ready. I'll text back the words 'You're stronger than you think,' and when you get that text, you'll go to this address." She scribbled an address on the back of a business card and slid it to me. "It has to be those exact words because your father may notice that you're missing, and when he does, he's going to check everything."

"So it has to look natural," I said. "It has to look like I ran away."

"You ready for that?"

"I think so," I whispered.

"Do not tell the girls."

"I won't."

"I'm serious, Lenora. The last thing you want is for them to send a Russo or Marchetti out there to ruin your days of peace."

My heart skipped. "You mean Rocco?"

"Dean, Rocco, or Michael." She shrugged. "It's all the same. They're hunters, you know, but it's not animals they hunt."

"What does that mean?" I asked quietly.

"It means you better lie low, enjoy yourself, and make sure no one finds out you're gone."

"But Rocco's so nice," I said, stuck on the hunter thing. "He's always smiling and laughing."

"The charming ones are the most lethal." Mom took her last sip of coffee.

The aftertaste of her words bothered me the rest of the day. It wasn't like I thought Rocco was a saint. . .but a hunter? What did that even mean? I pushed it aside. It didn't matter. That wasn't going to keep me from wanting one night with him. There were no strings attached, so whatever he did wasn't my concern.

CHAPTER FIVE

Rocco

SOME PEOPLE HATED GETTING THEIR HANDS DIRTY. I WASN'T ONE of them. The way I saw it, if I could torture and kill potentially innocent people for the government, I could do the same to scums who had tried to take advantage of my father. It was how I got sucked into this business, to begin with. I was home on a paid two-week vacation, and Dad had to collect some money he was owed. On our way over, he told me about Neil Kemp, the former boxer turned wife-beater and child abuser who now worked as an enforcer for another family. Dad just wanted the money owed, and information about the man Neil worked for. He didn't give a fuck about what kind of man Neil was or the things he'd done to innocent women and children, but I did. It was where the joke about me being a vigilante started. Maybe I felt it was a way for me to pay for the atrocities I'd committed overseas—a way for me to call it even in the eyes of the universe. I watched as my father tied the man up. I watched as he got in his face and questioned him. I watched as Neil laughed and spit blood on my father's shiny shoes. I watched him not say anything about who he worked for.

After about an hour, I suggested to my father that I take over. His expression was priceless—he had no idea what I'd done after my time in the Marines. When I began waterboarding, clipping nails, restricting airways, and ultimately getting Neil to break, my father was shocked. He gathered his answers, and then I slit Neil's throat—that hadn't been part of the plan. As we left, he stared at me with admiration and unease. Afterward, I told him what I could about my job, which wasn't much without having to kill him—rules and all. He urged me to return home and work with him, and I did after I finished my contract.

Somewhere along the way, even torturing these people got boring. Once you'd heard ten men's tortured sobs and pleas, you'd heard them all. They were all the same. They started cocky, boasting about the things they could do. Two hours into the questioning, they changed their tunes. Suddenly, they were sorry for what they'd done. They were begging for the second chance I'd never give them. Lately, I'd been letting Matti and Nico collect on my behalf. They were both young and so bloodthirsty, you'd think they'd lived horrible lives and would never guess that they were raised by good people in quaint middle-class neighborhoods, white picket fences and all. Nico's dad was an enforcer, but that didn't mean he was a bad person.

Matti's grandfather was revered in organized crime, but his dad went on to become a district attorney. I'd seen some shit in my life, but not even I could wrap my head around how his son ended up working with me. They did several things for us, from driving to security to this. Where I was now with my businesses, I didn't need to be out here at all, but once in a while, for the right cause, I felt the urge to get my hands a little dirty. This was the second time I was sitting in a car with one of these clowns this week.

"Maybe you need to get laid, Roc. Get rid of the pent-up tension in a healthier way."

"Mind your business." I glared at Mattia.

"Serious question," he said. I took a breath to reign in my annoyance. "Do you ever lose control and stab one of these people a million times?"

"No."

"No?" He sounded surprised.

"In the beginning, sure. Overseas, I'd lose my shit all the time."

"Why not anymore?"

"I pride myself in maintaining control of my emotions. It's what separates me from the Mattias of the world, who want to start a bar fight every time he has one drink."

He scowled. "I don't do that."

"You're young. You're allowed to do that." I shrugged.

"Do you have nightmares of the shit you did overseas?"

This fucking kid was really starting to get on my nerves with his questions, but I'd just told him I controlled my emotions, so if I snapped, he'd have something on me, and that was never going to happen. Besides, it was a fair question.

"Not anymore," I said. "I don't dream at all."

"Really?" His brows hitched. "My boy Connor just got back. He's Navy. He's really fucked up from being in a submarine for nine months. He can't stop having nightmares. He can't even look at the ocean."

"Tell him to go see a therapist."

Matti laughed. "You're joking."

I glanced at him. "I'm not."

"You go to therapy?"

"This is my therapy."

"Torturing people?" His voice hitched, and I bit back a laugh.

"Yep, so shut the fuck up and focus before I add you to my list."

He sat up in his seat, eyes widening. He was quiet for ten seconds before he broke the silence. That was the thing about him. He never shut up. "I still think you should get laid."

I glared at him. "You're starting to piss me off. You know that?"

"I'm your favorite." He grinned. "Admit it, you'd rather come out with me than Nico."

If I saw this kid on the street, I'd think he was a fucking pretty rich boy with the way he dressed and looked. Most of the time, he dressed like he was going to Easter mass, with khakis,

polos, and shit. I'd joked with him that one of these days, I would
try out the look and see if it worked for me.

"Fine. For the sake of honesty," I said, looking over at him.
"I'd rather you both fuck off."

"Shut up." He laughed. "You love us."

"Focus, Matti." I leaned forward in my seat, and he did the
same.

"I don't even know what I'm looking for." He paused. "Or
who."

"You don't know Wally Baker?"

"The guy who burned down the bodega on 79th?" He
frowned. "Isn't he in jail?"

"He's out."

"Didn't he rape someone?" His frown deepened.

"Yeah, his daughter."

His face scrunched up. "What a sick fuck."

"I know."

"Why the fuck would they let him walk?" Matti asked quietly, and I knew he would call his father to ask him the same
question.

"That's our justice system for you." I shrugged.

"So you're gonna torture him because he raped his
daughter?"

"I'm gonna torture him because he still owes me a grand,
and I'm still pissed that he stole a bottle of Pappy from the shipment he drove from Kentucky a year ago."

I drummed my thumbs on the steering wheel. "And I'm
gonna kill him because he raped his daughter."

He let out a whistle. "Who pissed in your Cheerios?"

"Your mom."

"Fuck you, man, that's not funny." He scowled.

"Why? Because I fucked her?"

"You're disgusting."

I smirked. I hadn't fucked his mom, and I never would, but

she was newly divorced and openly flirted with me in front of him a few times, so I had fun with him about it. She was hot and all, but that shit complicates things, and I respected Mattia. I'd probably never admit it to him, but I respected him. He was a good kid. An idiot sometimes, but still a good kid. And he was loyal, which was rare these days.

I squinted and spotted Wally walking out of a tavern. "Let's go."

We locked the car and walked over, looking around to make sure no one was watching us. I didn't care if random people on the street saw us. They'd never be able to identify us. It was early afternoon, so they'd have a clear view, but people had faulty memories. Tonight, they saw a red car; tomorrow, it was purple; and the next day, it could've been yellow. Besides, in this part of town, you could kill a man in front of an audience, and no one would say shit. What I cared about were the petty drug dealers around here who would no doubt tell their bosses that they saw me. That could very well start a problem. Most of them knew we were "going legit." They also knew that was kind of bullshit. We didn't fuck with drugs anymore, though, so they had nothing to worry about. We'd never been in the drug game, but ever since the fentanyl bullshit, we vowed to steer clear. No one wanted to be responsible for the death of a college kid or finance bro.

"A little early to get piss drunk, don't you think?" I smiled when we reached him, and then I smiled wider when Wally's face drained of color.

"I told you I would get it to you by Friday." He put his hands up in defense.

"Oh, you're going to magically find a bottle of Pappy?" I crossed my arms.

"I told you already! I didn't steal it."

"Sure." I grabbed his arm. "I'm already bored of this conversation. Let's go."

When we got to the truck, Matti tied Wally's hands behind

his back and bound his ankles as he cried. He was piss drunk.
That didn't make for a fun time, and I'd have to cut the torture
short because I didn't have much time. As we drove to the warehouse, I thought about what I could do that was simple and
would hurt him enough to make him suffer before I killed him.
Matti spent the ride switching radio stations until he found a
station that played the kind of music that can only be enjoyed
if you're on drugs. Matti needed to pump himself up for things
like this. I just needed a body to fuck up.

The drive was short. I passed the meet-up spot where I'd
left my things earlier and drove to the next block. A few years
ago, the guys and I decided to buy four blocks of warehouses.
Not because we needed them but because we liked the privacy,
and if there was ever a day that we were raided, they'd have to
look through countless empty warehouses before they found
our meet-up. Even if they had found that they'd have nothing
on us, anyway, unless it was illegal to have a man cave in a warehouse (it wasn't). The torture chamber, as Matti and Nico called
it—because on top of being young idiots, they were also nerds—
was hosed down and bleached every week. Even on weeks that
it wasn't used, we bleached it. Our bodies were disposed of in
one of Dean Russo's crematoriums near his funeral home. If we
wanted to make money just offing people, we were a one-stop
shop. That wasn't our thing, though. I pulled up to the warehouse, Matti got down to roll it open, and I drove the truck in
and killed the engine.

"Chain him up." I rolled the door down and switched on
the overhead lights, squeezing my eyes shut.

I'd bought them from a guy who installed professional
lights—football, baseball, etc. Their brightness was the reason
I bought them. Unfortunately, it blinded all of us for a few seconds. By that time, he was chained up with nowhere to run.
Wally started to cry. So disappointing. I hated when they were

under the influence. I shrugged off my jacket and shook my head as I walked over to him.

"This is your problem, Wally," I said. "You don't know your limits. Not with stealing, not with women, not even with your children."

His eyes opened wide at that. "No. She lied. She was lying!"

"I'm sure she was." I put on my gloves and examined my table of instruments. I had somewhere to be in an hour, so I needed to make this quick. Quick and painful. I looked over at Matti, sitting in a chair, texting. Fucking kids. "Mattia, whenever you're ready to work, let me know since you're the boss."

"Shit, sorry." He dropped his phone and stood up quickly. "What should I do?"

"Strip him."

"Of his clothes?" Matti balked. "Like, get him naked?"

"That's what stripping someone usually means, yes."

He took a breath and walked behind me. Wally started to panic, screaming apologies, promising he'd never do it again, that he'd leave town and never come back, yada yada yada. I would have put something in his mouth, but I wanted to hear his screams. When I turned around, Wally was completely naked, and Matti looked like he was trying not to gag. Wally's pleas were getting louder, but they were already lost on me. I walked to the wall near him and looked up at the tanks to ensure they were full, then checked that the temperature was just right.

"Who adjusted this to forty-five degrees?" I asked, turning the knob down to forty.

"Ah, shit, that was me," Matti said, "I couldn't remember the temperature it was supposed to be, so I Googled it, and it said hypothermia can happen with water at forty-five degrees. It seemed about right."

I shut my eyes briefly. This kid was Googling shit. I didn't even want to know what his search history looked like, and for everyone's sake, I hoped the FBI wasn't interested either.

"If Google says forty-five, you do forty. It's torture, not a day in the fucking lake." I looked at Matti, who nodded. "And be careful what you search for on the internet. You know Big Brother is always watching."

I looked at Wally from this angle. Some people got out of jail stacked; he wasn't one of them. You could see the bones in his ribcage. He'd already pissed himself, which was unfortunate. I checked the time. Fuck. I had thirty minutes. I pulled the lever and smiled as the cold water fell over Wally, and he thrashed. The chains were the best kind of music. The chains, his screams, his gargled pleas as the water went in his mouth. It was all a thing of beauty. There was so much water in the tank that I could drown him without moving him. I thought about it. I'd done it before, but I had other plans for this asshole.

"Stop," he screamed when he managed to gasp for air. He tried to say something else but started choking on the water again.

I switched off the water and waited until he stopped moving and screaming before turning on the air conditioning. He let out a strangled sob when he felt the breeze coming from the vents. As his pleas for mercy rang out, I grabbed my favorite knife that could slice through a bone-in New York strip without effort. Rosie had shown me the knife when I had gone over for dinner, and I had immediately purchased one for myself. She had asked me three times if I'd used it for meat, and every time I smiled and said I had—but I never told her what kind of meat it was. Dominic knew, though, and Wally would as well in a few seconds. I grabbed the scissors at the last minute. Matti was bouncing off his heels next to me like he was set to fight some kind of boxing match, but my glare made him stand still immediately.

"Please," Wally said, hiccupping. He was shivering uncontrollably now. "Just please."

"Was that what your daughter said to you, Wally?" I walked over and stood directly in front of him. With the scissors, I cut underneath his left pec. He cried out, still shivering, the chains clanking above his head.

"Did she beg you to stop?" I put the scissors near his mouth. "Honest answers only."

"S-s-s-s-he did."

I nipped his bottom lip, slicing it right in half. He screamed again, crying louder now, the blood seeping down his chin, to his chest, to the floor between my boots.

I pressed the tip of the scissor against the left side of his face. His eyes widened, and he looked there to see what I'd do next. "What did you do when she told you to stop? Did you stop?"

"N-n-n-n-o," he wailed. "It was a mistake."

"A mistake." I took the scissor away. I looked over my shoulder and heard Wally exhale in relief. I smiled. He was such a fucking idiot. "Can rape be a mistake, Mattia?"

"No, sir."

"Hm." I let the scissors fall with a clank and looked at Wally, still shivering, still bleeding. "He says rape can't be a mistake."

"I-I-I-I-I'll apologize," he said. "I'll g-g-g-g-o back to jail."

"Oh, you'll apologize." I laughed. "Matti, he's going to apologize for raping her."

Matti snickered behind me. "Sick fuck."

I tossed the knife I'd had in my left hand and caught it with my right. His eyes widened even more, which seemed impossible. Maybe I should cut one out. Yeah, maybe I would. I set the tip of the knife on his Adam's apple and poked his chest with it as I dragged it down.

"You know what we do to men who don't know where to keep their hands?" I asked. "To men who steal?"

"W-w-w-w-hat?" he asked, then screamed, "No! Don't cut off my hands. Not my hands."

"Nah, don't worry. Your hands are safe, Wally."

"T-t-t-hank you." His teeth were chattering so hard I was sure he'd chip a few of them.

"It's pretty cold, isn't it?" I grinned, cocking my head to look into his light blue eyes. He was having trouble keeping them open. He tried to nod. "Matti, be a good host and switch off the air conditioning. Mr. Baker is cold."

Mattia did as instructed and backed away again, probably didn't want to dirty his boating shoes.

"Let me give you a little tutorial," I started, bringing the knife to the center of his chest and setting the tip on it. He shook uncontrollably, teeth still chattering. "The crime for stealing would be to cut off your hands, but I already told you I wouldn't."

"T-t-t-hank y-y-y-y-ou."

I traced the tip of the knife lightly, drawing some blood as I dragged it down to his pelvis again. His eyes widened even more. He shook his head rapidly.

"N-n-n-n-o."

"No? No, what?" I frowned.

"P-p-p-p-please. D-d-d-d-o don't."

"You haven't told me what you did with the Pappy,," I said. I stabbed his pelvis right over his dick.

His jaw wobbled. "I drank it."

Holy fucking shit. If he'd said he sold it, I might have been lenient, but this piece of scum did not deserve a drop of that bottle. I brought the knife higher and slashed a line across his stomach. His scream was deafening. Blood didn't just trickle out of him; it spilled like a dam opening up. It really was a good knife.

"P-p-p-p-"

"Please, what? You told me your daughter begged for you

to stop, and you didn't," I said, holding the knife in a steady grip as I made my way lower. "You told me it was a mistake."

"I-i-i-i-t was."

"Well, I'm about to make a mistake, too." I smiled at the look of horror he gave me when he realized where the knife was. "Maybe you'll learn from this mistake and not repeat it in your next life."

I sliced his dick off in one go. His screams bounced off the walls as blood cascaded down his legs. I stepped back to admire my work. It wouldn't kill him, but it's the price he paid for raping someone. Behind me, Mattia started to heave and throw up. I stared at Wally, watching the shivers become uncontrollable shakes, hearing the sounds of the chains rattle louder and louder. God, the human body was something else. He'd lost all this blood, and he was still alive. I moved forward and stabbed him on both sides of his stomach and, lastly, hit his femoral artery. Blood spattered all over me.

The chains stopped rattling. I groaned as I turned around and looked down at myself. I should've worn my other boots. I walked over to the bucket of disinfectant next to my table of instruments, dropped the knife in it, and then walked back to the lever. I pulled the lever and let the cold, angry water cascade over him. I pulled it again to switch it off and shook my head, looking at Matti. "That was boring, but it'll have to do."

Matti gaped at me, still holding his stomach.

"Come on, Matt. You've seen bad shit."

"I've never seen a man's dick cut off." He gagged again.

"You know what Gio's cousins would do?" I glanced over and smiled at the horrified face he was making. "They would've made him eat his dick."

Matti set a hand on his stomach and started heaving.

"Call Tony. He won't have a problem cleaning this up." I walked over and patted his shoulder. "I'll leave the truck. I have somewhere to be."

I took a deep breath when I walked out of the warehouse and headed to our meet-up spot. I'd have to bag everything I wore and drop it off here so it could be taken to the crematorium. I was fucking pissed about my boots. I stripped just inside the door of The Place to not dirty it. We hated when there was blood in here. Once I was done bagging it, I grabbed my black suit and headed to the shower. Normally, I would have skipped Giuseppe's party, but I looked forward to seeing the Principessa again.

CHAPTER SIX

Rocco

LENORA DE LUCA WAS A FUCKING VISION. I WAS GLAD THIS WAS where I saw her again after so many years, because if she'd walked into my new bar, I would have charmed her and had her back against the brick wall in under ten minutes. She kept looking at me like I was her next treat, so I knew she'd let me. I pushed all those thoughts away and focused on Dean and Lorenzo's conversation. Every time her throaty laugh filtered through the room, my cock stirred. I'd thought it last night when I saw her in that fucking see-through dress, but tonight she was even sexier. Tonight, she was wearing a satin dress in deep green. It was looser than last night's, but it had the same effect on me. I knew every man in this room, except for her family members, was picturing her naked.

Who could blame them?

I noticed that she didn't smile at them, not really anyway. She gave them a polite smile before she turned away. Our eyes caught, and I waited for her to look away, but she didn't. She didn't smile either. She looked a little nervous—and turned on— which turned *me* way the fuck on. I could easily school my face to look nonchalant and unaffected, but no one would fault me if I checked her out. Soon, she'd be married and whisked away to Italy, and I'd probably never see her again unless there was a funeral. I took a sip of my drink to rid myself of the sour taste left in my mouth.

She was promised to Adriano Salvati. Thirty-six years old. Duke Adriano to those who properly addressed him, which would not be me. He walked around with an air of importance as if his title wasn't just there out of courtesy. There was no legality to his title. He couldn't do anything with it besides try to impress American women because, let's be honest, women here flocked to those kinds of men. I doubted the women in Italy would, considering they knew it was all a facade—a stupid one, at that. Adriano Salvati held no power in any arena. If you believed the rumors, which I never fucking did, he was so well connected in the world of organized crime that he could make anyone bend to his will. I didn't buy it. To me, he was as phony as the title he hid behind. A little boy trying to play a part, which I guess was what most of us were doing.

"I thought you were on a killing ban for a year," Loren said, looking at my knuckles.

"It was a one-off." I smiled.

"You broke your own rule then." Dean raised an eyebrow.

"I was training Mattia," I said. "What was I supposed to do?"

"Let him kill whoever it was," Loren said as if it were obvious.

"Matti's still learning. He needed a demonstration. It went well, considering he threw up his lunch."

Loren's face pulled. "I don't even want to know what the fuck you did."

I shrugged. "Your loss."

"My favorite thing about you is that you can stand here, all happy-go-lucky and shit, after your torture sessions," Dean said, eyes smiling.

"Lessons." I raised an eyebrow.

"Fuck off." He laughed.

"Can we get back to the topic of our shipment? Just because it hasn't arrived doesn't mean it was stolen," Loren argued, snapping me back to their petty argument. "It just means the captain is slow as fuck."

"It was stolen," Dean said.

"How can you be sure?"

"Because I have someone on that ship."

"Who?"

"Don't worry about it," Dean smirked.

I took a sip of my drink and looked away because I knew if I didn't, I'd start laughing my ass off and ruin his little ruse. Russo and I were a lot alike. Admittedly, I had a better sense of humor. Not saying he wasn't funny as fuck, but his humor was sarcastic while mine was. . .well, I wasn't sure what mine was. I just liked to laugh. Laughing was the only thing that kept me sane most days. Otherwise, I'd probably go on a murder spree. That was how it was with me. You get Funny Rocco or Killer Rocco, so I tried to find amusement in everything. Lately, I'd been trying harder to eliminate Killer Rocco altogether. I blamed my brother for that. His latest Ted Talk about life, where he told me I was headed down the same path as our miserable father fucked me up. Therefore, I put myself on a "no-killing ban" to prove I could do it. I wasn't sure if Mikey really gave a shit. He probably wanted a year-long break where he wouldn't have to call me every night when the NYPD found a body. He wouldn't find this body, but I wasn't happy that I'd only made it six months before breaking the ban.

Nevertheless, Russo and I were a lot alike. Many of our military contacts overlapped, making it easy to share intel. I would never know how he'd managed to get the contacts he had because I'd never ask. Sometimes questions were better left unanswered. When you ask someone a question, you're allowing them to ask one back, and I would rather not talk about my time working for the CIA's dirty secret company. I didn't get into specifics about that job–NDA and all– and wouldn't want to talk about it with these guys, anyway. They understood street war and going after men who were doing worse shit than they were. Not to say they hadn't seen some awful shit. Of course, they had. But they'd only killed within reason, following some fucked up moral code our ancestors created. The man I killed last month should've been on death row, as far as I was concerned. I felt no mercy in taking him out. The shit I'd done for the government was horrifying. Shit I'd take to my grave, regardless of how ironclad the NDA I'd signed was, because thinking about it made me feel shame. The experience was helpful to me now, so I shouldn't complain. In the past, Russo made most of his money finding people. These days, he made it by making people disappear. The man on the ship was one of his. . .clients, so to speak, which was how he knew exactly what was happening. It was also how I knew he was fucking with Lorenzo.

"Russo." I laughed. I couldn't help it. Loren was so fucking anal about things, which made him an easy target for shit like this. He never bought into any of it, but lately, shipments were being stolen, so Dean's little joke was plausible. "Was the shipment purposely stolen?"

It seemed counterintuitive to steal our shit, but it wasn't. If the rest of the crew thought they were on the same side, they'd slip up and make their intentions known, giving us the names we needed. That was one of the many reasons a couple of "our" guys always traveled with our shit. Dean didn't answer my question, but his eyes lit up. It didn't even take Lorenzo a full minute before understanding dawned on him.

He shot Dean a glare. "You asshole. Why didn't you tell me? I was about to call Enrique."

"Professor Ricky knows. He has a helicopter waiting just in case," Dean said.

Professor Ricky. I snorted. Enrique had a good sense of humor, but I was sure he'd hate that nickname.

"Does the woman at the funeral home have you so worked up that you have to resort to dumb jokes?" Loren raised an eyebrow at Dean.

"Fuck off, Costello." Dean scowled.

I pressed my lips together to keep from laughing. Russo was

probably damning the day he let it slip that the owner's daughter was now running the funeral home he temporarily owned. According to him, she'd been "such a bitch" from the beginning. Dean owned the place now, but the previous owners were still running it and planning to buy it back from him when they could. They hadn't told their daughter any of this.

"So no one was trying to steal it?" Loren asked, making sure.

"They were, which is why we stole it first. The guys said Boston was behind it," Dean said.

"Jesus Christ. Again with Boston." I groaned. "We need to send men there. The agreement we have now clearly isn't working."

"We have a decent working relationship with them. Why fuck it up?" Loren asked.

"Because they're trying to steal shipments from us." I shot him a look.

"Unsuccessfully," he said.

"They're still trying," I huffed. "It's disrespectful."

"Don't worry about Boston. After this cargo, they'll know we're onto them. We need to worry about Chicago," Loren said. "With Joe gone and Gio here full-time, we left it pretty open."

"Russo owns Chicago." I lifted my glass slightly toward Dean.

"Times are changing," Dean said, shaking his head lightly. "Costello's right. Charles is dead. Joe is gone. Gio's here. The only person we have over there is Petra, and people know not to fuck with her, but she's not *us*."

I let out a breath. He wasn't wrong. Petra was a certifiable bad bitch, but a bitch is the only thing the men over there saw her as. How they could ignore the fact that she could kill them in under a minute, I didn't know, but they were constantly pushing her buttons, trying to see how far they could go. So far, they'd been unsuccessful at every turn.

We were all silent when Loren spoke up again. "What if Boston and Chicago are working together?"

"Huh." Dean's brows pulled. He was quiet for a moment. "I think I'll go over there and visit my godkids this weekend. Show my face around a little."

He took out his phone and excused himself as he started dialing. I watched as he lowered the phone to say hello to Cat, who was walking in our direction, and then he was off. Russo wasn't wrong. Times were changing. Many old guys from families in other cities were already handing their kids the keys to the throne. It was what my father did with me and what he did with him. The difference was that these kids were still young—a lot of them were in college. That part wasn't disturbing. If my kid went to college, I'd want him as far away from this shit as possible. From what I'd heard, though, these kids were reckless. Reckless and flashy. I said this aloud, making Loren laugh.

"That was us not too long ago."

"Us?" I raised my eyebrows. "Maybe you, Mr. Law School. I was in the trenches at that age, and then. . ." I shook my head, letting out a breath.

"Maybe you're right," he said. "Your father did drop that loan shark business of his on you from one day to the next." I pulled a disgusted face at the mention of loan sharking. He laughed. "Why did you give that shit to Nico again?"

"I have no interest in playing bank for people who will never afford to pay me back." I shrugged.

Loan sharking was a vicious, dirty cycle. I may be a shit to people who owed me money, but I wasn't about to terrorize good families who had dug themselves into a hole while trying to attain the American dream. Fuck that. I'd terrorized enough innocent people for this lifetime and the next.

"I'd still be a full-time lawyer if I could," he said, lost in deep thought. He was so full of shit I almost spit out my tequila.

"Yeah?" I raised an eyebrow. "You'd rather work crazy hours and leave all the money you're making on the table?"

At that, he grinned. He liked to act like he wanted to be a stand-up citizen but couldn't because of who his father was and what the expectations were. It was all bullshit. There was no way he'd be making the money he made if he'd stuck to being a full-time lawyer. The only thing Lorenzo Costello loved more than money was the person walking up to us.

"I knew I'd find some handsome gentlemen here," Cat said as she reached us, giving me a quick kiss before Loren wrapped his arms around her.

"You better be talking about me and only me," he said as he pulled her against his chest.

"Are you a gentleman?" she asked, eyes sparkling as she looked up at him.

"I can be," he said, lowering his voice as he bit her neck. "Or I can be what you *really* want me to be."

She laughed. I rolled my eyes. Getting married made these men fucking pussies. It was ridiculous. Dean and I were the only two left without partners, and we usually commiserated while they acted like teenagers. Neither of us would admit that being around them all the time made it hard not to want what they had. Sometimes. Most of the time, all the PDA just annoyed me. Cat and Loren were still having a moment, so I looked away again. I'd never been that way with Crystal. At the thought of her, I inwardly cringed. That was a bad call from the start. Normally, cutting ties with a woman meant going back to my old ways—working, drinking, working out, and fucking whoever I was attracted to that night. That usually lasted for about a week before I got bored.

It wasn't like I wanted to jump into another relationship. The whole fiasco with my ex was tiring enough. I was just being more careful about who I sank my dick into. Sometimes I envied Gio's situation. I mean, a gorgeous woman shows up at

your door, tells you you're already married to her, and ends up
being your dream partner? His arrangement was the only one
I'd seen work out. My parents had an arranged marriage, much
like Lenora's situation now. The women always bickered about
being told who to marry, as if any man wants to be forced into
marriage. It was just the way things went for some people in this
life. Even kings were used as pawns.

The laughter I'd been trying to avoid all night got closer,
and I looked up to see Dominic, Rosie, and Lenora trying to
escape the group they'd been speaking to. When I got here an
hour ago, Lenora had been sandwiched between her father
and husband-to-be, so I'd made it a point not to look in her direction. If I did, Giuseppe would call me over and talk my ear
off all night. I'd already interacted with Dominic's old man the
other day. We drank his expensive bourbon, smoked my expensive cigars, and talked about life—his favorite topic, which was
ironic, considering. I enjoyed hanging out with Giuseppe. He was
a psychopath, but he sometimes reminded me of my father, and
he told me stories about times they'd shared. He treated me like
I was one of his sons, which felt nice. That was another reason I
didn't want to stand anywhere near Lenora while he was around.
He'd probably read my thoughts, and since they involved soiling
his virgin daughter, he'd kill me before the night was over. As
if he knew I was thinking about him, he looked over at me and
met my gaze, smiling and lifting his glass. I returned the gesture.
His attention was taken away by Rosie, who went up to greet
him. He opened his arms and kissed her on each cheek, smiling
from ear to ear as he spoke to her.

I looked away and focused on Dominic and Lenora, who
were headed our way. I tried to look away from her. I tried to tell
my eyes to look at Rosie, who had joined them, but I couldn't
force my eyes away from Lenora. I let my gaze fall over her body,
taking in every single curve I could make out in that dress. When
our eyes met, hers were glossed over. It did absolutely nothing to

help the situation in my pants, which confused and annoyed the fuck out of me. I'd been around plenty of beautiful women. I'd been going to strip clubs weekly with Mattia, Nico, and Marco. How the hell was Lenora fucking De Luca making me hard without touching me?

"Took you long enough." I looked at Dominic because if I looked at his sister any longer, he'd catch on faster than his father, and the outcome would be the same—me at the bottom of the Hudson.

"Rosie had rehearsals," he said, giving me a half-hug. "That dancer I told you about was there tonight. You should've gone with us."

"Dominic." Rosie slapped his chest. "I told you to leave Marissa out of this."

"I think she'd be good for Rocco," he said, looking over at Lenora. "Did you think she was pretty?"

"I guess." She shrugged and looked away, biting her lip like she was uncomfortable, which, for unknown reasons, amused the hell out of me.

"Is she hotter than Rosie?" I asked Dom, keeping my eyes on Lenora to gauge her reaction. Her jaw twitched. She looked right at me and glared. Oh, she *was* jealous. I bit back a smile. Fuck. Fuck. Fuck. This was too good, but it was also really fucking bad. Two more days. Two more days I'd have to deal with her, and on both days, we'd be surrounded by people who would undoubtedly kill me if I made a move, so I was safe.

"No one is hotter than Rosie," Dom said loudly like he was making a fucking announcement in the middle of this engagement party. Rosie shook her head in exasperation when some heads turned our way.

"Quiet down, Dom. Yes, Marissa is hot," Rosie said. "I don't think she'd be good for you. She talks about herself too much."

"Red flag." I took another sip of tequila. At that, Lenora smiled, though she looked away quickly to hide it.

"Could be a good thing," Loren said. Cat rolled her eyes.

"She doesn't ask questions, though," Dom said. "Isn't that what you said? She talks so much about herself but never asks questions about anyone else."

"Okay, maybe a yellow flag," I said.

Lenora's jaw ticked again. I tried to hold back a smile, but it was impossible. Normally, I stayed away from jealous women. They annoyed the fuck out of me with their false accusations, and they were always false. I barely had time for one woman. I couldn't understand why they'd think I'd make time for two. After Crystal, I stayed away from women like that, but seeing Lenora's reactions made me feel something. Jealousy looked hot on her. Everything seemed to look hot on her.

"What kind of women do you like?" Lenora asked, her eyes widening like she was shocked she'd asked the question.

"What do you care what he likes?" Dom asked. My heart started beating faster.

"I can't ask a question?" she raised an eyebrow at him.

She was wearing a lot of makeup, but I saw her blush. Or maybe I was imagining things I wanted to be there. I stopped my train of thought, trying to remember what I had to eat and drink today and whether or not I'd smoked any pot. I didn't smoke pot often, but it would be the only explanation for me acting like a horny teenager around this girl. Maybe I'd smoked pot last night with Nico and Matti while at the strip club. I didn't remember much of last night, but I was sure it was like every other night I'd gone out with them. They'd hang out at Scarab, help me put up frames and install light fixtures, and then we'd go to the strip club and drink. They'd go to the back rooms with some women while I sat in the front, scrolling through my phone and idly watching the women dancing on the pole. It wasn't that I didn't enjoy watching them, but we'd gone so many times that I was on a first-name basis with most of them. I'd seen them in plain clothes, so the illusion was gone. I wasn't one of those people who sat there picturing myself fucking my friends. I'd gone down that road before. No thanks.

"Are you asking what type of woman I like to fuck or what type of woman I would settle down with and marry?" I asked once Dominic stopped bickering.

She swallowed hard. "Is there a difference?"

"I mean, I wouldn't die for any women I've fucked." I tilted my head. "If I meet one worth dying for, I'd marry her on the spot."

"On the spot." Loren laughed. "I'd pay to find this woman."

"And you're a cheap bastard, so that's saying a lot," I replied. He flipped me off.

"How would you know?" she asked. "How would you know she's worth dying for?"

My heart did a little skip that made me pause because *what the fuck?* When did that question start making me feel shit?

"I have no idea," I answered. It was the truth.

"You'd just know," Dominic said.

I looked at him. "Yeah, but you're a weirdo. You knew you wanted to marry Rosie when you were fifteen."

"How's that weird?" Rosie asked.

"Did you think you'd marry Dominic?" I raised an eyebrow.

"At fifteen?" Her brows rose. "Fuck no, but that's because he was screwing all the cheerleaders."

"I would've dropped every single one for you, and you know it." He shot her a look. "You were too busy dating my brother."

"Oh, God. Here we go." I took a bigger gulp of tequila. Loren and Cat said the same thing and also took a big gulp of their drinks.

"So it's never even crossed your mind to die for someone you were. . .hooking up with?" Lenora asked quickly, staying on topic. "Do you have a type?"

I was grateful for her questions because the last thing we needed was Dominic staking his claim on Rosalyn as if he hadn't done so a million times already. Annoying as fuck, I tell you. I wasn't entirely sure how I was supposed to answer her. How was I supposed to explain that I'd met enough women to know I would never meet the one I'd die for? Therefore, this conversation was inconsequential. I humored her anyway because I couldn't say no to Dominic's sister and could tell she was naive enough to believe in real love, despite having to marry a man she didn't love.

"Nope, I don't have a type." I took another sip of tequila.

Dominic snorted. "You definitely have a type."

"I don't think he does," Rosie said, brows pulled slightly as she thought about it.

"He likes older women," Cat responded. My eyes flicked to Lenora just as she rolled her eyes. I felt my lips twitch but held the smile back.

"Sometimes I like them a few years younger than me," I said.

Lenora's eyes shot to mine. I swore I could see her breathing quicken. I needed to stop looking at her. I would tell her she was my type if my friends weren't here. It wasn't a lie. Tonight, she was my exact type. Fuck. Maybe I had a death wish and didn't even know it.

"Speaking of younger people," Dominic started. My knee-jerk reaction was to tell him that his sister wasn't that young, but I stayed quiet because *what the fuck*. Dom looked over at her. She was blushing now. "Nora wants to work at the bar."

I blinked.

"Dominic." Lenora gasped.

"What? You haven't asked him, so I'm doing it for you," he said.

"I could have done it myself." She pursed her lips.

I frowned. "You want to work at Scarab?"

"Only for one night," Dom said.

"Why?" I asked, sounding exactly as confused as I felt.

"Because she took—" Dom's words were cut off.

"Because I took classes from one of the best mixologists in the country, and I want to show off my skills even if it's just for one night," she said, glaring at her brother. "I can speak for myself. You don't have to act like pàpa."

"I do not act like him," he snapped—it was a sore subject, which made sense when your father was a fucking monster.

Rosie set her hand on Dom's arm; as if she worked magic, he instantly calmed down. She looked at me. "Maybe she can do the soft opening."

Oh, ho ho. I think not. "We already have a bartender that night."

I didn't care if I was being an asshole. I couldn't have Lenora in my space. I could barely stand to have her in front of me in a room filled with people. And this was *me*; someone trained not to react to anyone in any situation. Grown-ass men had screamed in my face in every kind of weather imaginable. I'd questioned and tortured people for hours. *And this was who was getting under my skin?* I needed to pump the brakes on this now. Being alone with her would be catastrophic. I could feel it in my gut, and gut instincts were never wrong.

"Oh, my God. Look who's here," Rosie said, gasping. They all turned their attention to whoever she was talking about, but my eyes remained locked on Lenora's.

"It'll only be for one night," she said, lowering her voice and batting her lashes, sending my thoughts straight to the gutter. "Only for the family and friends night. It's not like I'll be able to do much more, considering I'm getting married."

She rolled her eyes. I wasn't entirely sure why Giuseppe wanted to marry her off so quickly. Still, we suspected it had to do with the land Adriano's family-owned, territories untouched by crime families. Most of it was near ports. It would be fantastic for business. According to Loren, this marriage would probably triple Giuseppe's profits. The fucker. I pushed that to the forefront of my mind. She was getting married. And she was Dominic's sister. And she was Giuseppe's daughter.

"Why did you take mixology classes anyway?" I stirred the ice in my glass.

"Why did someone, who is about to marry a duke, take mixology lessons?" Her smile was small, making her look shy. Innocent. Delicious.

"Yeah."

"I guess for the same reason I went to university and double-majored in Business and Sociology. Am I going to use those degrees? No, but it stupidly gave me a sense of freedom." Her face crumpled a little. I hated it. "You wouldn't understand. After all, I'm 'just a woman,' as every man in the room likes to remind me."

"That's offensive." My brows hitched.

"What is?" She raised an eyebrow back at me.

"You're insinuating that I'm a misogynistic, sexist pig."

"Aren't you?" She raised an eyebrow and waved a dainty hand in a circle. "Look around."

I did look around, mostly because I was still taken aback by what she'd said. She couldn't seriously think I was misogynistic. Or her brother. Or Gio. Or any of us. We were surrounded by boss bitches who made it very clear that without them, our ships would sink. Looking around the room, I understood what she meant. I knew most of these men; they were exactly who she thought they were. I didn't like her implication that I was like that, though.

"So you're assuming I'm like that because your father is?"

"And because you're in the same line of work. You are the company you keep and all that," she said, pressing her mouth together as if she wanted to shut herself up but couldn't.

"I . . ." was at a loss for words.

"My brother, Gio, and Loren are like that."

My brows pull together. "No, they're not. At all."

"Right. So, you think women belong everywhere you do?" she asked quickly.

"Absolutely."

"Above or below you?"

"That sounds like a trick question." I couldn't help the smirk on my face. She blushed fiercely as if realizing what she'd said.

"You know what I meant." She frowned. I couldn't help it. I laughed. This was adorable. On top of being drop-dead gorgeous, she was fucking adorable. She pursed her lips and added, "I don't find you funny, you know."

"That's a shame because I find grown-up Lenora quite entertaining." I winked and took the last sip of my now watered-down tequila.

Again, she blushed. For a moment, I let myself just look at her, taking in her big brown eyes, high cheekbones, and thin nose. Her face was a work of art. Her curves were distracting. Her skin was flawless. If I were to build my ideal woman, she would look like Lenora. I remembered where we were and who she was and forced my eyes back to hers. She shivered slightly as if I'd touched her in all the places I'd imagined, and fuck, wouldn't that have been fun?

"The party starts at nine," I cleared my throat. "Make sure you're at Scarab around eight, so you can be acquainted with the bar."

"Will you be there at eight?" she asked, licking her pouty lips slowly. Christ. I needed to get out of here.

"I'll be there."

"Good." Her smile was blinding. "As far as alcohol, does the bar have a lot of variety?"

"We have more than most," Lorenzo said, joining the conversation again. He was the one overseeing the shipments of alcohol. The one Dean had "stolen."

"If you need more rum, Isabel can always get it," Rosie said.

"True. Jamaican Mike can drive it over," Cat added.

I shot Loren and Dom a look that said *put an end to this conversation now.* Mostly because we didn't know who was listening, and Mike's place had already been ambushed once and raided again. It had gotten so bad that Russo had to start shipping our shit to the morgue. That's another story for another day. Lorenzo's eyes widened back at me, and I had to bite back a laugh. He wanted *me* to say something to his wife? Pussy. These men were feared in the streets, but at home, their wives inspired the fear.

"We agreed you wouldn't talk about the alcohol ring in public, remember?" he said, bringing his hand up to her face. "It's for your protection."

Cat laughed. "This isn't the Prohibition Era, Lorenzo. Running rum from Brooklyn to lower Manhattan is not illegal."

"You two know better than anyone that you shouldn't talk about our business publicly," Dom said.

"We'll stop talking about 'your business,'" Rosie started, air quoting the words, "when you two stay out of ours."

Loren frowned deeply. "We don't get in your business."

"So you don't go over every freaking contract I sign?" Cat asked.

He chuckled. "I'm a lawyer, babe. I can't help it."

"Right. And you two magically show up at night when we're rehearsing with our *male partners*?" Rosie raised an eyebrow.

"Or female. We don't discriminate," Dom said with a smile that vanished quickly when Rosie glared at him. "You stay too late and take ages to text us back."

"Because we're working," Rosie said. "Besides, we have bodyguards with us at all times."

Dom sighed heavily, throwing his head back. Loren shut his eyes and held the bridge of his nose. This was the part of relationships that I was not envious of. I felt a hand on my forearm that warmed my entire body, and I looked over at Lenora. What the fuck was that?

She dropped her arm quickly, eyes widening as if she felt it too. "Do you have special drinks planned for the soft opening?"

"Nope. The bar is yours for the night. You can do what you want."

"Thank you." Her smile widened even more, if possible, and I felt the warmth travel to my chest.

Heartburn, probably. I needed to leave. I looked around for Dean and spotted him speaking to Giuseppe and Angelo. All the big bosses were here except for Joe, who was waiting until the last minute to fly in since the IRS was looking at him for tax evasion. Funny how our country works. He'd killed and had people killed, burned down businesses, and imported and exported weapons, but they only wanted to get him because of his taxes.

"Well, this has been a blast but I'm going." I set my empty glass on the nearest empty surface and looked at my watch.

"Where are you off to? A strip club with Nico?" Dom asked. Lenora huffed and looked away. She fucking huffed. Hopefully, I was the only one who heard it. Maybe so, since Dominic didn't react.

"The night is young," I said. I was going to work. I had no fucking intention of going back to the strip club, but I needed to become an asshole for Lenora. It would be the only way to create distance.

"You're not going to stay for the big announcement?" Rosie asked.

"*I* don't even want to stay for that announcement." Lenora groaned, looking around. At least I don't have to entertain him, " she muttered when she spotted Adriano talking to a group of women who looked like they'd drop everything and go home with him. "At least I don't have to entertain *him*."

"I'll be at Scarab. Call me if you want to come by for a cigar later," I said to the guys and waved a big goodbye to everyone. I smiled at Lenora. A friendly smile, nothing more. "See you tomorrow, Principessa."

I walked away quickly. I needed to get out of there before the engagement announcement was made. It was awkward enough that I had a constant hard-on for the bride-to-be. It would be fine, though. Tomorrow, she'd get to Scarab at 8, I'd get some work done while she came up with cocktails, and then it would be over. Maybe I should tell Veronica to come over at 8. She lived close enough and her wife was out of town for work anyway.

"Rocco." Lenora's voice rang through the hotel lobby, bringing back my indigestion. I stopped walking and shut my eyes. This was not happening right now.

"Yeah?" I turned around. Fuck. Even the way she walked was turning me on. I needed to put an end to this. I stepped aside to let a family walk to the elevator and stood behind two marble columns.

"I just wanted to say thank you," she said, stopping in front of me.

Too close to me. She smelled like rose petals. I wanted to inhale her. My eyes dropped and I could see her pert nipples. Jesus, I needed to leave. Why was she cornering me? She tilted her head to look me in the eyes, and I fought the urge to lean over and lick the spot where her pulse beat.

"You don't have to thank me." I plastered on a friendly smile. "Anything for you, Principessa."

I saw her face shift from politeness to something else. She seemed flustered, aroused. She took a step closer to me. My heart felt like it was about to burst out of my chest. What was she doing? Didn't she know she was playing with fire? Hadn't she been warned to stay away from men like me? She flattened her hands on my chest and I felt them gliding up until they reached the lapels of my blazer. There was no way I could deny the attraction between us. I kept my gaze fixed on her deep brown eyes, waiting to see what would happen next. And then something I could never have predicted happened: she grabbed the lapels of my jacket in both hands, stood on tiptoes, and kissed me. Her lips were soft and full, and even without tongue, the sensation of them on mine made me groan with pleasure.

I didn't kiss her back. As difficult as it was to restrain myself, I wouldn't. But I couldn't resist biting her lower lip. Her responding moan traveled straight to my cock. I almost lost it, then, almost gave in. I didn't, though. I didn't let her deepen the kiss even though I wanted to grab a fistful of her hair and accost her mouth. I wanted to pin her against the column, lift that dress to her waist, and fuck her until her throat was strained from screaming my name. But she wasn't for me. She was meant for the man inside the doors behind her. I wasn't sure what the marriage agreement entailed, but knowing how men in the old country operated, I assumed she was still a virgin and was to remain one until marriage. Instead of giving in to my desire, I remained still. I didn't even trust myself to bite her lip again. If I did, I wouldn't stop.

She pulled back, took her hands off my jacket, and let out a harsh breath, brown eyes searching mine. If she apologized for what she'd done, I'd be pissed. She didn't but the sadness was clear in her eyes. I hated myself for putting it there, but she had to know this couldn't happen. I would have pretended I wasn't attracted to her if I were a better man. Then again, if I were a better man, I wouldn't want to fuck my best friend's little sister. But I'd never claimed to be good, and certainly not *better*. At least, not where morals were concerned. I would try, though, because it wouldn't be fair to anyone for me to break this girl's heart, and that was exactly what would happen, because I knew if she did this again, I'd cave. She was too tempting, and I'd never been one to deny myself anything. I brought my hand up and ran my thumb underneath her lip, wiping her smeared lipstick. I cupped her chin to tilt her neck.

"Go back inside, Lenora." I brushed my lips to her ear and heard her take a breath. I lowered my voice. "Don't do that again, unless you want me to spread your legs and fuck the virtue out of you."

I bit back a smile when I saw the utter shock on her face as I walked away.

CHAPTER SEVEN

Lenora

COULDN'T STOP THINKING ABOUT HIM. I TRIED, BUT IT WAS USELESS. When he pulled away from the kiss I gave him, I thought he would tell me he wasn't attracted to me or remind me that I was Dominic's little sister. I'd lifted the armor around my heart in anticipation. I hadn't expected him to say dirty things to me. I didn't expect I'd be going back to my parents' penthouse and locking myself in my room, so that I could touch myself with the image of him between my legs. I'd never done that before. I'd never touched myself with a particular person in mind. Even thinking about Rocco now brought an ache between my legs. He'd promised to fuck the virtue out of me if I kissed him again. I knew he meant it as a warning, but all it did was make my heart beat out of control at the thought of kissing him again. How many times would it take before he kissed me back? *Oh my God, was I assaulting him?* That thought made my heart drop. I thought about the night again, about the secret looks we gave each other, the tiny smirks he directed my way, and the hard-on I felt against me when he said the words he said. No. I may be naive about some things, but I knew when a man wanted me, and Rocco Marchetti wanted me. Whether or not he'd do something about it was a completely different story.

I needed to snap out of it before I reached Scarab. I needed to keep my head in the game. Tonight, I'd mix drinks, mingle with the New York families, and pretend everything was going well. Enrique was the only one I could speak to about tomorrow's trip, and even though he'd probably be around tonight, I knew he wouldn't bring it up. He may have been Lorenzo's best friend and part of their chosen family, but my mom was paying him way too much money for him to say anything. My driver parked directly in front of the black door, and while he got out to come around and open my door, I looked at the building. I hadn't expected the bar to be here, but seeing it made sense after Rosie said it was "hidden in plain sight." That was precisely it. The driver opened my door and said hello to the security guards. He walked inside to ensure it was safe. As if Rocco's bar wasn't the safest place in New York.

"You may go," I said as I stepped inside.

"Your father said I needed to stay put."

"My father is on a plane," I said. "Besides, you and I know I'll be safe here."

He seemed to consider that before walking out and letting the door shut between us. I turned around and looked at the place. The lights had already been dimmed. Scarab was much bigger than the unmarked front led on. It was beautiful and looked like every bachelor's dream cave, with dark furniture and artwork in gold frames. I took another step away from the door, my heels tapping as I walked down to the bar, my eyes scanning all the bottles. Lorenzo wasn't exaggerating when he said they had everything. He didn't say it looked like the library from Beauty and the Beast, sliding ladder and all.

"Do you like it?" Rocco asked, his voice rumbling as he stepped out of the dark hall next to the bar.

My heart tripped over itself when I saw him. He wasn't wearing a suit tonight but a black short-sleeved t-shirt and pants. Every single muscle in his body was on display. I licked my lips as I checked him out. I tried hard not to, but it was impossible. He was so fucking hot. I tried to snap out of it and answer his question, but when I met his eyes again, he was smoldering, and I forgot how to breathe, let alone speak.

"You need to stop looking at me like that," he growled, turning my insides to mush.

"I can't help it," I said quietly. His eyes seemed to darken even more. I'd never shamelessly flirted with anyone. Maybe I should have been embarrassed, but Rocco wasn't a stranger. And I'd always had a crush on him. "I've always looked at you like this."

"Not like this." He stepped closer but still far enough apart to avoid touching.

"Maybe my crush has developed into something more. . .lustful," I said, my lips twisting into a smile. "And in case you hadn't noticed, I'm all grown up now, Roc."

"Trust me, I fucking noticed." He let out a dark chuckle, his hooded eyes taking me in slowly, leaving fire in their wake. His eyes were on my legs when he groaned, biting his lip, a sound that hit me between the legs. "Why are you wearing that?"

"Because it looks good on me," I said. "I can handle working in a dress and heels."

"I'm not sure *I* can handle you working in that dress and heels." His gaze fell on my left hand. "No ring yet?"

"I left it at home." I looked away briefly. "It's worth more than my life, according to Adriano."

"Hm." His expression hardened. "I thought dukes were supposed to be romantic."

"In fairytales, maybe." I laughed, then saw his bandaged hand. "What happened?"

"Work hazard," he said.

I walked toward the bar, our arms brushing as I tried to move past him. My heart skipped when I heard his sharp inhale. Was it possible that he felt this too? I couldn't imagine. He'd practically called me a virgin last night, which wasn't far from the truth. I never knew what my father would do if he discovered I'd had sex with someone before marriage. I walked around the bar and let out a breath as I leaned against it, pushing my tits up slightly.

"Jesus Christ," he muttered.

"You don't have to fight your attraction to me," I said.

"Trust me, I do."

"I bet you're attracted to many women and don't fight it with them."

He was quiet for a long moment. I wasn't sure what I was expecting him to say. Probably something straight out of one of the romance novels I loved to read. He could say he'd never been this attracted to any of them. He could say he wanted to have me for himself. Anything was better than his silence.

"I don't know what you want me to say to that, but this needs to end, Lenora." He gave me that serious look again, the one he gave me last night, right before he said dirty things. I braced myself. "Do I want you? I think that's obvious, but nothing can happen between us. You have to know that."

"Because I'm Dom's sister, Giuseppe's daughter, or because of Adriano?"

He let out a rough chuckle. "Take your pick."

"They'd never find out, so those are stupid reasons for something not to happen between us." I pushed off the bar and crossed my arms.

"Spoken like a brat who's used to getting her way."

"I don't always get my way," I said, annoyance shooting through me, an ingrained reaction from all these years I'd been told that. "I'm marrying a man I don't even know." I let out a breath. "I'm attracted to you and want to do something about it."

"What is it you think you want, Principessa?" he asked, taking one step toward me, and then another, until he was directly in front of me. He set a finger underneath my chin and tipped my head up. I forgot how to breathe again. "Do you want me to fuck you on this bar?" He took another step until our chests touched, making it clear that he was hard. All over. He ground into me, his cock at my stomach. I bit my lip but the moan still escaped. "Do you want me to pry your legs open and eat your pussy?" His voice was so low and his eyes as dark as his promises. "Is that what it'll take to get this out of your head?" He took a step back and dropped his hand. "I can assure you that if I fuck you, it'll only make things worse when you marry."

"You mean because I'm going to end up having mediocre sex for the rest of my life?" I huffed out a shaky breath. "I don't want to get married without ever having experienced good sex?"

"How do you know we'd have good sex?"

"I just do."

"Well, then, you're free to use your imagination when your husband fucks you and pretend it's me." He turned to walk away.

"One time," I said, my voice so quiet I was sure he hadn't heard me, but then he stopped dead in his tracks. "We have sex one time, and that's it."

"Have you ever had sex with anyone?" He turned around.

"Not exactly." I licked my lips. His eyes flared. "I want you to be my first."

"Jesus." He ran his fingers through his hair and shook his head as he looked down at the ground. "I can't be your first, Lenora."

"Why not?"

"Because it isn't right." He pinned me with a stare, the intensity in his eyes making me shiver.

"Please, Rocco."

"Don't beg," he said. "Never beg a man for anything."

I frowned. "I thought men liked it when women begged."

"The only time I want to hear a woman beg is when I'm fucking her, and she wants to come."

"Oh, God." My heart pounded, and my face heated. "I. . .I want to do that."

"Lenora." It was a warning.

"I'm trying not to beg," I whispered. "I really, really don't want Adriano to be the first person to fuck me." I waited when he didn't say anything. I asked, "Will you do it?"

"I don't make impulsive decisions."

"Is that a maybe?" I held back a smile.

"It's not a yes, it's not a maybe, and it's not a no." He let his eyes rake over my body again, groaning when he was done with his appraisal.

"But you want to," I said, needing confirmation.

"What I want is inconsequential," he said. "Your brother would hate me for this. Your father would kill me for this."

"They won't find out."

He snorted. "Famous last words."

"Give me your phone." I stepped in and stuck my hand out to him, waiting. He did as I asked, slowly, as if trying to change his mind about it. He watched me put my information in it and dial my number so I would have his as well. I handed it back with a smile. "There. When you're ready to. . ." I swallowed and whispered, "fuck me, you can get ahold of me."

"You have no idea what you're asking for." His lips twisted.

"I know exactly what I'm asking for."

He grunted, turning around. "Get to work, Lenora. The crowd will start spilling in soon."

It was a maybe.

CHAPTER EIGHT

Rocco

WHOEVER SAID OPENING A BUSINESS WAS FUN CAN SUCK MY DICK. I had several business ventures, none of which I'd call legitimate. I mean *I* would, but the law, my accountant, and the IRS would beg to differ. Scarab was the first entirely legitimate business that I could call mine. The planning stage was fun. I brought in world-renowned designers. As fun as that part was, it was also expensive. It was all expensive. It would have been cheaper to get another location, but this place had a significant history. It had been owned by my father and used by the old crime bosses as a meet-up spot. It was where they conducted business and indiscretions, meeting their girlfriends here. It was entirely off-limits for their wives, though, which was probably why one of them set the place on fire over twenty years ago. It had been abandoned since, which was why it needed significant restorations. Restorations that were bleeding my bank account, something Lorenzo's cheap ass reminded me of every time he stepped in here and spotted a new addition to the place.

Dad left the bar to my brother and me, but since Mikey's a homicide detective and doesn't want to be in business with people who sometimes commit homicide, he signed it over to me. Scarab was no longer a meeting place for bosses but a members-only club. There was a long waitlist, but it was open to anyone who wanted to dish out ten grand a month. I was going to charge more, but after much deliberation, I figured ten grand was a good starting number. People agreed. My website crashed within thirty minutes of putting up membership applications. Rosie joked that this would become a glorified Raya, and as I combed through the list, I was starting to see why she'd said it.

People finding a partner here was the least of my problems right now. I was nervous about tonight. I was worried about this weekend. I needed everything to be perfect because if there was anything worse than a Karen, it was a rich Karen. Half of the men on the membership list were that person. They'd never complain to me personally, but they'd run their mouths on their social networks and that would fuck up my numbers. I glanced at the monitor and saw Lenora on the third step of the ladder, reaching for a bottle of gin. I sat back in my seat, enjoying the view but not the hard-on I instantly had. Her dress was too tight and too short.

There was no way I'd be able to keep men from staring at her tonight, which was fine. As far as I was concerned, they could look as long as they didn't touch her. She stepped off the ladder slowly, biting her lip as she examined the bottle in her hand. I wanted nothing more than to bite and suck that lip into my mouth. I stifled a groan. She was so unexpected. Since I'd heard from her brothers how sheltered she'd been, I figured she would be quiet as a mouse. She wasn't quiet, and she wasn't afraid to ask for what she wanted, which was a major turn-on. I wondered if she'd been this forward with the guys at her boarding schools or in college. The thought instantly made me see red. I didn't want to think about her with other men. I didn't want to think about her, and tonight, I wouldn't. Dominic knew me well enough to pick up when I was attracted to someone. That meant I needed to stay away from his sister while he was around.

"It looks nice," my brother said as he looked around.

"Thanks."

"*Really* nice," he added.

"You sound like you didn't think it would," I said.

"I didn't." Mikey grinned.

I shook my head. "Thanks for coming. Dom had a bet going with Loren that you'd back out and not show up."

"When have I ever not shown up to any of your friends and family things?" he asked.

I nodded and gulped my drink to relieve the sudden discomfort in my throat. Because my mother died when I was fifteen and my father wasn't around much afterward, Michael took the role of my parent. That meant parent-teacher conferences and calls from the school. He'd been overseas for some time, which made it tricky, but he always pulled through. Because of him, I could live alone from the age of sixteen without being put in the system.

"These days, you hide the fact that you're my brother," I said, lowering my glass.

"Only from the authorities." He brought his glass of tequila to his lips.

"You *are* the authorities."

"Not quite." He chuckled. "How is the membership going so far?"

"We're fully booked through the end of next year."

"Holy shit. Really?" His eyes widened. "You're still charging ten grand a month?"

"Yep."

"Damn. That's a lot of money."

"Money you could be lining your pockets with." I winked, taking another sip of my drink.

"Nah." He grinned. "I have enough on my plate without worrying about the DEA or the IRS or any fucking government department on my back."

"This is one hundred percent legit." I set my glass down on the table between us.

"I don't want to hear it, Rocco."

"Okay, Michael," I said, mimicking his stern voice. "How's the separation coming along?"

"As expected. Elizabeth is trying everything in her power to get me to stay, not because she wants me, but because she doesn't want to explain things to our social circle."

"Is she using the dog as an excuse?" I asked, shaking my head when he nodded. "I told you not to get a fucking dog."

"She can keep the damn dog. I just want out. She's suffocating."

"Yeah, but you knew this, and you still moved in with her!"

"Her father's the Chief of Police."

"Even more reason to run the other way."

"Easy for you to say. You haven't had a serious relationship since. . ." He frowned. "Do you count Crystal as serious?"

I shot him a look. "Until she tried to stab me in the middle of the night."

"To be fair, you did cheat on her."

"I did NOT cheat on her. Why would I lie to you about that?" I asked. "I went to *Oui* to interview girls since Dominic couldn't, and suddenly I'm a big cheater."

"You let one of the women give you a lap dance." His brow raised.

"She accosted me."

"Right." He snorted.

"I was sitting behind the desk reviewing her file, and suddenly she was on my lap, showing me what she could do. I pushed her off, and Crystal only found out because I was trying to do the right thing and told her about it." I looked at him. "This is why you have to lie. Honest people are prone to be attacked in the middle of the night."

He laughed, shaking his head. He can't argue there. I may be many things, but I'm not a cheater. Cheating takes too much energy and time that I don't have. I explained that to Crystal, but she chose not to believe me. She became so obsessed with catching me in the act that she started following me. That was when I ended things. No pussy was worth my peace of mind. Well, maybe Lenora's, since I hadn't been able to stop thinking about it since I saw her, even though I knew it would bring me hell. If not from Dominic, definitely from her father. If not from the two of them, Adriano would find a way to punish me for sullying his wife. He had some of Giuseppe's men doing his dirty work and hid behind his title and wealth. It wasn't surprising that Lenora didn't know the kind of man she was marrying.

"I met someone," he said after a moment.

"You met someone?" My eyes snapped to his. "Is that why you finally decided to grow some balls and leave Elizabeth?"

"No. Maybe. I don't know." He exhaled.

"And you're sitting there calling me a cheater?"

He laughed lightly. "I haven't cheated. Not physically, but I can't stop thinking about her, and it's unfair to Elizabeth."

"Tell her. She'll yell at you, throw out your clothes, or let you peacefully walk away. My money's on the second option. She doesn't like messy things."

"I'm pretty sure she's the one who's been cheating. For months, I've heard her talk on the phone late at night."

"You've been sleeping in separate rooms for months," I pointed out.

"True." He took another sip of his whiskey. "Ray died."

"What?" The change of subject nearly gave me whiplash. "When? How?"

"Two nights ago. 'Natural causes'," he said, using air quotes.

"It wasn't me," I said automatically. I wish it had been me, but I never got a chance to pay him a little visit in Ireland, where he'd run once he caught wind that I was looking for him.

"I figured since you haven't left the country. Still, he's dead." Mikey shrugged. "He was the last one."

I nodded slowly, letting that sink in. We'd been looking for the home invaders that killed our mothers for years. Ray Batiste,

Hubert Grant, Aaron Molina, and Bert Michaels. Those names will forever be ingrained in my brain. Dominic and I dealt with the three of them. Ray was the only one who got off easy. He had a knack for making bad decisions, so one of them was bound to catch up to him. I let that sit for a moment. They were all dead. Did I feel peace? No. If anything, I felt rage building.

"What?" Mikey snapped. "I know that look. They're dead, Rocco. Dead."

"And you're fine now? You're at peace with it?" I searched his eyes and saw the second of hesitation. "Exactly. The person who was pulling the strings may not be dead."

Someone had killed my mother, Dominic's mother, and Rosie's mother. Someone had sent those men to rip our worlds apart, and for what? Territory. That was what everyone agreed on. Territory and power. We'd narrowed it down to the Irish and the Russians. They were the ones who'd zeroed in on some of our businesses while our fathers were distracted. Dominic and Gabe were sent to Italy to be with Giuseppe, who was remarried but still inconsolable in his own way. He'd always said their mother was his true love. *The one who got away*, he'd said, which was why he was always reminding Dominic not to fuck it up with Rosie. Mikey, Dad, and I visited and stayed in Italy that summer, and it had been dreadful. My father died looking for the men responsible for the murders. Mikey became a detective because of it. I'd joined the military, was recruited by another agency, and later, became part of the family business my brother refused to partake in.

"Whoever pulled the strings is probably dead by now," Mikey said.

"Maybe. Maybe not." I sat back in my seat.

"It could have been Joe."

His suggestion made me shoot up in my seat and look around, ensuring no one heard him. I glared at him and whispered, "Joe is one of us. One of ours."

"You sure about that?" He leaned in as he whispered back. "He faked his death and came back like the second coming of a twisted version of Christ. He's ruthless enough."

"Mikey." I stared at him in disbelief. "He was Dad's brother. *Our* uncle."

"Not by blood."

"Yes, by blood," I snapped. "We swore an oath with our blood. That means something."

"I'm not saying it doesn't." He scooted to the edge of his seat, his knees hitting the table between us. "They weren't like you guys. They said they were brothers, swore an oath, and still stabbed each other in the back any chance they got."

"They didn't kill their people. Whoever set that up targeted wives and mothers. *Their* wives. *Our* mothers," I said. "They would never do that. *Joe* would never do that."

"Joe's wife was the only one who remained unscathed by the attacks."

"Because they didn't live in Providence."

"So? If I were trying to make a statement like that, I'd attack everyone, even those out of town." He took a sip of his drink. "They tried to come after Angelo and Giuseppe in freaking Italy, Rocco. *Come on.*"

"It makes no sense, Mike." I shook my head. "It can't be Joe."

Joe *had* taken more territory after it happened, but was he capable of murdering innocent women? No. He'd known those women since they were born. He'd known my mother longer than he knew Giuseppe or my father. They'd all grown up together. It had to be someone in Providence. It had to be someone who knew exactly where we lived and everyone's schedules. Besides, Joe wouldn't have wasted his time killing our mothers just to take over a few measly territories. God, fuck Michael. Now that he'd planted the seed, I knew it would be hard to dig it out.

"Who's that?" he asked. I turned my attention to where he nodded, needing to twist my body to follow his line of vision.

"Who?" I asked, knowing damn well who he was referring to. I'd purposely made myself turn my back to her when I sat here.

"The gorgeous bartender."

My jaw ticked. "Lenora De Luca."

"No shit." He looked at her again, then at me, mouth hanging open, and then back at her. "No. *Shit.*"

"Yeah, so maybe stop looking at her like that. You look like a creep."

"A creep?" He laughed. "How am I a creep?"

"Because you're too old for her."

"Thirty-six isn't old."

"It's too old *for her*." I glared at him again, then looked back at Lenora. "I knew I should've told her to cover up a little. Dom's not going to be happy when he sees this spectacle."

"Yeah, I'm sure Dominic, who's at the bar having a drink with Rosie, is the reason you want her to cover up." He scoffed.

"Stop looking at her," I snapped when I found him still watching her.

"Alright. Jesus." He laughed, shaking his head. "Isn't she engaged to be married to a thirty-six-year-old?"

"Yeah. So?"

"I'm just saying. I'm not too old." He hid his smile behind his glass.

"Do you want to start a fight?" I asked, knowing he was baiting me but unable to stop myself from reacting. "Is that why you're doing this?"

"Nope, but I am enjoying your discomfort." He grinned. "You can't blame me. You're either all business or all jokes, never anything in between. Never this. You never gave a shit what Crystal wore."

My lips twisted. I wanted to argue or tell him that I wasn't a misogynistic, sexist pig, unlike some of these guys, but I couldn't. I couldn't because that was exactly how I was acting about

Lenora. I thought I didn't care if anyone looked as long as they didn't touch her, but seeing how Nico and Mattia crowded her space and how she threw her head back and laughed each time they said something, made me see red. Suddenly, I had the urge to run up there, hoist her over my shoulder, and get her the fuck out of there. As if she felt my gaze, she lifted her eyes and met mine. Even from here, despite the low lights and people between us, I saw her inhale deeply, and fuck, I felt it heavy on my chest.

"It's nothing." I turned back around.

"Nothing." He chuckled. "Welcome to hell, little brother."

I wondered if he was talking about the new woman he'd met or Elizabeth. Either way, he was one of two people who could see right through me, and he'd done it in two minutes. Dominic was the other, and that was the one I worried about.

CHAPTER NINE

Lenora

"**Y**OU LOOK BEAUTIFUL AS ALWAYS," ADRIANO SAID, LIFTING MY left hand and kissing it. I wasn't sure if he was talking to me or the rock on my finger since that was where his eyes were.

"Thank you. I wanted to speak to you," I said quietly.

"In private?"

"Preferably."

He grabbed my hand and led me across the room where fewer people were. He turned his back to everyone else—a stance the men in these events took so that people wouldn't interrupt them. It was like wearing headphones in public, a universal sign not to be spoken to. That move made me realize that Adriano was as much a part of La Cosa Nostra as the rest. He may hide behind a title, but he was definitely in this life. I took a deep breath and looked at him. I'd decided I needed to speak to him about this, and honesty was the best policy.

"Can we delay the wedding?"

He arched an eyebrow. "Again?"

"Only another year."

"Year?" he asked, eyes wide. "I can't. I need to marry. I need you to have my children to secure the future of my estates, my land."

My jaw dropped. "I'm not going to have children right away."

"Did you not read the contract?" His smile was slow, but where it was usually kind or at least placating, this one was off. It sent a shiver down my spine. "You will have one child in our first year of marriage. Another, the second or third—I'll give you the option. Don't worry. You will get one million dollars for each child."

Don't worry? I brought a hand up to my neck to loosen the invisible noose. I was sure another woman would have been happy about that arrangement, but the cost was too high. I knew this marriage had nothing to do with me, but it didn't make me feel less sick to know they'd discussed this at length with lawyers present. I knew this happened back in the day, but we'd come so far. Stupidly, I thought we were past the times when a group of men got together and discussed what a woman could and couldn't do with her body. A child with Adriano? *Two children?* My stomach felt utterly hollow. I lowered my hand from my throat.

"Will I be able to bring my horse?" I asked.

"From America?" he asked. I nodded. He shook his head once. "No. I'll get you a new horse if you want a horse."

"I already have one," I said quietly. "It'll help if she's there. She'll help make me feel less alone."

"No." Adriano's eyes pierced mine. They were such a dark shade of brown that they almost looked black. "You will have servants and children and make friends with the women in my world. You will never be alone."

"But—"

"You will bring nothing from America. You will start over in Italy and be an excellent Italian wife. I was told that your mother's culture is much like ours. It's the only reason I settled for a. . .you." He waved a hand in the air as he spoke. "I was told you would be a young, subservient wife and that's what I expect."

I opened my mouth and shut it a few times. What could I even say to that? I couldn't yell at him. I couldn't tell him I was none of the above. I couldn't know that being raised in the States shaped me to be my own woman. If I said any of those things, my father would be furious. I felt sick.

"What else do you need to speak to me about?" He glanced at his watch, exasperated with me.

"Nothing," I said brokenly. If he noticed, he didn't care.

"Good." He turned and walked away.

I observed him walking away, his hands swaying back and forth as he confidently strutted in his high-end attire. He smiled and laughed with a group of men he had reached, but it was all a front. He was cruel and controlling and wouldn't let me take Aanya with me. My mouth began to quiver as I stood there, so I quickly faced the wall and wiped the tears away. After taking deep breaths to help me calm down, I turned around to meet my mother's eyes. I could feel her compassion even from the other side of the room. I could feel her arms wrap around me and comfort me with just one look. I bit my lip to keep it from wobbling. She gave me an imperceptible nod, telling me she'd be there when I needed her. She took her eyes off me and looked at my father with a smile as he spoke. I stood there a second longer until he put his arm around her and brought her to his side. She'd said their marriage was based on mutual respect and love. From this angle, I could believe it. Still, I wanted a union with spark.

CHAPTER TEN

Lenora

I WAS IN MY BROTHER AND ROSIE'S KITCHEN, HOLDING A GLASS OF WINE for Rosie's birthday party. They'd rented a house nearby for the event since Dom and Loren had made it very clear that they didn't want strangers in their homes. When I asked Gabe who these unknown guests were, he finally looked up from his phone, his mouth twitching. We shared an amused look. They only hung out with each other. Maybe Rosie's dance friends were strangers.

"Let's say one of the guys brings a woman they're dating around," Gabe explained. "She'd be considered a stranger."

"Who would be a stranger?" Rocco asked.

My pulse raced as I heard his voice, and my stomach filled with butterflies when I glanced over and our eyes locked. He put two cases of beer on the counter, then came over to greet us—a side hug for my brother and a kiss on the cheek for me. As he backed away, I noticed his tiny smile just before he grabbed things from the bags in his hands—a bottle of whiskey, a carton of orange juice, Sprite, and Little Debbie Zebra Cakes. It was such a strange addition to the rest that I had to laugh.

"Is there a children's party going on?" I asked.

Rocco raised an eyebrow. "You don't like Zebra Cakes?"

"I've never had one."

His mouth dropped. He looked at Gabe. "You're a terrible brother."

"I don't eat them either." Gabe laughed. "Roc, maybe you can answer this question for us. Nora wants to know why you guys throw parties in other people's houses if all you do is invite the same people you've been hanging out with your entire lives."

"We don't like strangers in our house," he said, still putting away the things he brought. He knew every cabinet by heart, which showed how much he visited.

"Did you invite any strange women?"

Rocco looked up from his task. "No, but Nico and Matti might have."

"So you're afraid a woman will stake out the house and rob it later?" I asked, brows pulling.

"You don't think women are capable of thieving?" Rocco raised an eyebrow. "That's very sexist of you, Lenora."

My face heated. "That's not what I meant. I just don't know any women like that."

"Of course, you don't, Principessa." Rocco cocked his head, giving me a lopsided smile that made my world tilt with it. "You hang out with the elite while the rest of us do your dirty work for you."

"Rocco." It was a warning from Gabe.

Rocco shot him a look. "It's not a big secret."

"I'm not a child, Gabriel." I looked up at my brother, then at Rocco. "Back to my point, my father would never hire a woman."

"Yeah, because your father is. . ." Rocco stopped and let out a chuckle, shaking his head. "I already told you we're not like him."

"Dom has women managing his businesses. Gio's right hand is a woman. Rocco has women spies, for Christ's sake," Gabe stated, and my stomach coiled with unwarranted jealousy. "Just because Dad's stuck in the old times when women did nothing but birth kids and cook doesn't mean we're all like that."

"That's what Adriano expects of me," I whispered.

Neither of them had a readable expression when I looked at them. They looked like they didn't know what to say and weren't sure if they should even try to comfort me.

"How do you know?" Gabe asked, his voice low as if he was speaking to a child.

"He told me. He said he heard I was 'submissive,' whatever that means." I looked over at Rocco, whose jaw twitched. "And he said he heard I'd make the perfect wife. He also said he wouldn't allow me to take Aanya to live with us." My voice broke on that last part.

"Oh, Norie." Gabe sighed, stepping forward and wrapping his arms around me. I let myself be cocooned by him. He wasn't a wall of muscle like Rocco or Dominic, but he was still much larger than me and made me feel safe. "I hate that you have to do this."

"Yeah." I sighed, pulling away. I needed to get out of this kitchen before I started crying over Aanya again. "I'm going to go change for the party."

I didn't say anything more after that. What could I say—that I may or may not have a way of getting out of this marriage by resorting to blackmail? God. I wished I could tell him. Gabe was less judgemental than Dom, though I knew if I told Dom, he'd have a fleet ready in an hour to protect me. I couldn't rely on either of them, though, because it would make them complicit, and while I was pretty sure Dad wouldn't hurt me, I couldn't say the same about them. They had rules to adhere to. Even Gabe, who worked in finance, had somehow involved himself with organized crime. Dominic refused to talk about it.

Whenever Dominic talked about it, he got upset. It was understandable since he sacrificed a lot for Gabriel to attend college. Gabe was the type of guy parents wanted their daughter to bring home. Meanwhile, Dominic was the broody, tattooed bad boy. Well, former bad boy. A perpetual smile had replaced his permanent grouch since he'd gotten with Rosie.

When I arrived at the room I'd been assigned to, I lay on the bed and stared at the ceiling. I usually didn't stay the night since my parent's estate, where Aanya lived, was only a fifteen-minute drive from here. Despite theirs being a magazine-worthy estate, I preferred this house. It was still a mansion, but somehow Rosie and Dominic had made it feel warm and cozy, like a home. Loud laughter woke me. My eyes popped open as I sat on my elbows and looked around. It was dark out now. I must have overslept. I reached for my phone and noticed two missed calls and a text. The text was from Emma, Cat's sister, who I hadn't seen yet. She lived in Florida now but flew up pretty often—the perk of having a boyfriend who could fly planes.

> **Emmaline: I'm here and want to see you! Rosie said you were taking a nap. COME PARTY WITH US. when you're ready!**
>
> **Me: be there soon**

I tossed my phone down and stood up, following the sound of the voice I thought I heard earlier. It was coming from the balcony. Unsure of who or what to expect, I held my breath as I walked closer to the french doors.

"Nah, I'll be there," he said.

Rocco. The voice on the balcony was Rocco. I moved the curtain aside. He was standing on the right side of the large balcony connecting these two rooms. I vaguely remembered coming out here last time and saying it reminded me of Romeo and Juliet. My pulse raced. Was he staying next door? I wondered if he'd be alone or have a roommate. The house was huge, but they had more friends than rooms, so a roommate was possible. I pressed myself against the glass to get a better look at him. He had something in his hand. A cigarette, maybe? I didn't even know he smoked.

He laughed again, and I wondered who he was talking to. A woman? I pushed the thought away immediately, but that thought made me unlock the door. At the sound of it, he stood up straight, told the person he'd call them back later, and dropped the phone on the cushioned chair next to him. When I opened the door fully, his stance was wide, as if he was ready for a fight. He was wearing a black t-shirt and jeans. I assumed his hair was wet and slicked back from a shower, and those piercing blue eyes were burning into me. The balcony smelled like weed.

"You're looking at me like that again, Principessa." He brought the joint back to his lips and took another puff. He exhaled slowly as his eyes raked over me. I walked closer to him. His mouth pulled up slightly when I stood in front of him with my arms crossed, hoping he couldn't hear how fast my heart was beating.

"I already told you I've always looked at you like this," I said.

He nodded, his gaze running down my neck and exploring my body before his eyes met mine. The fire in them was palpable. He took another puff and offered it to me, a challenge in his eyes that made my mouth pull up slightly. He thought I was *so* innocent, and maybe I was in many ways, but not with this. After all, I'd been at boarding school my entire life. What did he think we did for fun? I took the joint from his hand and inhaled. I tilted my head up to exhale the smoke, and he made a sound that rumbled through me. When I looked at him again, his eyes were on fire.

"You're staying in there?" He jutted his chin toward my bedroom. I nodded. He chuckled, shaking his head. "Of course you are."

"Will that be a problem for you?" I took another puff, tilted again, exhaled, and looked at him with a coy smile. "Will you not be able to contain yourself?"

His eyes darkened. "Do you want me to?"

"You know I don't."

"How can someone be so innocent and so fucking sexy at the same time?" he asked so quietly that I wasn't sure he was even talking to me.

The next time I inhaled and looked up to exhale, his mouth was on my neck. It was so unexpected I almost choked. He kissed and sucked his way up to my ear, and my legs turned to jelly. I held his thick forearms to steady myself as he explored my neck, the sensitive spot behind my ear, and dragged his mouth down to my clavicle, licking the dip between. I held on tighter and inhaled sharply when one of his hands palmed my breast. I was wearing a silk purple wrap blouse. He tugged the knot I'd made to close the blouse with his other hand. His touch made me feel like I was on fire. He was tugging on the knot when his phone buzzed. Just like that, he was off of me. The joint fell out of my shaky hand as I tried to catch my breath. I pressed a hand to my chest, willing my heart to chill out. He looked perfectly composed. He was completely unaffected by what had just happened as he answered the call.

"Yeah, I think she's still here," he said. "I'll knock on her door and walk her over now."

He disconnected the call and took a huge breath as he pocketed his phone. "Let's go, Principessa."

I could only nod and follow him. We met Nico in the kitchen, and he decided to walk with us, which meant we couldn't discuss what had just happened. In my head, I chanted that it was fine. It was. I'd been mentally and emotionally preparing myself for failure on the Rocco front, which was not very De Luca of me, but the way he kissed me and the heat in his eyes when he looked at me. . .he wanted me.

CHAPTER ELEVEN

Rocco

"THERE WERE TWO CASES OF HAVANA CLUB MISSING," I SAID, checking my phone to see if there was an update on this mess.

"No shit. You're sure about that?" Dom asked.

"I ordered three, and only one arrived, so I'm sure."

"Were they stolen?" Dom asked.

"I think they were. Loren wants me to let him know before I make accusations." I scowled.

"Damn. Will one box be enough to hold you over?"

"Definitely." I checked my email and saw one from Veronica about a private event. "We've been splitting the boxes between my place, Gio's, and Dean's."

"It won't be a big deal. We'll get some boxes from Isabel's," Gio said, putting an arm around his wife.

I nodded. It wasn't like everyone ordered it; I just didn't like running low on supplies. I needed to stop thinking about it. I read the rest of Veronica's email. She wanted to bring some of the employees from Oui to Scarab for a special event. I'd have to sit down with her and Dominic to discuss this.

"Hypothetically speaking, what would happen if Lenora doesn't marry the Duke?" Isabel asked Dominic.

My ears perked up. I pocketed my phone and waited for Dom's answer. Only because I was curious, not because it mattered. I didn't want to marry Lenora. I decided I would give her what she wanted and move on. I thought about the balcony and her taste when I licked her neck. It was lemon and vanilla and fresh. She might look like an angel, but a little devil was inside her, and I was dying to unleash it. The thought of having her underneath me, on top of me, however, I could get her, was making me hard again. I was such an asshole for thinking about fucking her as I stood next to her brother.

"You mean if my father called the wedding off?" Dom asked, "Or if she somehow disappeared?"

"Is there a difference?" Isabel asked.

Gio snorted. "Huge difference."

"If my dad calls the wedding off, he'd bear the repercussions. I don't know what that would mean, but no one messes with Giuseppe, so I doubt there will be any," Gabe said. "If Lenora 'disappears,' Dad will lose his shit, and Adriano will wreak havoc."

"Why? It's not like he's in love with her. He doesn't even know her," Emma said.

"Not everything is about love, Emmaline," I said, smirking when she flashed me her middle finger.

"Adriano is a lot like my father," Dom said. "He gets off on possessing things. Right now, he thinks he owns the almighty Giuseppe De Luca's daughter. It may not mean much here but in Italy? That's huge."

"Not to mention, he's been bragging about how pure she is to everyone and how he might deflower her in front of them," Gabe said, clearly disgusted. A spark of anger shot through me.

"Where'd you hear that?" Dom asked, his voice low and controlled. "Where the hell did you hear that, Gabriel, and why are you just telling me now?"

"Because I know how you get, and as much as I would love to stop this wedding, you know it's impossible without going to war," Gabe said. "She's going to be his wife."

"So that means he should be able to do whatever the fuck he wants to her?" Dominic asked, still composed, but the veins in his neck were throbbing. "Because she's his wife, he should be able to deflower our *little sister* in front of people? What the fuck, Gabe?"

"Who's everyone?" I asked, my high officially gone, the relaxed feeling replaced by quiet rage.

"Adriano throws these huge parties," Gabe started.

"Orgies," Gio said.

"Orgies that you and Dom used to attend," Gabe said, raising an eyebrow.

"Fun times." That was Isabel. She sounded more amused than upset.

"Gross." That was Rosie.

"Watch it." Dom glared at his brother. He looked down at his wife and said, "I was eighteen and only went once."

"Oh, fuck off. You two weren't even together and Rosie knows you weren't a saint," Gabe said. I could feel Dominic was a second away from pulling his gun on his brother, so I stepped in.

"Gabe," I snapped. "Just tell us what the fuck you heard."

"I went to one of those parties last time I was there and spent most of my time in the cigar room. I was talking to a friend when I heard a group of men talking about how Adriano bragged about Nora's. . .virginity."

"Did they know who you were?" I asked.

"I doubt it. It was a masquerade type of thing." He waved a hand around his face.

"What does Adriano gain from this marriage besides being able to say he married Giuseppe's daughter?" I set my drink down carefully. If I didn't, I'd break the glass.

"He gets a cut of whatever Dad uses his land for. Getting access to the ports will be huge for Dad and Adriano with his forty percent cut," Gabe explained.

"Forty percent?" Dom nearly shouted, then lowered his voice. "The fuck? Dad agreed to that?"

"Why would Adriano need that money?" Isabel asked. "He's a duke. I mean, we drove by his castle when we were there."

"It's a bullshit title," Gio said. "Those guys don't have money."

Isabel still looked confused, as did Rosie and Emma.

"They only own whatever land was passed on, and every generation keeps getting rid of more and more of it to maintain those castles and that lifestyle," I explained. "Adriano needs this."

"Desperately, from what I heard," Gabe said, pursing his lips. "So Nora's stuck with the creepy, sick bastard."

"The creepy bastard who thinks taking a younger woman's virginity gives him bragging rights," Rosie said, scowling.

"There you are," Yari said loudly as she came up and hugged Rosie, Isabel, and Emma. She said hi to the rest of them before coming up to me. I looked at her expectantly to see what would come out of her mouth today. "You ready for me tonight, handsome?"

"Yari." Rosie's tone was a warning, but she couldn't help her laugh. I had to laugh as well because this woman was relentless.

Yaritza was Rosie's best friend. She also worked at Oui, the escort company Dominic owned. It had been a complete coincidence. Before Rosie and Dom found each other, Yari always flirted with him. Now that he was taken, she'd moved on to Russo and me. It was all in good fun, though. Not that I didn't think she'd fuck either of us if we suggested it, but her flirting was all in good fun. The first few times, I considered hooking up with her, but I didn't want things to get weird since she was Rosie's friend. I nearly laughed at myself. I didn't want to hook up with Rosie's friend, but I was salivating over my friend's sister, like that made any sense.

"I'm just offering my services." Yari winked and stood

next to me. She pulled my arm to say something in my ear. I was already expecting dirty words, but she asked, "Who's that tall guy talking to that hot girl?"

Heat shot through me instantly because, in my opinion, Lenora was the only hot girl on the other side of the pool. I straightened and looked over at the man in question. Nico was talking to Lenora, who was looking straight at me. I frowned and looked at Yari. "That's Lenora and Nico. You haven't met Nico?"

"Damn. *That's* Lenora? She's gorgeous," she said, looking at Dominic and Rosie and back at Lenora. I couldn't verbally agree, so I said nothing. Yari slapped my arm with the back of her hand. This was her favorite way to get our attention. "Wait, that's Nico, the driver guy?"

"Sure." I laughed, wondering what Nico would think about that job description.

"When did he get hot?" she mused, linking her arm through mine.

"You're probably confusing him with Marco," Isabel said.

While they talked about our soldiers and drivers and who they thought was hot and not, I focused on Lenora. Even across the pool, I could see the fire in her eyes as they narrowed. Yari yanked my arm again and pulled me down, but my attention remained on Lenora's face. She scowled a little, and my cock twitched in response.

"Who is *that?*" Yari asked, pointing at the other side of the yard. I couldn't help but laugh.

"Man, I really hope I never have a daughter," Dom said, "Especially one like you, Yari."

"Fuck off." Yari's eyes lasered on Jimmy. "But really, who is that?"

"He plays for the Jets," I said.

"That's the NFL player? The Jimmy guy?" She gasped and looked at Rosie. "That's the one you were dating?"

"She never dated him," Dominic snapped, looking at Yari like he wanted to strangle her.

"Yup. That's Jimmy." Rosie smiled. "See? This is what happens when you go MIA."

"Damn." Yari pulled my arm. "Introduce us."

"Go introduce yourself." I pulled my arm away.

"He's seeing someone," Dom said.

"Oh, Yari doesn't care. She just wants to f—" My words were cut off by her hand over my mouth.

If Lenora had done this, I would have licked or bit the palm of her hand. Shit, if Yari had done this last week, I would have done it, but now, my eyes were on Lenora, who was getting more visibly upset by the second. I didn't like it. The jealousy was cute when we talked about whether or not I liked older or younger women. Yari was here in the flesh, though, and I didn't want Lenora to feel threatened by her in any way. Not that she should. No one in this party had anything on Lenora. Besides, she was too good. I wanted to make her smile. And scream my name.

I yanked Yari's hand from my mouth.

"I just want to meet the man my best friend almost gave her heart to," she said.

"Yaritza," Dominic warned.

Yari ignored him. She lived for this shit. She was just as bad as Gabriel, trying to make Dom jealous as if it took much to poke the bear when it came to Rosie. Last week, I told Rosie she looked good in some white jeans, and Dominic looked at me like he wanted to murder me.

"I did not give him my heart. I almost checked number five off the—" Rosie's sentence was interrupted by her husband.

"Okay, that's enough. You wanted me riled up?" he asked, dipping down and lifting her in his arms like a bride on her wedding night. He buried his face in her neck and made her yelp.

"Dominic." She slapped his chest. "You know we're joking."

"And you know I hate those jokes." He shot her what he probably thought was a stern look and then shot Yari a real stern look that promised death if she kept going.

"Okay, I'm going. Can you let Rosie down so she can introduce me to him, or is she no longer allowed to talk to him?" Yari asked, raising an eyebrow.

"Of course, she's allowed to talk to him. Contrary to popular belief, I don't control her life. And Jimmy's a friend." Dom winked as he set his wife down.

Rosie grabbed his face and kissed him before taking Yari's and Isabel's hands in hers. Isabel automatically grabbed Emma's, and they headed off. They looked like they were about to skip into a fucking musical, holding hands like that. Gabe followed them off to greet his finance friends who had arrived.

"It's like she wants my blood pressure to go up," Dom said under his breath.

"You're the moron who falls for it every time." I shook my head.

"I don't fall for it. I know I have nothing to worry about, but the image still pisses me off." He picked up his glass of whiskey and took a sip. "Onto business."

"Yeah. Where's Russo?" Gio asked, looking around the yard. "And Cat." He frowned as he took out his phone and texted one of them.

"Russo's at the funeral home, probably trying to figure out what coffin he wants to bury the woman running it in," I said.

Dominic laughed. "I need to meet this woman."

"You and me both," I said. "Loren went down to the port

with Jamaican Mike and his crew. And Cat. . .I don't fucking know. She's your sister."

"And you didn't want to join Lor and Mike?" Dom asked, raising an eyebrow. "That's new."

"I was already here when they said they were heading over there. It would have taken me too long to catch up to them," I said because it was better than saying that I had seen his sexy as fuck sister sipping wine in his kitchen when they called, and there was no way in hell I was leaving.

"Huh." Dom looked at me a moment too long before turning to Gio. "Should we send some of our soldiers?"

"I already did," I said.

"Oh." Dom smiled. "So, *that's* why you're here."

"Yep." I took a sip of the whiskey I'd been babysitting.

When I looked back up at Lenora, she was talking to Matti. Nico and Mattia reminded me of Dom and me when we were younger, which was why I saw red when Mattia set his hand on Lenora's shoulder. She looked over at me and smirked. Oh, so now she was trying to bait me. I raised an eyebrow. She stepped away and took her phone out of her back pocket. Mine buzzed a moment later. I took a step back from the guys and looked at it.

Lenora: maybe he can be my first

Heat traveled from my ears to my toes. If I were smart, I would encourage it, but Matti was a fuckboy, and the thought of him touching the innocent Principessa made me sick. The idea of anyone touching her made me sick. She'd already put the idea in my head, and now we had to follow through. I looked up and caught her watching me. I remained fully composed as I typed out my message.

Me: dont you fucking dare

Her mouth tipped up.

Lenora: what would you do if I ask him?

Again, my body went hot. I looked at her. She raised an eyebrow. I had a love-hate relationship with this saucy side of her.

Me: fuck around and find out

Lenora: like you'd care

I knew she was probably fishing for compliments or trying to see if I said anything about Yari. I didn't bother responding. What the fuck was I supposed to say? Was I supposed to tell her that I cared? Did ripping Matti's and Nico's limbs off if they dared to touch her constitute as caring? Fuck. That alone told me that I shouldn't fuck her, much less be her first. It would only complicate the shit out of things, and the last thing we needed was more complications when things were finally settling down. I looked up again and saw her smiling up at Matti. It took everything in me not to charge over there and snap his neck. Yeah, I was doing this.

CHAPTER TWELVE

Lenora

I HATED SEEING HIM WITH OTHER WOMEN. I HATED HEARING ABOUT him with other women. I'd been at this party for two hours now, and I no longer wanted to rip Yari's head off because she moved on to Jimmy and then Nico and kept talking about how hot he was. I thought that would be the end of that, but then Gabe's finance bros arrived, and one of the women they were with introduced herself as Crystal. I knew instantly that she was Rocco's ex, so I saw red all over again. I thought I was too young to have issues with my blood pressure, but this party was proving otherwise. Crystal was a little shorter and curvier than me, and she used those curves to her advantage. The black dress she was wearing looked like it was drawn on. The jeans and blouse that made me feel confident before suddenly made me feel like the prude I was. She was the opposite of me—which should've been fine since he said he had no type, and I knew he was attracted to me—but I still felt the sting of jealousy.

"Don't start baiting Rocco," the guy she was hanging onto said. He'd introduced himself as Reid. "I'll be six feet under before I can do my next line."

"Please. Rocco isn't jealous," Crystal said.

"Really? He looks like he would be," another woman said.

Crystal scoffed. "I could have fucked Reid in front of Rocco, and he probably wouldn't have batted an eye. He's probably the least jealous boyfriend I've ever had."

"And the best in bed," the woman said.

"Tammy, can you shut the fuck up?" That was Reid.

"Reid is the best," Crystal said, and I believed her with how she was clinging onto him, but then she looked at Rocco, and I got mad all over again.

I focused on Nico and Mattia, who talked about cars and engines. I rewound the conversation. She'd said Rocco wasn't jealous, which was odd. He was jealous earlier when I was pretending I'd hook up with Mattia. I would never have done it, but I wanted a reaction out of him, and even though his composure remained completely stoic, his texts and burning eyes told another story.

"He's fucking hot," Tammy said. I was beginning to hate her.

"He's emotionally unavailable." Crystal clicked her tongue against her teeth.

"You're just saying that because you tried everything to get a rise out of him and never got one." Tammy laughed.

Crystal sounded like she didn't care, but even though she was holding onto Reid's arm, she was eyefucking Rocco. I decided I'd had enough of this party and this crowd. I'd be long gone in two weeks and never have to see most of these people again. I grabbed my phone and started walking. I thought it would be fun to mess around and make Rocco jealous, and it was, but not at the cost of me losing my mind in the process. The logical part of me screamed that I should stop the madness, that it was best if I didn't give my virginity to Rocco or anyone else but Adriano. That idea repulsed the other part of me. It didn't matter. I was done. If I felt this way and Rocco hadn't even kissed my lips, imagine how I'd feel if he slept with me. I'd have to endure years of jealousy and longing while I stood by a man I'd never love. And Rocco would move on because that was what men like him did.

I kissed Rosie goodbye and told her I was exhausted, then said bye to everyone else and snuck out the side door that led to my brother's house. A little garden sat between the houses.

I'd only seen it during the day, but at night it was breathtaking. They'd strung little lights throughout. It almost felt like a fairytale. I startled at the loud slamming of the gate behind me and increased my speed. I hoped Dominic hadn't told Nico or Mattia to escort me back. Dominic's overprotectiveness was the only reason Dad let me stay here without his security. I heard movement behind me but kept going. I was near Dominic's gate when an arm grabbed me from behind, and a hand covered my mouth. Instinctively, my body tightened in readiness to fight or flee. I was ready to struggle against the person's grip until I heard his rough voice.

"Not a sound, Principessa," Rocco said near my ear. My heart was still pounding wildly, but I sagged against him. He let go of my mouth but kept his hand on my stomach to keep me from moving.

"You scared me." I elbowed him twice. Hard. He didn't even make a sound.

"Why? Were you expecting Nico?" he asked, dropping his voice in a way that made my entire body shiver. "Or Mattia?"

"Were you expecting Crystal?" I spat out. "Or Yari?"

"Hm." The sound vibrated through me as he bit my earlobe. I shut my eyes hard. "Is the Principessa jealous?"

"No."

"No?" He chuckled, another sound that vibrated through me. "It sounds like you might be."

"Are you jealous?" I countered. "You didn't want me going home with any of them either."

"What if I am?" He growled. It sent a shiver through my body. I was about to speak again when his hand moved down, and he started unbuttoning my jeans. He slipped his hand into my underwear as he bit my earlobe, and my legs started to tremble. "Shh."

I inhaled sharply as his hand brushed against my mound. He murmured something, his voice low and husky as he said he approved of my "freshly waxed pussy." I was so entranced by the moment that I forgot to breathe as he delicately explored my folds.

"Oh, my god." I gasped as he pushed his fingers into me. My breathing was ragged as his hand moved. His thumb rubbed my clit as he thrust the others in and out of my opening. It felt like his fingers were everywhere as he touched my pressure points.

"Fuck. You're so wet, Principessa," he murmured against me.

"Rocco. Please." I arched my back, wanting more. Needing more.

"Hmmm, that's right. This is where you beg." His lips brushed against the back of my neck as he removed his fingers and began to massage me up and down, my breath hitching each time he brushed against my clit. I only took five exhales before pleasure shot throughout my body. I sank back against his chest, breathing like I'd just run a mile. He took his hands away from my jeans, refastened them, and then smacked my butt hard. "Go to your bedroom."

I didn't need any further encouragement. I pushed aside all thoughts of Crystal and Yari from my mind. Rocco could have chosen any woman from the party to bring home with him, but he picked me.

CHAPTER THIRTEEN

Lenora

I'D GONE STRAIGHT TO MY ROOM, SHOWERED, AND CHANGED INTO the lingerie I had with me. It was a white lace bra, panties, and a garter set meant to be worn on my wedding night, but since it was the only thing I had that was remotely sexy, I was using it tonight. I sat in the center of my bed, waiting. First, I lay on my side, then sat up and crossed my legs. Then I faced the other way so my back was facing the door that led to the balcony. I wasn't sure what position would look the sexiest. I must have fallen asleep waiting because the sound of a door clicking shut woke me. I sat up straight in bed, pushing my hair out of my face. So much for all the rehearsing. Rocco stood by the door in a faded red t-shirt and gray sweatpants. His eyes hooded as he walked over to me. My breath hitched.

"Fuck." He stood right at the edge of the bed. The lights were off, but we could see each other well enough because of the lights on the balcony. It didn't take much light to see the obvious erection in his pants. He didn't touch me, he just stared, and I wondered if I was supposed to do something.

"Am I supposed to. . .do you want me to. . ." I started moving to get on my knees, but Rocco tapped my knee and shook his head. I stopped immediately.

"Good girl." His mouth pulled into the most sinful grin I'd ever seen. He reached over and tipped my chin up, looking into my eyes with such intensity that a shiver rolled through me. "Tell me if you want to stop at any point."

"Am I. . .am I supposed to, like, use a safe word or

something?" I asked, feeling myself go hot all over with embarrassment. When he chuckled, I tried to look away, but he pinched my chin and made me meet his eyes again.

"If you want to stop, you say stop." He searched my eyes. "Okay?"

I nodded, breathless already.

"I need you to tell me you understand."

"If I want to stop, I say stop," I whispered, unable to find much strength to put behind words. My body remembered what those fingers did to me outside, and I was already going under again.

"Lie back."

I did so immediately, uncrossing my legs and lying flat on the bed. He hungrily surveyed my body, devouring it with his eyes. His lips were drawn in a tight line as he reached for the garter on my left thigh. Slowly, he slid his finger underneath and then suddenly yanked. I gasped as an electric shock shot through my thigh. Our eyes locked as he did the same to my right side, and I jolted again, my breath coming in short ragged bursts as the heat between my legs intensified.

"Was this meant for your husband?" he asked. "For you to wear on your wedding night?"

I nodded, unable to speak, unsure if he wanted me to.

"But you wore it for me," he mused, sliding both fingers underneath each garter and pulling the elastic higher off my leg. I braced, knowing the snap was coming, but still yelped when it hit my thighs.

Rocco's expression hardened to a solemn mask as he regarded me with a newfound intensity. I felt my heart racing as I tried to comprehend the many facets of this man. I had to remind myself to stay focused and not let my emotions lead me astray. I had wanted him since I was a child and couldn't believe this dream had become reality. His hands slid up and down my legs, tracing my thighs and ankles until his thumbs found a particular spot on the inside of my legs, which caused me to let out a loud moan of pleasure. I kept my eyes open, watching his expression as his hands roamed upward, my stomach contracting against the calluses on his hands. Rough yet gentle, like the man himself. When he reached my breasts, he squeezed them through my bra, his eyes dilating as he watched me arch against him, begging for more without words. He pulled back, standing straight, and shook his head again.

For a moment, I thought he was regretting this and was going to tell me he couldn't go through with it. I opened my mouth to say anything that would get him to touch me again, but the intense look in his eyes when they snapped to mine made me shut it.

"Turn around, Principessa," he said, his voice low, gravelly.

My heart flipped as I turned onto my stomach. I laid my head to the right, then to the left, then to the right again, unsure of what the fuck I was supposed to do with it. Without looking back, I knew he was probably laughing at me, but I waited quietly, nonetheless. He slapped my right cheek hard. I gasped loudly.

"Ass up," he ordered. "On your hands and knees."

I squirmed. He slapped my left cheek. Hard. My throat made a sound, something between a gasp and a strangled moan. I looked over my shoulder, biting my lip to keep from moaning again just from the fire in his eyes. He opened my legs wider and stood between them. I felt him on my ass as he reached for my hair and wound it in his hands, pulling me up until I was on my knees with my back against his chest.

"You like this, Principessa?" he asked low in my ear. "You like it when I slap your ass? When I pull your hair?"

I tried to nod, but his hold on my hair was too tight.

"Tell me."

"Y-yes, I like it."

"Hm." He let go of my hair so quickly that I had to catch myself from completely flopping on the bed.

I was about to look over my shoulder again, but suddenly his body was looming over me. He kissed the back of my neck, a gentle peck that made butterflies swarm inside me. With open-mouthed kisses and licks, he made his way down my spine. It was almost impossible to stay still. When he got to my lower back, I shimmied, needing more. More. He bit my right cheek, then my left. My arms shook as I tried to keep myself up.

"Such a perfect body," he said as he began to undress the lower half of my body, taking off my stockings and garter.

A soft hiss escaped his lips as he pulled my thong down slowly. I couldn't tell if he was taking his time to savor it since it wouldn't happen again, or if he wanted to allow me to halt him should I choose. My temperature rose as he set his hands on the back of my legs and trailed them up my backside, cupping my ass firmly. Then I felt a lick between my cheeks, and my body jolted forward in an instant. He clasped both hands around my hips and pulled me back towards him.

"Relax," he said, and I did immediately. His hands worked to unhook my bra, the last piece of clothing I had on. I was completely naked on display, and he was still fully dressed. "Turn around."

I submitted to his command and collapsed onto the bed, my body shaking with anticipation. His hands were on my breasts, kneading, and then my nipples, squeezing and tugging as I writhed in pleasure. I struggled to hold back the moans that threatened to escape my lips as the pressure in my core began to build. He wasn't even fucking me yet. He was playing with my breasts, and I was ready to come again.

"Has anyone played with your nipples, Principessa?" He kept kneading, kept pinching, and twisting. I could barely breathe as exhilaration shot from my spine to my toes, but I managed to nod. His expression never wavered as he came down and took my left nipple into his mouth.

"Oh. . .my. . .God," I whispered, my back arching off the bed.

"You like that?" He moved on to the other and did the same, biting it as he pulled away. He looked amused at the sound I made when he pulled away from me. "You want more?"

"Please."

My breath hitched as I felt his scorching hot lips and hands exploring my body. He nibbled each nipple before he descended further, raining kisses down on my stomach. His tongue delicately traced around my belly button before his lips started a slow path to the spot between my legs. I could feel the anticipation radiating off of him, but I clamped my legs shut out of instinct. He pulled back and looked at me with a feral glint.

"Open." His eyes burned with the command. I shook my head, biting my lip hard. I felt tears prick my eyes, though I couldn't understand why. Maybe because it was too much, this felt like sensory overload. "Lenora."

"I can't," I whispered.

"Has anyone done this to you before?"

"No."

"What's the problem?" He set his hands on my knees and began drawing slow circles with his thumb as he waited for me to answer.

"I don't know."

"Are you embarrassed?" he asked, eyes softening when I nodded. "Oh, Principessa." He chuckled, shaking his head. "You wanted me to be your first, didn't you?"

"Yes." I wiped my eyes quickly.

"Do you still want that?"

"Yes," I said quickly. "I want you."

Another ghost of a smile. "Open your legs, Lenora. I want to taste you."

My pulse jumped. Shakily, I managed to open my legs for him. I felt so vulnerable. I was so naked. He was so dressed. No one, besides my doctor and wax technician, had ever seen me like this. In boarding school, no guy would come near me. In college, the few guys I could sneak into my dorm shoved their hands down my pants and fumbled around while I did the same to them. Only one of us got off every time, never me. This felt too personal. Rocco went down on his knees and pulled my body to the edge of the bed. I watched as he kissed the insides of my thighs and made his way to my core.

"Such a pretty pussy, Lenora," he said, his breath tickling my folds.

It was the last thing he said before his mouth was on me. The stroke of his tongue lit a fire inside of me, unlike anything I'd ever known. With it, he stroked my clit and my folds, moved down to the opening, and fucked me with it. My hands flew to his hair as he moved back to my clit. He groaned against me, grabbing my ass and lifting me. I watched him devour me as he made noises of approval in the back of his throat. It was almost too much. My grip on his hair tightened, and I began to roll my hips.

"You like fucking my mouth, Lenora?" he asked, his voice low.

My eyes widened as I nodded and gasped again when he hit a specific spot. He made another sound of approval as he pulled my clit into his mouth and sucked, his eyes finding mine as he flattened his tongue against me with enough pressure to bring me to orgasm. My legs trembled, and my head thrashed side to side as I squeezed my eyes shut and rode out the wave; all the while, he continued to lick me. He stood slowly, kissing my thighs and stomach, pulling my nipples into his mouth again as his fingers stroked me where his mouth had just been. I was sensitive when he rubbed his thumb on my clit, but when he dipped one finger inside and then another, I thought I might explode. He pulled back to look at me as I gasped and moved my hips with his rhythm.

"You like fucking my fingers?" he stopped pumping his fingers suddenly, and I gasped for air.

"Yes," I breathed, moving so he'd continue.

That earned me a wicked grin. He pressed his thumb against me again and, this time, went straight to that magic spot. As I thrashed on the bed, coming against his fingers, he brought a hand to my mouth. In the back of my mind, a part of me panicked at the thought, but that was pushed away when my eyes rolled back as he pulled another orgasm out of me. When I opened my eyes to look at him, he watched me with unmasked desire as he licked his fingers. My face heated, and that earned me another wicked grin. I reached for him, needing to touch any part of him—his face, his hands, anything—but he stepped off the bed, completely out of reach. He pulled his shirt over his head and let it fall to the floor. I sat up on my elbows, heart pounding as I drank him in. There were light scars on his sides and chest as if someone had taken a knife to him. The scars did nothing to ruin his perfectly sculpted body, but I instantly wanted to find the person responsible and kill them for hurting him like this. As I ogled the lines of his chest and muscled arms, he lowered his sweats and stepped out of them. His cock was hard and thick, and I knew there was no way he would fit inside me, as he set his hands on my knees. He'd break me in half. I must have stared at it for too long, because he squeezed my knees to get my attention.

"It'll fit," he said, as if reading my mind.

"How?" I asked, my words a rasp from not using my voice. He shot me a lopsided grin that melted my insides, but he didn't respond.

"Sit up."

I did.

"On your knees."

I did. The position put my face right in front of his cock. I licked my lips, wondering how it would feel in my mouth. I looked up at him.

"May I?" I whispered.

"Fuck." He sunk his fingers into my hair and gripped me at the nape so I'd look him in the eyes. "You want to suck my cock?"

"Y-yes." I licked my lips.

His grip tightened. "Say it."

"I want to suck your cock."

A devilish look swept over his face as his voice lowered. "Now, ask me."

"M-may I suck your cock?"

His smile was filthy. "Now, beg me."

"Can I please, please suck your cock, Rocco?"

"Jesus fucking Christ." He exhaled shakily, eyes flaring as he loosened his grip. I brought a hand around it and pumped it once. Twice. He cursed under his breath, grip tightening. "Suck it or don't, Lenora, but if you keep looking at it with your innocent eyes, I'm going to shove it down your throat, and you're not ready for that."

Pleasure spiked through me. I pressed my legs together as I leaned in and licked from his balls to the tip, my tongue swirling on the head before I took him in my mouth. There was no way I'd be able to fit all of him, but I did the best I could, licking and sucking. I looked up and found him watching me, a look of wonder amid the fire. It made me take him deeper.

"Fuck. Yes." His grip tightened. "Just like that." He thrust into my mouth. "Good girl. Just like that."

I squeezed my legs together, feeling myself getting wetter with each praise. I didn't know why that turned me on so damn much. Or maybe it was just the way he said it to me. He pulled me off suddenly and growled as I licked my lips around my mouth.

"Lie back."

I did, getting on my elbows to watch him again. He reached down and grabbed a condom from his sweatpants, one hand on his dick, pumping as he looked at me with those cloudy blue eyes.

"You don't know how fucking hot you look right now." He

bit his lower lip and shook his head as he opened the condom and slid it over himself.

I wondered if he brought it for me or if he always carried one around just in case. I pushed that thought away before it made me irrationally upset. He spread my legs open further, bringing his fingers back between them, his face inches from mine.

"I don't know how much more I can take," I whispered, gasping as he hooked his finger and found that damn spot again. My back arched as he pinched my right nipple. The familiar warmth spread through me again. I began to move against his fingers as the pressure continued to build.

"Let go," he said, a command that shook my body.

"Oh, fuck. Fuck. Fuuuuuck."

He positioned himself between my legs, kissing my jaw and my chest. I held my breath when I felt the tip at my entrance. I knew it would hurt, and he was so big that it would probably hurt even if I weren't a virgin.

"Try to relax," he said, pushing inside. He shut his eyes and stopped. "Jesus fucking Christ."

"What?" I searched his face. He looked like he was in agony.

His eyes flew open. "I should probably tell you this before I'm completely inside you."

"What?" My heart stopped thinking of what the hell it could be.

"I've never fucked a virgin."

"Never?" I felt my brows pull. Could that even be possible? How? He'd been a virgin once.

"You're my first." His lips twitched a little as he rocked his hips slowly against me. "And fuck. I don't know if I can go slow."

"Then go fast."

"I'll hurt you if I go fast. Just give me a minute." He breathed out and pushed inside a little more.

A jolt of pain shot through me. I squeezed my eyes shut as

if that would lessen it. He spread my legs wider, pushing deeper, deeper. Tears sprung from my eyes as I bit my lip to keep myself from making a sound. He seemed to sense this and reached for a t-shirt I had draped over a pillow. He wound it and put it in my mouth, smiling at whatever I looked like. He thrust in a little deeper and caged me as he lowered himself.

"Scream for me," he growled in my ear as he pulled out and thrust in one go. I screamed. He hissed. "Fuck, you're so tight."

He kept thrusting slowly in and out, and I could tell he was holding himself back. The way his muscles roped and his face pinched, I knew this wasn't how he normally fucked. If my tears were any indication, I didn't think I could handle him going faster. He brought his hand between us and began rubbing my clit as he moved.

Pleasure replaced the pain, and he moved faster, going deeper each time. I moaned loudly around the shirt in my mouth and whimpered at the loss of him when he pulled out again. He kept his eyes on me as if trying to memorize what brought me pleasure and pain. He thrust hard, all the way in, knocking the wind out of me with the force, and started to fuck me. My body bowed off the bed as I screamed against the t-shirt.

"More?" he asked, slowing down and pulling out again. Eyes wide, I nodded frantically. His mouth tugged. He thrust in all the way again, I clenched around him, and this time, he was the one who shut his eyes and groaned. "God damn it, Lenora. I want to draw this out for you, but you're too fucking tight. Fuck." He groaned as he thrust into me again. I wrapped my legs around his hips, telling him I wanted more. He let out a forced laugh, his blue eyes clouding as his hand found my clit again. I gasped.

"You feel like fucking magic." He pinched my clit and swiveled his hips, giving me that devious smile again as if he knew what it would do to me. Limb by limb, my entire body tightened. He leaned down as he swiveled his hip again.

"Come for me, baby," he growled into my ear, and I lost it.

My body spasmed out of control. He hissed and muttered things I couldn't make out as he pumped into me a few more times. I felt his seed fill the condom inside me, but little white dots clouded my vision as the aftershocks of my orgasm rolled on. He set his forehead against mine and took a harsh breath, then another.

"Jesus Christ, Nora," he breathed.

Somehow, I smiled at him and said, "You've never called me Nora."

Then my eyes shut, and I fell asleep.

CHAPTER FOURTEEN

Rocco

BRUNCH WAS JUST AN EXCUSE FOR PEOPLE TO DAY DRINK WITHOUT being judged. I hated it. The food situation was fucking stupid. It was Rosie's birthday, though, and she loved brunch, so here we were, sitting in a little Brooklyn restaurant that was hipster central, eating fucking waffles with a side of french fries. The birthday girl smiled wide as she set a mimosa in front of me. She was already drunk. I took it only because I loved her and pretended to drink even though I hated pulp.

"I'm going to get us some real drinks," Dominic said, slapping his napkin on the table. "The acidity is killing me."

Thank fuck.

I looked up and caught Lenora's eyes for the first time today. She blushed and looked away. I brought the stupid mimosa to my lips to hide my smile. I'd returned to my room as soon as she fell asleep last night, and after tossing and turning for an hour, I went right back to eat her pussy one last time. I wasn't sure any amount of food or drinks would ever rid me of her taste. No amount of pussy would rid me of the memory of it. Any of it. I was a bastard for taking her virginity. Even as a virgin, I'd had no interest in fucking one. Lenora was different, though. She was in an abnormal situation, being married off to some stranger. I didn't blame her for wanting to give this piece of herself to someone of her choice. It just happened to be me. It was practically a favor. I kept telling myself that this morning when I woke up with my cock hard, ready to walk over there and fuck her again. It was a one-off. Or three-off, if you counted me eating her pussy and fingering her that second time as a different occasion. I heard my friends talking around the table, but I was replaying the night, the sounds she made and the conversation we'd had afterward.

"How are you so. . .unaffected by all this?" she'd asked.

"What do you mean?" I stilled at her words. Was this the part where she asked me for more, and I told her that more would never happen?

"Like, despite everything you've been through, you're not angry all the time," she said.

My brows rose in surprise. I got that question all the damn time, but I didn't expect it from her. "I'm not happy all the time either. You just haven't seen me when I'm angry." I shot her a look over my shoulder. "Count that as a blessing."

"Still." She sighed. "How are you happy at all?"

"Why wouldn't I be?" I turned to face her but stayed on this pillow while she stayed on hers. "Happiness is a choice. Why would I choose to be angry?"

"No one wants to be angry. We just are." Her brows were pinched. "How do you make that choice despite everything?"

I realized she was probably asking so she could have this in her arsenal when she married that douchebag, but I didn't know what to say. I didn't have time to sit here and recount all of the shitty years I'd gone through before getting to the place I was at now. I didn't want to tell her that I used to be very fucking angry all of the time, and the only thing that helped was using people as punching bags. If she was going to keep one image of me, I wanted it to be this one but saying I was happy all the time was total bullshit.

"I was angry for a long time. I still am sometimes, but I don't let my demons control me. I

don't let them win. I've trained myself to be happy the way I trained myself to disassociate when I need to do shit I don't want to do. It's not an easy choice to make, but it's better than the other option."

She set a hand over my heart. *"Do your demons ever come out? Like when you. . .deal with people?"*

My mouth twitched. "Yep."

"Is that when you let yourself be angry?"

"I guess it depends on how much money they owe me." I smiled at the way her eyes widened even more.

"Oh."

"Oh?" I smiled. "Just 'oh'?"

"I know you have to do bad things, but you're a good man, Rocco Marchetti."

I could tell she meant it, but I was done talking. I trailed my hand down her body until I reached her cunt. Her breath hitched. I knew she was probably sore, but she opened up her legs for me anyway. Blind trust was the only term I could think of when it came to her. She offered me blind trust. I didn't deserve it, but fuck, who was I to turn it down?

Fuck. I needed to stop thinking about what happened, but the smell of her, the taste of her, the feel of her was too fucking good. She had the kind of pussy I could easily become addicted to, which was exactly why I wasn't doing it again.

I set the glass down and sat back, still watching her. She was wearing a top that looked like it belonged in the 1800s, all tight around the waist, with strings in the back and her tits nearly spilling out of the top. It would be easy to take one out and suck on it. Her eyes found mine, and she shimmied in her chair as if she could hear my thoughts. I felt myself smile and forced myself to look away. My eyes landed on Yaritza, who was using her cellphone camera as a mirror to fix her hair. Lenora had been trying to be nice to her all morning, but I could tell she was still bothered by how Yari acted around me last night. Usually, I'd leave it alone and let Lenora jump to whatever conclusion she wanted. I didn't like explaining myself to anyone, especially jealous women. Call it after-fucking remorse, but I suddenly wanted to explain myself or at least let her know there was nothing there.

"Any luck with Jimmy?" I asked Yari.

"He's too nice." She pouted at me. "I told you I need a bad boy, but you won't give me the time of day."

"You have serious issues." I laughed and looked over at Lenora, who was frowning and looking down at the menu like it had answers to all her burning questions. She seemed troubled this morning, and I didn't like it.

"That took forever." Dom set a drink down in front of me and one in front of his brother as he took a seat and looked at Rosie. "What time is Cat's show tonight?"

"Eight. Emma is picking up Enrique at the airport," Rosie said, typing on her phone. "Isabel and Gio are home already. Dean wants to hold a meeting tonight."

"Says who?" I asked. How the hell did Rosie know this, and we hadn't even gotten a text?

"Dean is at their house, and he just told Loren, and Loren told Cat, and Cat told me." She raised her brows like it was apparent.

"I won't go," Dom said, setting a hand over hers. "It's your birthday."

She smiled. "You can leave me alone for a few hours, Dom. I won't mind."

The server came back with our food. He kept flirting with Lenora and staring at her tits, driving me crazy. What the hell was wrong with me? I took a breath. Her magic pussy. That was what was wrong with me. It was the only reason I took my phone out and texted her.

Me: stop smiling at the server

I saw a smile touch her lips as she typed.

Lenora: jealous?
Me: let's not do this again

She looked up at me and raised an eyebrow—a challenge. My jaw tensed. No, fuck that. I'd reached my limit with the little jealous games last night. The last thing I needed was for her to openly flirt with the server. When he returned and set a glass of water in front of her, she smiled wider, batting her lashes at him as if he'd just given her a gold brick. My fingers worked like I was possessed.

Me: don't push me, Principessa. You won't like the outcome

It was the closest thing to admitting that I was jealous. She didn't respond to the text, but her smile was blinding. I shouldn't have texted her. I shouldn't even care if she smiled at the server, but I was sulking at the thought of another man's hands on her. I took a breath and cleared our text messages. She'd be married in less than two weeks, and then another man would have his hands on her for the rest of her days. There was nothing I could do about that. I opened up the group chat with the guys. It's a bullshit excuse for a text chat, considering there are no real conversations. I typed out a text asking what time the meeting is. When I finished, I checked the numbers for Scarab last night. I'd been there for opening night on Friday, but since it was Rosie's birthday weekend and John wasn't working at Gio's club, I'd paid him a generous amount of money to go to Scarab and run it. I'd also asked him to find me a manager. John was good at that shit.

Dom's phone started buzzing. He looked at it and frowned but answered immediately. "I thought you were leaving town?"

Lenora stiffened. I watched her as she looked at her brother. Dom just kept saying a series of "uh-huh" and "no fucking way" and "Nah, that's impossible" over and over. When he hung up, he let out a whistled breath.

"What happened?" Lenora asked, sitting up straighter.

"Someone broke into the Connecticut house," Dom said, brows pulled.

"How?" Gabe asked.

"When?" I asked. "Last night?"

"He doesn't know."

"He wasn't there?" Gabe asked.

"No. He got there yesterday and noticed a few things missing."

"A few things like what?" I asked. Giuseppe's homes looked like art galleries. Anything a robber would have stolen would be worth millions.

"Who would do that?" Rosie asked.

"He'll find out soon enough. He has cameras everywhere," Gabe said.

"He's going through the footage of the last month. It's going to take a while," Dom said.

"Wow," Yari breathed. "I've only met him once in passing, and he was nice to me since I was with Rosie, but even I know not to mess with that man."

"Excuse me," Lenora said, setting her napkin on the table. "I have to go to the restroom."

I looked at the front of the restaurant and ensured a guard was there. There were two in the back where the restrooms were, so I knew she'd be safe, but I needed to know why she suddenly looked uncomfortable. Who was she texting? Had they scared her? I texted my brother.

Me: Call me

My phone rang a second later. "Mikey's calling. Be right back."

"What's going on?" he said when I answered.

"Nothing. I needed an excuse to get up from the table. Thanks for calling."

"Since when do you need excuses to do anything?" He stayed quiet, waiting for me to answer. When I didn't, he said, "Roc, I don't know what you're up to, but you better be fucking careful."

"Who said I'm up to anything?"

"Your silence."

I groaned. "I'll be careful, Dad."

"I'm serious, Roc."

"I know you are. It's nothing to worry about. Listen, I have to go."

I hung up the phone as I reached the bathrooms. I'd deal with my brother later. The bathrooms were all unisex, so I tried each of them. Only one was locked. I knocked on that one.

"I'll be right out."

"Open the door."

I couldn't hear it, but I swore she caught her breath. I waited. Waited. I knocked one time, loudly. "Now, Lenora."

She unlocked the door. I stepped in, shut the door with the bottom of my shoe, and locked it behind me. She was looking down and sniffling, so I gave her a minute. When she looked up, it was obvious she'd been crying—mascara clumped and puffy lips. I hadn't kissed her last night. I wasn't sure why, but I regretted it as I jerked off this morning. Seeing her lips like this, all I wanted to do was kiss her. So I did, because what the fuck difference did it make if I crossed another line? I stepped forward, cupped her face, and brought my mouth down on hers. I meant for it to be hard, but our lips moved slowly. Her tongue sought mine first and I granted permission immediately, deepening the kiss, holding her face closer to mine, lifting her ass with my other hand, and slamming her back against the wall as the kiss turned frenzied. Fuck. I was already hard and having difficulty remembering what made me come after her. I pulled away.

"What's wrong?" I asked against her lips.

Her eyes welled with new tears, her lip wobbling. I backed away and let her set her feet on the ground. Tears didn't bother me. I'd made grown-ass men cry. Crystal was always fucking crying, and it annoyed me most of the time. Seeing Lenora cry didn't sit well with me. She was already going through enough and was too innocent to suffer.

"Tell me." I lifted her face so she'd look at me. Tears slid down her face, and I leaned down and licked them before they reached her mouth. Even that tasted good. Jesus.

"You shouldn't be here, Rocco," she whispered.

"Tell me what's wrong."

"I. . ." she shook her head, averting her eyes. "You shouldn't be here."

"Lenora."

"I'm fine," she said, closing her eyes and taking a deep breath. "I'm fine."

I stared at her, feeling completely out of my depth. For all I knew, I was the reason she was crying. Did she regret last night? My chest felt heavy at the thought because if that was the case, I couldn't help her. I couldn't give back what she gave me, what I willingly took, and if I were being honest, I wouldn't even if I could. Maybe that made me a selfish bastard, but she'd trusted me. Would they check for her hymen? Was that what she worried about? Fuck. It would make perfect sense if she were worried about that.

"Is this about last night? Do you regret it?" I asked.

"What?" Her eyes flashed to mine. "Of course not. Last night was special for me. I would never regret it."

"It was special for me too." She bit her lip and tried to turn away. I cupped her face and held her chin so she'd look at me. "What is it?"

"You've had sex countless times. I'm sure a lot of them were special. That will be my only special time."

"Lenora." I closed my eyes briefly to take a breath.

I had done a lot of fucked up things in the past and accepted guilt for them all, including the ones I had tucked away and tried to forget. Breaking this girl's heart wasn't something I wanted to add to that list. She was too pure and deserved better. As I opened my eyes, I found her waiting for me to say something else. I knew she wanted some kind of declaration of love or some bullshit that I couldn't give her, so I gave her the truth.

"None have been as special as last night. I mean that," I said.

A quiet sob left her lips. Unable to see the pain any longer, I wrapped my arms around her and set my chin on her head.

"I can't do this," she whispered, and I knew she was talking about her wedding.

"You're so strong, baby. You can do anything," I whispered against her hair, inhaling her scent once more before I pulled away.

She reached up, grabbed my face, and kissed me. It was a soft yet demanding kiss that made my insides quake with something terrifying. It felt like a goodbye. I'd always hated goodbyes.

CHAPTER FIFTEEN

Rocco

"WHAT HAPPENED WITH MY SISTER THE OTHER NIGHT?" THAT was Dom's voice behind me, nearly giving me a heart attack with his question.

My hands stilled on the deck of cards I'd been shuffling. My stomach squeezed. *What happened with his sister?* Motherfucker. He was going to try to kill me, and even though I could have him on the ground in ten seconds, I would have to let him kill me because what I'd done was unforgivable. I hadn't reached out to Lenora because I wanted to give her space. Quite frankly, I wanted to get away. I felt Dean's eyes on me, and I wanted to tell him to go to hell. However, I kept my head down and played cards as if I were unaware he was addressing me. For all I knew, he could have been speaking to Russo.

"Marchetti," Dom snapped.

My stomach squeezed the way it did before the interrogations I'd done. And like I'd done before every single one of them, I emptied my thoughts and kept my cool. I turned around and looked at Dominic, my partner in crime, a man I'd known since the day I was born. Twenty-eight years of friendship, of sharing everything from test answers to women. Never in all of those years had I lied to him. I hated that I would have to start now, but I quickly slipped into mission mode.

"What are you talking about?" I asked. "What night?"

"Any night." He ran a hand through his hair. "At the bar, at Rosie's party. Any night. Yari said she saw her speaking to you. What did she say?"

Of course. Fucking Yari. I frowned. "Nothing of importance. She told me about school and bartending and clarified that she didn't want to get married."

"Fuck." He kicked the chair next to me. I sat perfectly still as I assessed him. He looked at me again, a wild look in his eyes he only got when he was about to lose it. I set the cards down and stood up slowly.

"What the fuck happened?" I asked with a calmness that I did not feel.

"I. . ." He took a breath.

"Spit it out already, De Luca," Dean said behind me.

"She's gone."

The entire world seemed to stop at that moment. I blinked. I assessed his posture, the situation, and the words he'd just spoken. I didn't trust myself to speak yet. I needed one more second. Thankfully, Gio couldn't keep his mouth shut and asked for me as he walked back into the room.

"Who's gone?" He took a sip of the homemade lemonade Rosie had sent. Fucking homemade lemonade in a mob house.

"My sister," Dom shouted. "She's fucking gone."

"What do you mean go—" I started, but Dom's wild eyes cut off my question.

"She left. She grabbed a bag and left, and no one knows where the fuck she is, and my father is losing his everloving mind."

"Fuck," I breathed, sitting my ass back in the seat.

I thought about the kiss in the bathroom of that restaurant and how it felt like a goodbye. She meant it as such. She knew she'd be leaving and said goodbye without actually saying it. I figured it was because she was going to marry that asshole, not because she was going to. . .

"Did she run away?" I asked.

"Was she kidnapped?" Russo asked at the same time.

We both looked at each other then, my confused eyes

turning lethal, his questioning ones turning into more questions. I turned to Dom.

"No, she wasn't kidnapped." He laughed sharply, taking out his cell phone.

The five of us hovered over the screen. Even before he pressed play, I felt something twist in my stomach because I knew that the hallway led to Giuseppe's home office, and Lenora was at the end of the hall. He pushed play, and we watched as she hurried into his office. In the next clip, she looked like she was searching everywhere for something until she sat and sagged down into her father's chair. Her body moved until she hit the floor, and there she was for a long time. From this angle, we couldn't tell exactly what she was doing, but when she finally stood back up, she had two things in her hand: a notebook and something small.

"She stole my father's ledger and USB drive," Dom said, pushing the side button on his phone as he started to pace again.

I sat back in my chair.

Dean sat back in his.

Lorenzo and Gio both took a fucking seat.

No one spoke.

Stealing from Giuseppe De Luca was a death sentence, and I wasn't sure how he'd apply that to his daughter, but considering that he'd killed his older brother with his bare hands, I didn't like the odds. Would he kill her? Maybe not. Would he hurt her? Fuck yeah, he would. My mind raced, trying to figure out how he could hurt her and how I could stop it from happening. He'd already fucked up her life. The last thing she needed was for him to fuck it up more.

"Have you spoken to her mother?" I asked, finally breaking the silence.

"Her phone is off. Her mom's in surgery."

"Hypothetically speaking," Dean started. "I assume your

father already has all his men looking for her. What will happen once he gets ahold of her?"

"Fuck." Dom's eyes squeezed shut as he sank into his usual seat. "I can't think about that."

"What about Adriano? Does he know about this?" Gio asked.

Dom's eyes opened and formed slits. "As soon as my father realized what was missing, he called Adriano and told him she'd run away."

"Fuck," Loren breathed out, speaking for the first time.

I couldn't breathe, let alone speak, so I stayed quiet.

"His men will go after her," Dean said. "Adriano won't let her make a fool of him."

Dom's phone buzzed. From the way his eyes widened, it could only be his father or his sister. He answered without indulging us. He listened. Nodded without saying anything. Listened.

"Okay," was all he said as he hung up.

We waited.

He took a deep breath and let it out. "The USB drive has a tracker."

"And?" I asked calmly.

"She's in Florida." He looked me square in the eyes. His were filled with a concern I hadn't seen in a long time. "We need to get to her before they do."

BECAUSE I'M YOURS

CHAPTER SIXTEEN

Lenora

I DROPPED MY BAG BY THE DOOR, LOCKED IT, AND LET OUT A BREATH as I turned around and looked at the apartment. It was part of a hotel, a "room" she bought from the owner. All of their "rooms" were fully furnished apartments. Mom's faced the beach. Deep down, I understood why my mother couldn't share this with me, but it still hurt. How long had she had it? Who had she shared it with? I looked around, searching for answers to those questions. She had pictures of us in the bedroom: my fourth birthday, me with Aanya on the beach, and one with my parents at their vineyard as we toasted my graduation. I set that last one down and sat at the edge of the bed, thinking about how long it had been since I had seen them.

Some sort of code to my father's ledger made it impossible to understand. I thought it was the initials of people who owed him money and the amounts, but I couldn't be sure. I hadn't even tried to look at what was in the USB drive. I was going to on the flight over, but I was terrified of what I'd find. My father was not a good man. I knew that better than anyone, but that didn't mean I wanted proof. I'd taken this as a bargaining chip, not a way to throw its contents in his face. I stared at my bag for a long moment, weighing out whether or not I should look at what was on it.

I wondered why my father hadn't stored the ledger and USB drive in his safe, and I had two ideas: either he was so arrogant that he thought no one could ever steal from him, or he didn't trust anyone with this. All of us kids had the codes to the safes;

Dad kept some money and business contracts there, things that wouldn't hurt him if someone broke into the home. Home invaders would have found the ledger easily, but they wouldn't have been able to interpret it. The USB drive he had placed so deep in the bottom of the desk that it would take too long to uncover it. I knew Dad wasn't stupid. He'd know it was me soon enough. I was counting on that, though. After my mini-deliberation, I took a deep breath, grabbed my laptop and the USB drive, and opened the files.

CHAPTER SEVENTEEN

Rocco

I'D BEEN SITTING ACROSS FROM EMILE FOR TWENTY MINUTES, BUT IT felt like three days. My mind wouldn't quit racing, but I let him do his job without interrupting. Emile was one of the best hackers we knew and had worked with me for a private company that the CIA didn't want anyone to know about. I trusted him implicitly and knew he would do this job well. I just wished he did it faster. Dean was sitting next to me, waiting to hear from his contact. Giuseppe had the manpower to hunt down anyone, but he wasn't in his territory. Lenora would have already been found if he'd been back in Italy. We had the upper hand here. As we waited, I thought about Lenora and tried not to get upset again, but it was impossible. I was fucking furious that she'd just left like that without telling us. We would have helped her. *I* would have helped her. Fuck. I could have whisked her away and ensured that Russo made it so no one would ever retrace us. That made me pause. What the fuck was I thinking? I had businesses to run. I couldn't just disappear. I wanted to keep her safe but didn't want to disappear. I wouldn't do that for her, or anyone.

"I downloaded the camera feeds from the street and lobby." Emile looked at us over his laptop. "I'm sending you the files and deleting the feed."

I breathed a little easier.

"I'm having Carlos check the cameras from Pensacola to Marco Island," Dean said.

Emile let out a whistle. "That's a lot of territory. It'll take a while."

He wasn't wrong, but it was the only thing we knew for certain. Giuseppe had told Dominic that she was off the Gulf Coast of Florida. Dom was still trying to get ahold of Lenora's mother, but I'd grown impatient. I found out what hospital her mother was at and would visit her tonight. Dom couldn't leave without his father figuring out something was wrong, but I could. I just hoped her mother wouldn't throw her under the bus.

The nurses at Baptist Hospital were nice enough and led me to the waiting room of the wing that Lenora's grandmother was in. I'd told them I'd stay there until her mother came out. I told them it was urgent. I lowered the ballcap on my head when I spotted who I assumed was one of Giuseppe's men guarding the area. He blended in just enough with his jeans and a gray t-shirt. You would think he was just waiting for someone, but the way he walked said otherwise. He had a knife strapped to his leg. I couldn't see it, but I could tell. I wouldn't be surprised if he brought his gun in here, even though guns in hospitals were illegal and a bad idea for countless reasons. I didn't bring mine, but I didn't need one. I was the weapon. I kept my head down either way, because if they saw me talking to Mrs. De Luca, this plan could blow up in my face. I called Emile, who answered right away.

"I need the cameras on the second floor of the oncology building shut down," I said quietly. "All of them."

"On it." He hung up.

I kept my eye on the door. When it finally opened, Lenora's mother rushed out and saw me. Her face paled. I put both hands up to let her know I wasn't a threat, but she still calculated everything before she took another step. She was a sharp woman; she'd been married to Giuseppe long enough and was studying her surroundings, as she should. She put a finger up, and the man in jeans walked over. I cursed under my breath. I studied the man. He studied me. I knew I could take him down, but I also knew it would be a hell of a fight. Fuck my life. I didn't have time for that right now.

"He answers to me, not Giuseppe," Mrs. De Luca said as she walked over.

"Did he send you for me?" she asked quietly.

"No."

Something flashed in her face. Concern. Sadness. "For my daughter, then."

"No one sent me," I said. "I'm here on my own."

"Why?"

"A lot of people are looking for your daughter right now. It's best if I find her first."

She let out a harsh laugh. "Please. I know what you do. If I tell you where she is, you'll take her back to her father or worse."

"There are worse people than your husband?" I crossed my arms. "Enlighten me."

She blushed and looked down with a sigh. "Look, my mother is dying. Every minute I'm here with you is another I'm not with her."

"I'm sorry," I said. "Nothing hurts as much as losing a mother."

She swallowed and nodded as she asked again, "Why are you here? Where is Dominic?"

"Back in New York. We couldn't risk being followed."

"And you're sure no one followed you?" She raised an eyebrow. My eyes swung to the guard next to her, momentarily wishing he'd vouch for me so we can just get this over with. I knew he was a jarhead like me. That alone should be enough reason for him to vouch for me. He didn't.

"Look, Mrs. De Luca. . ."

"Sofia," she said.

"Sofia, I need to get to your daughter before anyone else does."

"What makes you think I know where she is?"

"Call it a hunch."

She studied me for a moment. I wasn't sure what she was searching for on my face, but I knew she wouldn't find it. I waited patiently for her next question or statement. She'd either try to quiz me to figure out if I was telling the truth about her husband not sending me, or tell me to go fuck myself. Either way, I was prepared. I wouldn't hurt her, but I'd need to plead my case until she understood that we were running out of time.

"Where's Russo?" she asked.

"Back in New York."

"You're here completely on your own?"

"That's what I said."

"Did you volunteer to come?"

"Yes."

"Why?" She studied me again. I knew exactly what she was asking me. As if to ensure I understood, she added, "Do you care about my daughter?"

Christ. I laughed quietly. I couldn't help it. I was going to be fucked in so many ways when this fiasco was done. If I survived Giuseppe, I'd still have to deal with Dominic's wrath. It was a fair question. It was also the only bargaining chip I had left to play with her mother.

"Yes." It was a simple enough answer and the truth.

She arched an eyebrow. "Does she know?"

"I . . ." I frowned. Did she know? She knew I wanted to fuck her, but did she know I cared about her? I thought of the bathroom that Sunday morning and decided she must have known I didn't go around holding women while they cried and promising them I'd take care of them. I cleared my throat and gave her another truth. "I think so."

"Do her brothers know?"

"No." I rubbed a spot on the back of my neck that felt like it was burning. I wasn't used to dealing with mothers, especially not the mother of someone I'd fucked. This was making me feel like I was fifteen all over again.

"She's getting married," she said with a sad lilt.

"I know," I said. "I know this is impossible for many different reasons. . ."

"Dangerous," she supplied. "It's dangerous. They'll kill you. Maybe not Dominic, but Giuseppe and Adriano will kill you."

"I know that as well."

"And yet, you came alone." She blinked a couple of times like she couldn't wrap her head around that.

"With all due respect, Sofia, I don't need backup."

She searched my eyes. "Are you willing to die for my daughter?"

"Yes." No hesitation. I felt as surprised as she looked.

"I'll tell you where she is." She took a shaky breath. "But you have to promise me, swear to me, that you'll keep her safe."

"You have my word," I said as she handed me a card. I looked at it. Naples. She was in fucking Naples. "Do you have someplace safe to go?"

"Do you think I'm in danger?" she asked, an edge to her voice.

"I think you know your husband better than I do, but I'd stay vigilant."

"I need to stay with my mother."

I looked at the man next to her and nodded. I'd told her I didn't need backup. If I told her she needed more security, I'd be a hypocrite and it would be a slap in the face to the man protecting her. I had no doubt she'd be safe. Giuseppe was a monster, but I knew he wouldn't harm his wife or his children. As I walked out of the hospital, I replayed our conversation. *Are you willing to die for my daughter?* I didn't hesitate with my answer, and as I tried to analyze it from every angle, giving myself an out,

I found none. Once upon a time, I'd been willing to die for my country. I'd always been willing to die for my brothers, bound by blood and shared secrets we'd take to our graves. I'd been willing to protect women I'd been with in the past, of course. If they were attacked, I'd defend them. I wasn't a fucking asshole. But die for them? Fuck no, I wouldn't die for them. Yet, I knew, beyond a doubt, that I would gladly give my life to save Lenora. She was too innocent for all of this shit.

CHAPTER EIGHTEEN

Lenora

THE WATER WAS WARM AS IT HIT MY TOES BURIED IN THE SAND. IT
was blissful here. The beach was pretty deserted. Few people
were fortunate enough to take random weekdays off to enjoy
this. I closed my eyes and laughed when I felt a splash on my
stomach. I'd been sunbathing when two little kids decided they
wanted to build a sandcastle beside me. I peeked my right eye
open and found one of them staring at me, his dark curly hair
covered in sand.

"What happened to your castle?" I sat up and leaned forward to wash the sand off my hands.

"It won't stay," the older one said.

I look at what they had to work with. They had two plastic
buckets, one red and one blue, and sea animal shapes—a dolphin,
a turtle, and a starfish. I hadn't been exposed to many children.
My older family members were much older, and all their kids
were in their twenties and early thirties. I knew Nadia and Tony's
kids, but it wasn't like I saw them often. I'd always said I wanted
to have kids at twenty-five. Now that I knew it was on the hori-
zon, I wanted to revolt against it. I looked at these two. One had
to be around five, and the other maybe six or seven. They were
cute and inquisitive, but it wasn't like my ovaries kicked when I
saw them. Rosie said whenever she saw a baby, she wanted one.
Each time she said it, my brother took her in his arms and acted
like she was something fragile to be worshiped. It was beautiful and depressing.

"Where are your parents?" I asked.

They both looked at the two beach chairs and pointed. I looked over, and their mother smiled and waved at us. I waved back with a smile. A man was lying on his stomach, his left hand hanging to the side, a book he'd been reading discarded on the sand. I assumed it was their father.

"Do you know how to build a castle?" the older one asked.

"Yes." I pressed my hands back into the sand and closed my eyes, tilting my face towards the sun.

"Can you help us build it?" the younger one asked, his little voice sounding too sweet to say no to.

I sighed and sat up, looking at the two of them again. They were relentless, these two. They reminded me of my brothers. "I'll teach you, but you'll have to build it yourself."

An hour later, I'd built two sand castles. When my stomach started growling, I told them I needed to leave. The sun was setting anyway. I would shower, open a bottle of wine, and order room service. I'd started watching 90 Day Fiancé and was hooked. As I set my things down in the room and kicked off my flip-flops, I took a deep breath, taking it all in. I'd only been here two days and was already dreading leaving. I was at peace here, away from everyone. I wish I could have brought the girls with me, their husbands, and Rocco. I bit my lip and beelined straight for the bathroom as I thought about him.

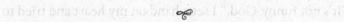

I was soaking in the tub when I thought I heard a noise. More accurately, I'd been touching myself soaking in the tub when I thought I heard it. I hadn't ordered room service yet, so I knew it couldn't be that. Maybe someone had checked into the place next door. I shrugged it off and returned to what I was doing, closing my eyes and thinking about Rocco between my legs as I moved my fingers between them. His blue eyes were on mine as he kissed down my stomach and settled between my legs.

He touched me and licked me until I was screaming his name. I gasped, arching my back and moving my fingers faster as I pictured him touching himself before he pounded into me, and then I was gone, my orgasm washing over me like a wave. I set a hand on my heart to calm it and got out of the tub. I dried off and wrapped a towel around myself and another on my head. The room was dark now, and the only light was that of the moon. It was all I needed, anyway, as I walked over to the bed and picked up the phone to order room service. I hung up when I was done and let myself fall onto the bed with an oomph.

"I have to say, the only thing that rivals you coming on my face is watching you make yourself come and chant my name."

At the sound of his voice, I screamed and sat up in bed. He turned on a floor lamp and remained seated in the chair on the side of the room. I set a hand over my pounding heart and backed up on the bed as I stared at him, unsure if this was real or a dream. It had to be a dream because how the fuck would he have found me? I thought about my mother's words and how she'd said they'd send a Marchetti or Russo after me. And there he was, sitting with his leg crossed at the ankle, wearing khakis and a blue polo that matched his eyes, looking like a fucking Ralph Lauren ad. My heart kept pounding. He raised an eyebrow.

"What the hell, Rocco?" I yelled. "What the hell?"

His mouth twitched.

"It's not funny. God." I set a hand on my heart and tried to focus on breathing, but it was impossible.

"You want to talk about things that aren't funny, Principessa?" He stood up, his amusement replaced by something that made my stomach clench as he prowled over. That was what his gait reminded me of: a prowl. A tiger's. A lion's. Some kind of fierce animal that was ready to pounce on prey. His expression was closed off. Serious. Scary. He stopped before me, and I craned my neck to look at him as he leaned over me. "It's not funny to disappear and not tell anyone where you are. It's not funny that you trusted me with your virginity and not with this. It's not fucking funny for you to be here living the good life while we're going out of our fucking minds with worry."

"Is that why you're here?" I asked, my voice as weak and shaky as I felt. "Because you were worried? Or are you here to hunt me down?"

"Hunt you down? That's oddly specific." He raised an eyebrow. "Tell me, Principessa. Did the person who told you about me tell you what I would do if I hunted you down?"

"No," I gasped, finding it harder to breathe.

He covered my throat with his hand. "Use your imagination. What would I do if I was hunting you?"

My eyes blurred with tears. "Kill me?"

"Kill you?" Amusement lit his blue eyes as he took his hand away. "And you think I'd kill you?"

"Maybe? I don't know." I squeaked. "God. Rocco, just tell me. What are you going to do with me?"

His smile was as feral as the animals that pounce. When he held my throat again, it was to pull me into a bruising kiss.

CHAPTER NINETEEN

Rocco

AFTER MY MOTHER WAS MURDERED, I BECAME A VERY ANGRY teenager. People thought I went into the military to follow in Michael's footsteps. The truth was, I had no option. I didn't know how to kill someone and get away with it. I was fighting anyone and everyone who got in my face. I got my ass kicked a couple of times because of it. Then, Mikey sat me down on the eve of what would've been our mother's birthday, and told me that if I didn't want to end up dead or in jail, I should join the military. "The Marines will be a good fit for you," he'd said. I listened, obviously, and was turned into a human weapon. Then, they turned me into a monster. I had a lot to thank them for. Having to learn to hold back and not unleash when I got angry was something I wouldn't have discovered how to do on my own.

Even when I went to laundromats and bodegas to collect a payment, I didn't unleash that version of myself. Even when I'd helped my friends execute their vengeance against whoever hurt their women, I didn't unleash him. Finding Lenora De Luca in a tiny red bikini having the time of her life made the monster roar, not because she was safe and had us worried. Not because one of her father's men could find her there at any moment. The monster roared at the thought of handing her over to that motherfucker Adriano. This unexpected, complicated reaction made me decide right then and there that I wouldn't. If I had to kill every duke and duchess, king and queen, and whatever other bullshit titles these idiots decided to claim for themselves, so be it. I wasn't doing it because I wanted her to be with me. I knew that would be messy and complicated. I was doing it because she deserved this freedom.

I'd been watching her for the better part of the day, trying to figure out the best time to make my presence known. I'd watched her play with the kids at the beach, building sand castles as they ran around her laughing. I'd called Dom to let him know I had eyes on her as I watched her from afar, her brown hair whipping around her face, her perfect body in that bikini, her smile and little claps when the kids got the hang of how to build sandcastles and did it without her help. My heart ached at the scene. Fucking ached. I'd gone into her room to wait for her. I was going to speak up as soon as she opened the door, but I just wanted to watch her for a little while longer. I was going to tell her when she went into the bathroom, but I was afraid she'd slip and get hurt, so I waited some more, giving her privacy to wash off. And then I heard her moan my name, and my eyes snapped up from the text I'd been writing my brother. I hadn't come here to hook up with her. I'd already told myself it was out of the question. I needed to keep this professional and take her to a safe place until we planned our next move. My name on her lips threatened to throw me over the edge, though.

That and the fact that she didn't trust me with this. She trusted me with her virginity, but not her safety? I went from turned on to angry in less than a minute. By the time she'd ordered room service, I had to shut my eyes and focus on breathing so I didn't explode. So, I sat. I waited. I finally made my presence known. I'd expected her to freak out, be angry, relieved. I didn't know. But fear? Fear of me? I hadn't expected that. When she said the word "hunt," I knew someone had told her some elaborate, bullshit story about me. And then she asked what I would do with her, so I kissed her. Hard. It took her a second to react, but when she did, she wrapped her legs around me, wrapped her arms around my neck, and kissed me back fiercely. I groaned against her mouth when I felt the heat of her pussy on the front of my shirt. The towel fell on the bed as I carried her in my right arm, my left hand reaching for the ridiculous towel around her head and tossing it. She pulled back for a moment, just a moment to catch her breath, and then her mouth was on me again. She kissed me like she'd let this scene play out in her head millions of times. Like she'd been ready for me to walk through that door. Fuck, I hoped she was ready. Not breaking the kiss, I sat down on the armchair by the french doors that led to the balcony, my hands gripping her ass cheeks as she continued to shove her tongue in my mouth to dance with mine. I pulled away this time and looked at her. Her skin was flushed, her lips puffy, and her eyes shone. I was going to fuck that mouth of hers. I'd fuck every single hole in her body if she let me.

"Are you scared of me?" I asked, watching her expression morph from awe to a confused frown.

"No."

"No?" I lifted an eyebrow. She looked away. I grabbed her chin and made her look at me again. She shut her eyes briefly. When she opened them, she looked a little sad.

"I'm sorry I said that," she whispered. "I know you wouldn't hurt me. I was in shock, is all."

I gripped the nape of her neck and pulled her lips back to mine. When we broke the kiss again, she lifted my shirt over my head and took my pants off. I planted kisses on her jawline, neck, and chest until I got to her tits and started licking and nipping those. She had the perfect little nipples and the perfect tits. I covered them with my hands and squeezed. She threw back her head and moaned as she rolled her hips over my hard cock.

"Oh god, " she said in a gasp as I continued playing with her nipples.

I was sure I could make her come like this, but I didn't want to. I wanted to make her come a million different ways, but right now, I wanted her to stay on top of me. I slapped her ass to get her attention. She gasped and straightened, her hands still on my chest.

"Ride my cock like a good girl."

"I don't know if I. . ." She looked down at my dick and back at me. I lifted and positioned her, not looking away from those beautiful brown eyes.

"Get on my cock and ride it, Lenora." My voice was gruff in my ears. She arched into me when I squeezed her hips.

Her hands grabbed the sides of the chair as she sank onto it slowly. My eyes screwed shut, and I threw my head back at the feel of her walls enclosing me. She was so wet. So ready. I looked at her again. Her face was pinched, and she bit her lip like she was in agony. I held her hips again, helping her go slow. I needed to remember that she'd only been fucked once—twice—for the first time the other night. This position was new to her. My heart was pounding hard when she finally had me fully inside her. Her eyes were watery, and she looked like she was struggling to breathe. If this had been any other woman, I wouldn't have cared to ask any questions. I would've pounded into her without care.

I reached up and cupped her face. "Okay?"

"You're too big," she whispered.

"You're already on me, baby." I kissed her, biting and sucking her bottom lip into my mouth. "Go slow if you have to."

I don't know why the fuck I said that. She set her hands on my shoulders and started rocking her hips slowly, coating my cock with her juices. She was driving me crazy with her sounds each time my cock hit her in a certain spot. I bit my tongue to keep myself from coming. She was so fucking beautiful. Her wet brown hair slowly curled as she moved. Her eyebrows pinched like she was concentrating on a fucking test and needed to pass it. Her eyes shone with a light I'd only seen the last time I fucked her. It was almost too much to bear, but I was an expert in endurance.

"Fuck," she said as she started moving a little faster. I took a hand off her hip and tweaked her nipple. "O-oh, my G-g-od."

"Keep moving just like that, Principessa." I pressed my mouth to hers again, a searing kiss that ran to my toes. "Fuck. Yes. Just like that."

"I'm gonna. . ." She was gasping for breath as she moved. I felt her tightening around my cock.

"Don't you dare, Lenora." I pinched her nipple hard enough to make her yelp. "Don't you dare come without permission." I took my hand off her nipple and slid it between us, pressing my thumb against her clit.

Her eyes widened as she shook her head frantically and stopped moving altogether. "I can't. If you do that, I won't be able—"

I slapped her ass. "Did I tell you to stop?"

"Rocco." Her moan was loud as she started to move again.

"Bounce on my cock." I moved my thumb in slow circles against her clit. When I felt her clench around me again, I stopped and smiled at the glare she shot me.

"This isn't funny." She hit my chest. "This is not fair, Rocco."

"Ah." That made me chuckle. "You want me to be fair, then."

"I want you to. . ." Her lip wobbled, and tears filled her eyes when I moved my thumb again, then stopped while I used my other hand to move her up and down on my cock. I was less than ten seconds away from coming, so I had to let her do it anyway, but her face, those tears of pure need. Fuck.

"What do you want, Principessa?" I bit her lower lip. "Tell me."

"You know what I want." She screamed when I took away my thumb and started pulling her with both hands on her hips, so her body was moving back and forth now, her clit hitting my pelvis, causing friction against her clit. I ducked down and pulled her other nipple into my mouth. She bit her lip, trying hard to hold back her orgasm. "Oh, my fucking. . .Rocco."

I took my hand off her hip and brought it to her other nipple, licking and tweaking them both. She stopped moving.

"Please, please, please." She was openly crying now.

I grabbed her hips again and began to move her, up and down, up and down. She stopped moving when I let her go and started gyrating her hips slowly.

"Move." I slapped her ass hard.

"Please." Her bottom lip trembled. I leaned forward and took it into my mouth again.

"Come, Lenora. Come all over my cock."

Her body shook as she finally let go, my name a scream from her lips as she threw her head back. I pulled out of her and pumped my cock once, twice, and came all over her stomach, her chest, and some of her chin. The doorbell rang, and we both snapped out of our post-orgasm haze.

"The food," she said, scrambling to her feet, swaying a little before she gathered her bearings. "Coming!"

"Again?" I smirked when she shot me a look.

"I have your come all over me. I can't open the door like this."

I reached for my shirt, stood up, and dressed her. It was long enough that it went to her ass. The doorbell rang again. I spanked her. "Go."

"Rocco." She shot me a look. "This isn't helping."

"Do you want me to open the door completely naked?"

"No." She scowled, looking down at herself where my come was slowly slipping down her leg. Fuck, that was hot.

I stood up, put on my briefs, and walked to the door.

"Rocco!" she hissed behind me, but I was already there, opening the door for the young man delivering her food. He looked at me, eyes wide as he looked down at my half-hard dick in my briefs and set his hands on the table he'd rolled over here.

"I just, I'll just," he started.

"I got it," I said. I reached next to me, where I'd left my

bag earlier, and pulled out some money. I handed it to him and wheeled the food in. "Thank you."

"N-n-no, thank you." He smiled wide and bolted to the left.

"Lenora, your food is—"

"I cannot believe you just did that," she said, standing in front of me. She looked like one of those cartoons with smoke coming from their ears. It was adorable.

I kissed the tip of her nose. "Don't worry. I gave him a good tip."

CHAPTER TWENTY

Lenora

H E WAS CRUEL, MAKING ME SIT AND EAT MY FOOD WEARING A POLO stuck to my chest because of his come. It was uncomfortable, and I wanted to wash it off, but each time I tried to stand, Rocco gave me a stern look and told me to finish my food. He stood up, wiped down the television remote with a wipe from a Lysol travel pack, and sat back down as he turned it on. I was curious about why he freaking traveled with Lysol wipes, but I wasn't going to ask.

"Aren't you hungry?" I asked instead.

"Nah, I ate. I need you to finish eating so we can talk."

"When did you eat?" I stabbed my french fry in the little ketchup bottle and popped it

into my mouth. The last thing I wanted to do was talk, but he was here for a reason, and I knew we had to get on with it.

"I don't know. An hour ago, maybe two? They make pretty good pasta in that little

restaurant by the pool."

My chewing stopped, then slowed, then I picked up the pace and swallowed the french fry. "How long have you been here?"

"Hmmm. . ." He was flipping channels, not even paying attention to me. "Right before you started building sand castles."

My jaw dropped. That was a long time ago. Had he been in the room while I soaked in the tub? I felt myself go hot at the thought.

"What?" He glanced over at me, looked at my plate, and took a fry. "What's that face?"

"You heard me in the bathroom, didn't you?" I whispered, grabbing a fry and swirling it in the ketchup.

"You mean when you moaned my name as you touched yourself?"

I looked at my plate and shoved the fry in my mouth. This was beyond embarrassing.

"Lenora."

I kept my eyes on the plate.

"Lenora."

My eyes snapped up. "What?"

"I've had my face in your cunt. There's no need for you to be embarrassed about that," he said totally nonchalantly, as if having his face between a woman's legs was something he discussed all the time with his lovers.

"I guess that's true." I frowned. My chest burned at the thought of him and his lovers—the past, future, and maybe even the present ones.

He sighed heavily, tossing the remote aside. "What now?"

"Nothing." I shook my head and swallowed back my jealousy. It was pointless anyway. "Does my brother know you're here?"

"Yes."

"How did you find me?" I started eating one of the chicken tenders.

I'd ordered chicken tenders, french fries, and a chocolate milkshake for dinner. If he didn't think I was young and inexperienced before, I was sure this meal would do it. I didn't care anymore. I couldn't afford to.

"The USB drive you stole from your dad," he said. "Where is it?"

My ears swooshed with the beat of my pulse. My heart slowed down. Oh my God. Oh my God. My father knew. My father saw me steal his things. I wanted that, didn't I? I wanted to use this as a bargaining tool. I wanted him to know what I was capable of. Now that it was happening and Rocco freaking Marchetti was sitting across from me, I wasn't sure I wanted that anymore. My hands shook as I set the half-eaten chicken tender down. He was looking at me expectantly. There was no point in lying.

"I hid it under the mattress."

He gave a nod and stood up. I stayed in the kitchen/living room area and waited with my heart in my throat. If he took this from me, I would have nothing. He could use this and me as blackmail. I could be his bargaining chip if it turned out he wanted something from my dad and I had to be honest. Everyone wanted something from my dad. Fuck. I genuinely didn't think any of this would blow up in my face. He sat down across from me again, looking through the ledger.

"Do you understand it?" I asked. "It looks like it's written in code."

"What was on the USB drive?" He looked at me, his blue eyes no longer caring, lustful, or even scary. They were just blank—another side of him I hadn't seen.

"I don't know."

"What do you mean you don't know?" he asked, letting out a breath. "You plugging that USB drive into your computer was how they knew where to look for you."

My heart pounded. "They're coming? My dad is coming?"

"Soon enough, they'll show up. His men. Adriano's men."

Oh my God. Fuck it all to hell. They'd kill me. Or worse. People feared death, but there were things worse than dying, and my father knew how to execute them. Adriano's men wouldn't be any better. For all I knew, he'd let them rape me. My leg bounced. I was fucked.

"They're going to kill me," I whispered.

"They won't."

"They'll do worse. They'll pass me around. They'll rape me. They'll let them," I said brokenly.

"No one is going to fucking touch you, Lenora." His eyes darkened. "What's on the USB drive?"

"I didn't look. I was going to, but I was too scared to." I bit my lip. "I swear that's the truth."

He gave a nod, shut the ledger, and stood up. "You'll finish eating while I shower, and then we're leaving."

My jaw dropped. "Leaving? It's already night."

He looked outside as if needing to confirm this. Instead of replying, he turned around.

"Wouldn't it be better if we left tomorrow? No one knows about this place. I mean, you just found out about it. It'll take my father at least another few days."

"You don't seem to understand how much trouble you're in." He turned slightly.

"I do understand. I just want one more night of peace." I looked at the tiled floor. When did peace acquire such a steep price?

"Fine. One night. We leave early."

I nodded, feeling a weight lifted off my chest, until I turned around and stared at the rest of the chicken nuggets. I couldn't eat anymore, suddenly terrified of what would happen. My father was supposed to be in Palermo while I was here. He wasn't supposed to find out I took something from him yet. I was supposed to spring it on him, not the other way around. I grabbed the phone Mom gave me and saw a series of calls from her. My stomach sank. I knew they wouldn't hurt my mother, but even bothering her with this would be awful. Her mother was freaking dying. Her mother was dying, and I was doing what? Pretending I could beat my father at a game he'd mastered long ago? God. I was so stupid.

Me: Is everything ok?

Mami: did Marchetti arrive?

I stared at the screen.

Me: YOU KNEW HE WAS COMING?

I dialed her number because fuck it. She answered on the first ring.

"You know he was coming?" I whisper-shouted.

"I was calling to warn you." She sniffled. My heart dropped.

"Oh no. Mom, did she. . .did abue—"

"She's gone." Mom sobbed into the phone. I'd never seen my mother cry. I'd never heard her cry. Hearing her break down like this and knowing I couldn't be there for her was heartbreaking. Not because I was the exemplary daughter but because she was alone. My mom had no one to help her get through this.

"I'm so so sorry," I said, my voice catching. "I'm so sorry."

"It's okay." She breathed in and out. "It's okay. Death is a part of life. It's okay."

I didn't know if she was saying it for my benefit or hers, but all I could do was let her speak. Nothing I said would lessen her pain.

She took another breath. "Stay with Marchetti. Don't move away from him for a moment, do you understand?"

"Y-yes. You told him where I was?"

"He was very persistent and cares about you, Nora." She sniffled again. "I have to make funeral arrangements. A funeral and a wedding that might as well be a funeral." She laughed tightly. "I love you."

"I love you too."

I stared at my phone until Rocco took it from me, placed it on the nightstand, and carried me to the bed. As he got in the bed next to me and pulled my back to his chest, butterflies erupted in my belly. I didn't want to be one of those who got clingy after having sex with someone, but being in his arms felt so right. When he kissed my neck and inhaled as I drifted off to sleep, I recalled my mother's words. *He cares about you.* If only that were enough.

CHAPTER TWENTY-ONE

Rocco

"**I** HATE LONG CAR RIDES," LENORA SAID BESIDE ME.

"It's only a two-hour drive."

"Still too long."

She'd cocooned herself in the seat, her seatbelt on the side of her right arm as she looked at me. I'd only looked at her twice in the ten minutes we'd been on the road and decided twice was enough. She was too distracting and I hated distractions. Her eyes were closed now. Three times. Three times I'd looked in twelve minutes. This woman was making me weak.

"Once, Gabe and I decided to drive from Connecticut to D.C. It was supposed to take us like seven hours. It took fifteen." She shuddered, squeezing her body tighter. "Never again."

"Why were you driving to D.C.?"

"I wanted to see the cherry blossoms and Gabe was bored. The flights were cheap, but he thought it was a better idea to drive. For bonding."

"Did you bond?"

She laughed. "If you consider him mansplaining the stock market and all of its issues bonding, sure."

I felt my lips tip up. When I looked over—the fourth time in twenty minutes—she was still laughing, and I found it impossible not to laugh along. Here I was on a rescue assignment, laughing. Admittedly, I hadn't been on many rescue assignments, but the one I could remember, I'd spent the entire time calculating exit strategies and going over the steps in my head. I couldn't even tell you who the fuck I rescued. That was how little attention I paid to them. When I was on a mission, I tuned the world out and focused. Lenora made that impossible.

"How were the blossoms?" I asked, looking at her for the fifth time.

"I didn't see them." She closed her eyes and shook her head. "We miscalculated and went the wrong weekend."

"You're joking."

"I wish I was." She laughed. "Gabe is so smart when it comes to his job, but he can be such a moron for regular life things."

"Tell me about it," I said. "When we were kids, we always got in trouble because of Gabe. He didn't know when the hell to shut up."

She sighed. "I wish I'd grown up with you guys."

"I don't."

Her smile dropped. "Why not?"

"I would've gotten into a lot more fights if you went to school with us."

"What, defending my honor?" She laughed.

"I would've probably fucked up any guy who looked in your direction for too long."

She grinned. "Because you're jealous."

"When it comes to you, I guess I am."

My heart clenched when her expression turned sad, and she looked out the window.

CHAPTER TWENTY-TWO

Rocco

"**H**ERE? YOU BROUGHT HER HERE?" ENRIQUE HISSED.

"Just for an hour until I'm sure the safe house is ready."

"Jesus fucking Christ." He shook his head and looked over at Lenora, sitting on the couch, resting her chin on her knees as she looked at the television.

It's set on some reality dating show, but her eyes were glazed over, and she was just staring. Dominic and Dean were on their way to the safe house, about two hours from here. Gio and Loren were staying back to make sure everything remained safe there.

"I have a USB drive that has some sort of tracking device. How can I strip it without stripping the contents?"

Enrique exhaled, running a hand over his buzz cut. It was the same haircut I had for years before I finally started letting it grow out. I still kept it short, but it was long enough to grab. He paced his kitchen back and forth as he thought about it, or something. I couldn't be sure what he was thinking half the time. He was a former military pilot and former FBI agent. Former, not because he was old, but because he'd taken Loren up on an offer he couldn't refuse. He was making enough money to afford this lavish mansion in Sarasota, with the beach steps away. It was his second home. His first was still down in Miami. That one was just as opulent. He shared them both with Emma, which was comical. He was a smuggler, and she was writing newspaper headlines about people who smuggled shit. As far as everyone knew, he was a private pilot, which wasn't *not* true. He was also pretty tech-savvy, which was why I was here now.

"Let me see it." He stopped pacing. The door opened as I reached into my pocket, and Emmaline walked inside, eyes wide when she saw me.

"What the fu—" She stopped when she saw Lenora on the couch, then looked at Enrique. "What. The. Fuck?"

"I'll explain later," he said.

She still hadn't recovered as she closed and locked the door, but she went up to Lenora, who started sobbing when Emma hugged her. My chest squeezed. I threw my head back and looked at the high ceiling to take a breath. When I looked at Enrique again, he was still waiting, palm up, for the USB drive. I took it out and handed it to him. He walked to the kitchen counter and examined it under the light.

"I'd have to uninstall whatever program they put in it, but that would require me to use a computer, and then they'll be able to track it to me." He set it down. "You'll have to go to a rest stop, open it there, and keep driving."

I crossed my arms and took a step back.

"Why do you want to know what's on it anyway?" he asked. "Wouldn't it be best to just give it back to Giuseppe?"

"That's not happening." My mood darkened when I saw Lenora still crying and talking to Emma, probably telling her everything she wouldn't tell me on our drive over here.

My phone buzzed. Seeing my brother's name, I felt myself breathe a little easier. "Yeah?"

"It's done."

"Thanks." I took another breath as he exhaled into the line.

"I don't even know what to say to you right now, Rocco," Mikey said in his serious dad voice. "You know this won't end well, and you won't be able to hide forever."

"I don't need to. I just need to buy time." I hung up and looked at Enrique again.

He looked over at Emma, back at me, and back at Emma. She hadn't even looked in this direction, but she gave Lenora a kiss on the head, stood up, and walked over to us.

"What?" she whisper-shouted to Enrique. "I can feel you staring."

"I wasn't staring." His mouth pulled up slightly as he opened his arms.

She rolled her eyes and melted into him. Fucking melted. Now, I'd seen it all. It wasn't that Emma was a bitch, but. . .yeah, Emma was a bitch. I'd seen them together countless times, but she was always off-talking to her sister while he was talking to us. This was weird. He leaned down and started telling her about the USB drive issue. She listened intently, her eyes moving between his as if she were reading a book. When he finished, he stood straight again and waited for her to say something. She pursed her lips. She looked at me with her light brown eyes as if trying to see into my brain and rip apart every thought. I almost smiled. She would have made a good interrogator. She let out a growl and tilted her head up before pinning me with that stare again.

"I'm only doing this because you're family, but I swear to God, Rocco, if someone shows up here and tries to kill us but fails, I will kill you."

I stared at her, unsure of what to say. Was she going to let me borrow a computer? What was happening?

"Fine." She looked at Enrique again. "But no more."

"No more, babe." He kissed her and walked away.

Emma went into the kitchen and poured two glasses of red wine, and walked back over to Lenora as I stood there wondering what the fuck had just happened. I didn't have to wait long. Enrique showed up with a black laptop that looked like it weighed ten pounds. He set it down on the counter, facing the television, so we had a clear view of Lenora and Emma, and pulled up a barstool. I did the same and sat beside him.

"This computer is almost impossible to track," he explained

as he turned it on. "Emma thinks I'm going to get killed if I keep using it."

"Would you?"

He shrugged. "I doubt it. My dad is pretty high up in the FBI chain."

I said nothing as the computer finally showed a blue page, and he typed in his login code. He opened a program and plugged in the USB drive. I was on edge as we waited. I'd looked at the ledger several times, and Lenora was right. He'd written it in some kind of code. Maybe Dom would be able to decipher it. Enrique clicked some things. Typed some things, clicked the enter button loudly, and sat back. I watched as green numbers and letters took over the screen.

"There. Now, the USB drive is untraceable no matter where you plug it in."

"How do we look at what's on it?" I asked. He clicked, opened a folder with more folders, and stood up. I looked at him.

"I'm not looking at what's on that thing." He put his hands up, backed away, and headed to the fridge.

"Pussy," I muttered under my breath.

He laughed. "Damn right. I've heard enough horror stories to fuck with that man."

I grunted in response and looked at the folders. The names were dates ranging from 1990 to now. I clicked 1990. More folders opened up. This was like a goddamn Matryoshka doll that never seemed to end. I clicked the excel sheet. On the left were what I assumed were initials; on the right, money—owed or paid, I wasn't sure. I clicked out and checked last year's folder. It also had an excel sheet. I clicked on the folder beside it, which was filled with pictures. I clicked one. Lenora smiling at a girl in school. Lenora threw her hands up in frustration. Lenora walking out of a building. They were all taken on different days. I knew he was stalking the shit out of her, but damn. I exited that one and went to another. This one was filled with pictures of

Sofia. He even had one of Sofia in a hospital room, sitting next to who I assumed was her mother. Jesus. I clicked the next one. Dominic. My heart stopped beating. There weren't many pictures of him, but still. He even had one of Dom holding Rosie's hand while they walked down a sidewalk. There was Gabe, too. Jesus Christ. This was a lot. I went back to the '90s folders and clicked a random one.

Carmela De Luca. My heart slowed as I hovered over the cursor on Dominic's mother's name. I couldn't click it. I clicked back and looked at all of the names. He was watching every single person he knew. My eyes stopped on Beatrice Marchetti. I stopped breathing. Next to hers was one with my dad's name. Next to his was one that said, "Marchetti kids." I clicked on my mom's. I couldn't click it. I wish I hadn't opened the file when I saw her face. My chest squeezed as I went through pictures of her. She was such a happy person. Such a kind person. I swallowed the lump in my throat and got out of the folder. I clicked the excel sheet in this one. I sat back and read the amounts, then the initials. Halfway through the sheet, I froze.

R.B.

A.M.

H.G.

B.M.

Next to each of their names was $10,000. I stared at that number, feeling a tingle start in my fingertips. It always started that way. Soon, I'd be consumed with rage—ten grand. I would have said it was a coincidence if I believed in those, but too many signs pointed at what I knew had to be true. I snatched the drive out and shut the computer. The three of them looked at me, all wearing the same confused look on their faces. I felt like a live wire ready to explode at any minute. I shoved the drive in my pocket and walked out the back door. I needed air. Holy fuck. I needed air. I made it to the sand before my legs gave out, and I sank to my knees.

Giuseppe De Luca was the one who put a hit on my mother. On Rosie's mother. On Dominic and Gabe's mother. All this time, I'd maintained that he was a monster but only to outsiders and never to women or children. All this time, he'd sat at dinner tables, sharing cigars and drinks while knowing he'd murdered my mother. How many times had he commiserated with my father? My father, who fucking broke after Mom was murdered. My fucking father, his brother, a man he always swore to protect. How many times did Giuseppe tell us not to worry, that we'd get our vengeance, that the people responsible wouldn't get away with it? I buried my hands in the sand and squeezed, a scream ripping out of me before I could stop. I was going to fucking kill him, but first, I would make him suffer. I took my phone out of my pocket and called Michael.

CHAPTER TWENTY-THREE

Lenora

ROCCO WAS LOSING IT. HE HADN'T SPOKEN A WORD IN THE TWO hours we'd been in the car, but I could tell he was trying hard not to snap. I'd never seen him like this. I wanted to ask what happened. I'd chased him outside, but Emma and Enrique held me back, telling me he needed a moment to himself. Emma told me to let him work it out on his own first and that he'd speak when he was ready. She'd know. Her brother was mercurial and did this often. Not Rocco, though. I'd never seen or heard anything about him losing his temper. My heart broke when I saw him sink to his knees on the beach and start to shake uncontrollably. When he came back inside, he was completely void of emotion.

That's how he'd been during the car ride, and I didn't know what to do. I felt that Emma was right; even a sound out of me could make him snap. I took my phone out and stared at it. I wanted to text Rosie, but I knew I couldn't. I didn't want to text my mom since she was going through so much crap already, and I didn't want to add to it. I was staring at a blank screen when a hand reached over, grabbed it, and tossed it out the window. It happened so quickly that I almost thought I'd imagined it. He closed the window and kept driving, his face impassive.

"What the hell, Rocco?"

His eyes flashed to mine. "No phones."

"That was a safe phone." My brows pulled. It was the only way for my mother to get in touch with me.

"No phone is safe," he said, his voice leaving no room for arguments.

I let out a sputtered breath and crossed my arms. I could've argued and made a stink about it, but I kept replaying the image of him on the sand and decided to keep my mouth shut. What had he seen on that USB drive to make him do this 180? Maybe I'd find out before my brother and Dean got to the safe house. I wasn't sure how far they were. I knew they were driving down from New York, but I didn't know when they left. I didn't even know where the hell I was. Before my trip to Naples, I'd never been to Florida. The only thing I had to go on was the highway signs, which didn't tell me much. The last sign we passed said Port Saint Lucie. Whatever the hell that was. I brought my knees to my chest, closed my eyes, and slept.

"Get up. We're here."

I heard the words spoken angrily in my dream. At least, I thought it was a dream until a door shut loudly and jolted me awake. I rubbed my eyes and yawned as I sat up and looked around. Wherever we were, it was pitch black. In front of the car, I saw Rocco walking toward a house with our bags in his hands. I unbuckled my seatbelt, slipped my feet into my slides, and got out of the car. As I shut the door, I realized pebbles covered the entire perimeter. Each step made a crunching sound as I walked to the house. We were in a very remote location, judging by the darkness and endless trees around us. The building stood two stories tall, mostly enclosed in glass, except for the parts shrouded by gray siding. It was a sleek, modern-looking structure with no curves or angles to its shape; even the roof was flat. Despite its plainness, it was beautiful—something you'd expect to find on an architect's Instagram page. Inside, Rocco flicked on the lights, switched off the alarm, and shut the door behind us, double-bolting it. I wondered how my brother and Dean would get inside if we were asleep.

"Grab onto something." He said it with such displeasure that I wasn't sure he was talking to me until he turned those cold blue eyes on me. A shiver went down my spine. What the hell was wrong with him? "Grab onto something," he gritted out, jaw tensing.

I grabbed the first thing I could reach: the post of the stairs. He pushed a button. There was a whirring sound, like a loud air conditioner, and the entire house was moving suddenly. My eyes widened as I looked around. It was like being in an elevator, like the freaking Bat Cave. A few things clattered where I assumed the kitchen was, but everything else seemed to stay intact. The house did a little rock when we stopped moving, and the whirring sound ceased. Rocco pushed off the wall and started walking further into the house as if that was normal.

"What the hell?" I said, following him as he checked the thermostat. He ignored me. I followed him into the kitchen, which was also completely sleek and dark. He looked in the cabinets, opened a door that I assumed was the pantry, and kept moving around to ensure everything was intact. He was pissing me off.

"ROCCO."

"What?" He was moving things around in the fridge, still ignoring me.

"Can you please look at me?" I asked, my voice breaking a little with the plea. I hated how I sounded, but I was confused, tired, and scared, and I didn't know what I'd done to deserve his ire.

He shut the fridge and turned to me. "What?"

I swallowed. "What just happened? Are we underground?"

"Yes." He searched my face, and for a second, I thought maybe his anger had dissipated, but his eyes were still cold, and his expression was still blank even as he studied me. "It's one of our safe houses. The safest since it's underground, and no one would know to look for it."

"What about the car?"

"No one comes out here. It's private property, but if they do, it's just a car parked in the middle of nowhere." He stepped away from the fridge. "Help yourself to whatever you want. I'm going to set the bags upstairs."

It was the most he'd said to me, and even though he sounded more like a drill sergeant, I was glad he was speaking. He walked out and left me staring. I didn't need Emmaline to school me on mercurial men. I'd grown up with a father and two brothers who lost their shit in a blink. I usually just gave them space until they'd calmed down. Something about Rocco's mood told me he wouldn't calm down, though, and of course, I wanted to be the one to pull him from the darkness that had taken hold of him. Instead, I gave him space. I made two sandwiches, ate one, and left the other for him. I cleaned up the kitchen and walked around the first story.

Abstract art decorated the walls, and it felt homey enough that we could stay there for months. I crossed my arms to fight a shiver at that thought. I'd never been claustrophobic, but the thought of being down here for that amount of time made me uncomfortable. There was a guest room with a bed and a bathroom but no frills. I spotted a small plaque on the wall and walked over to it. *Phil's Bunker—est 1957.* So, it had been a bunker at some point. I'd always pictured underground bunkers looking like someone's garage but with canned foods. This was not that.

Despite my nervousness, I still managed to drag my feet upstairs. My bag was peeking out of the first room to the right. Two other doors were open, both bedrooms, and the fourth one was closed—presumably where Rocco would be staying. I was afraid to turn the knob and find it locked, so I went to my assigned room and shut the door before I showered and changed into my pajamas—loose black shorts and one of Gabe's old Yale sweatshirts that fit me like a dress. I got into bed and turned on the television, flipping through channels to distract myself from thinking about what Rocco was doing in the room next door. Since I no longer had a phone, I depended on the clock next to the bed.

I had fallen asleep, only to wake up again at 3:30 in the morning. I went to the bathroom. I was brushing my teeth, washing my face, and applying lotion. I eyed the adjacent door, a Jack and Jill style, which Rocco had yet to use. It had been locked from the other side. I shut off the lights and contemplated getting back into bed, but instead, I went to search for him. Regardless of the response I got, I needed him to know that I was there for him. I turned the handle of his room, and it opened. The TV was on, and he sat shirtless on the bed with covers over his middle, holding a phone in his hand. When he saw me, he lowered his phone and looked at me.

"You need something?"

"I just. . .I wanted to check if you were okay," I said, hating the meek lilt in my tone.

He glanced down at his phone again, ignoring me. I didn't know if it was because we'd slept together or because he'd always been kind up until now, but something about his anger rattled me to my core. It was a quiet anger, the kind that festered until it exploded. I should have left the room and locked myself in mine as I waited for my brother. Instead, I took a step forward.

He looked up again briefly. "I'm fine, Lenora. Go back to bed."

"You're not fine." I reached the edge of the bed, still leaving a good amount of distance between us.

"Go back to bed." He sighed, going back to his phone.

I sat down at the edge of the bed. He ignored me and continued typing away to whomever he was texting. Maybe he was texting Dominic and acting this way so we could get used to not being near each other when he arrived. That was what I wanted to tell myself, but I knew there was more to this.

"Are you angry with me?" I bit the inside of my cheek and looked down at the white covers, forcing myself not to get emotional.

"Jesus Christ," he muttered. "No, Lenora, I'm not angry with you."

I looked up, meeting his gaze, shivering slightly at the coolness I found in it. I wanted to pout and scream and ask why he was treating me this way—like a stranger—after we'd shared so much, but I decided against it. I wasn't willing to let myself look as weak and helpless as I felt. I kept my eyes on his and searched his face for any sign of it softening. When it didn't, I stood up and walked to the door.

"Good night, then." I opened it, shut it behind me, and went to my bedroom.

I shut the door before diving into the bed. Only then did I let myself cry. After a moment, I took a few deep breaths and wiped my face. It felt good to let that out. Dad always said, "big girls don't cry" and "save your tears for something worth crying over." I'd stopped crying in front of him when I was eight. Crying was cathartic and healthy and something I enjoyed doing in private. I flipped over to my back and threw an arm over my face, laughing. I was ridiculous. How could I possibly think anything would change between us? I was still who I was and still engaged to be married. I don't know why I thought last night would change things.

CHAPTER TWENTY-FOUR

Lenora

I WOKE UP AT EIGHT, GOT OUT OF BED, AND TOOK A SHOWER. AFTER I brushed my teeth and put my wet hair into a braid, I walked back to the room to dress. My only clothing options in Naples were bikinis, shorts, short dresses used as cover-ups and crop tops, and one maxi dress I had left behind. I laid out my shorts, red bandana crop top, and one of the cover-up dresses, trying to figure out what to wear. In college, I had a friend named Marcy who would go to any lengths to get her crush's attention. If that meant walking around in a towel, she would do it. If I were like Marcy, I would have worn the maxi dress so Rocco could feast his eyes on me every time I bent over. The problem was threefold: I wasn't like Marcy, my brother would kill me, and Rocco was heartless.

I went with the safer choice—a crop top and shorts. Unlike Marcy, who ended up marrying that crush of hers, I had no future with Rocco, so it didn't matter if I wore this or a bag over myself. I stood in front of the mirror and assessed myself. The pointy part of the bandana went to my navel, so only my shoulders, back, and sides were exposed, and my shorts weren't scandalous. Because my time in the sun had turned my skin to burnt gold, I only needed to apply mascara and lip gloss. Giving myself a full once-over—my muscular legs, hips, small waist, size B boobs, and hair in a braid—I decided I looked fantastic. Honestly, fuck Rocco Marchetti. I wasn't here to impress him anyway.

I found him in the kitchen, standing over the stove. I was so shocked by the sight that I froze. He'd laid out a full spread on the island counter: a bowl of mango, chopped-up avocado, toast, scrambled eggs, a bottle of syrup, and whatever he was making now. Pancakes, I guessed from the smell. I wish I hadn't been as impressed as I was. Dad couldn't cook to save his life. He didn't even know how to boil an egg. My brothers cooked sometimes. Gabe's food was usually burnt or undercooked, so he ordered out often. Dominic was better, but he had a meal delivery service. When he did make something, it was with Rosie's help. Since I had no indication that he knew I was there, I leaned against the doorway and continued watching him. He was wearing a black shirt that molded to his broad back, so I could see his muscles tensing with every move. I saw his perfect profile when he turned to get something next to him. It wasn't fair that he was this good-looking. I pushed off the doorway but remained glued there. I didn't know what to do. Was I supposed to announce my arrival? There were two place settings, so I knew one of them was for me. Maybe he was over whatever he'd been angry about? Maybe he'd go back to the happy Rocco I knew. After all, he was the one who had told me that happiness was a choice he made every day.

"Take a seat," he said, stacking whatever he was making onto a plate.

I walked forward and sat in the chair, staring at the spread. He switched off the stove, turned around, and set down a plate with french toast. My mouth watered at the sight of it. He couldn't have known it was my favorite since I hadn't told him, but it was a nice coincidence. He took a seat. The chairs were far apart enough to guarantee we wouldn't touch, which was good. The less interaction I had with him, the better. That was the decision I made last night after I cried myself to sleep. Today, and for the remainder of my time with him, I'd treat him the way I treated Dean, Gio, and Lorenzo. Like a brother and not the guy I'd had a crush on my entire life. And for now, I wouldn't speak to him unless he spoke first. Did it suck? Yes. I was over it, though. Even when I felt his eyes on me, I refused to look. I stared at the avocado.

"Eat," he said.

I jolted a little and picked up the mangos, serving some on the plate. What I really wanted was the french toast. He went for that first, setting three pieces on his plate. I took it from him when he offered and served myself the same amount. He put syrup on his. I put syrup on mine.

"Thank you," I said before I started eating.

I had to break my no-speaking rule for that, because I couldn't not thank him. He said nothing in return. I cut into the french toast and ate the first piece. I closed my eyes to savor it better as it hit my tongue. I was dying to groan at how freaking good it was, but I didn't make a peep. I wanted to tell him so many things—*I would be in heaven if you made this for me every morning. I can't believe you know how to make it this good, this is the best french toast I've ever had, and I've had a lot.* Of course, I remained quietly impressed. Not everyone knew how to make it the way I liked it. People either overcooked or undercooked it. I'd tried to make it once, and despite the simple steps, it was a disaster. How the heck did he do it?

"My mom's recipe," he said as if reading my mind. I nodded in acknowledgment and brought the napkin to wipe my mouth after chewing.

"It's amazing." I ate another piece.

Despite everything I wanted to ask and say, we ate the rest of the meal in silence. I wanted to ask about his mother and what else he'd learned from her. I knew she'd been killed in that awful massacre when they were teenagers. I was young, but I remembered the day my brothers moved in with us. Rocco and his father visited not too long after. It was a somber time. Out of respect, I'd never asked my brothers about their mother unless they spoke about her first. I did the same with

Rosie, and I'd do the same with Rocco. It wasn't like he was in a talkative mood anyway.

When we were finished, I picked up empty plates and bowls and took them to the sink to wash. This was another simple thing I would no longer do when I married Adriano. I should've been happy about it. I mean, who likes chores? But I'd rather have a pile of chores and freedom than live like an imprisoned queen. I kept my attention on the dishes I was washing. Rocco didn't offer to help, but he did clean the kitchen, bringing something to the sink every so often. Each time he did, he stepped so close to me that I had to will myself to stay calm. The silence between us was consumed by weird energy: anger and lust. We hadn't looked each other in the eye today, but it was there. I felt it deep in my belly, and when he brushed against me to drop a used spatula in the sink, I had to hold my breath not to gasp. The sound of an alarm nearly made me drop the plate in my hand.

"They're here," he said. "Grab onto something."

I set the plate down, turned off the faucet, and gripped the edge of the white sink. He did the same, setting his hand right next to mine, our fingers touching. My heart started pounding, so I closed my eyes and inhaled his scent. I wasn't sure what soap he used, but he always smelled so good. Clean. Sadness washed through me when I opened my eyes and stared down at our hands. The alarm stopped, and it was then that the house started to move up. Light poured in through the windows. It was so bright that I had to squint. I hadn't realized how dark the house was until now. Maybe because Rocco had turned all the lights on. I couldn't live here for too long. No amount of lights in a house could ever replace sunlight. The house stopped moving, so we let go of the sink. At the sound of the door unlocking, I brushed past him. When I slung myself into his arms, Dominic hadn't even fully stepped in. The instant comfort it brought made me start crying. Here

I was, running away from our dad to blackmail him, something I set out to do alone, and now I'd dragged them all into it. I wanted to apologize and thank them simultaneously, but I couldn't speak.

"Aw, Nora. Come on." Dom let his bag thump to the ground and wrapped both arms around me. "It's okay. I got you. You're going to be fine."

That made me cry harder.

"I get it, Nora. If I were stuck with this asshole, I'd be miserable too," Dean said somewhere beside us. That made me laugh. I pulled back and wiped my tears.

"Hey. You okay?" Dom asked, searching my watery eyes. I blinked and nodded because I couldn't trust myself to speak without losing it again.

Dean shut the door and locked it. He didn't push the button to take us back underground like I thought he would. He must have read the question on my face because he smiled one of his lopsided smiles.

"I'm sure you could use a little sunlight."

"Yeah," I whispered.

Dean walked to the back room and dropped his bag at the door. "It smells good. Who cooked?"

"He did." I jutted my chin in the direction Rocco was standing. I still couldn't look at him. "Best french toast I've had ever."

"Ever?" Dom asked, narrowing his eyes like I was exaggerating.

"I'm dead serious."

"That's a big compliment coming from someone who would eat french toast for breakfast, lunch, and dinner." He tapped my nose and stepped away.

I glanced at Rocco, finally, and found him looking at me with an expression I couldn't quite decipher. For a millisecond,

I thought I saw warmth in his cold eyes. It was gone in the next blink.

"Damn, Roc. You must have stepped your game up today," Dom said, walking toward his friend.

He stopped just before he got to him and frowned. I looked over again. They were having a wordless conversation as they looked at each other.

"What's going on?" Dom asked.

Rocco sighed heavily and ran his fingers through his hair roughly, pulling the ends when he stopped.

"Oh fuck," Dom said. "Is someone onto us?"

"Not that I know of."

"Then what?" Dom assessed Rocco's face again. "Come on. Let's take a walk."

My brother and Rocco walked outside while Dean, who'd been in the kitchen, followed, still clutching the mango and muttering curses. They shut the door behind them, and I moved to the big window. My hands trembled as I wondered if Rocco had told him about us. I couldn't hear anything on the other side of the glass—it was soundproof, bulletproof, and probably hurricane proof too. All I could do was look for clues by watching their body language. While Dom had his arms crossed, Rocco seemed to be talking, and Dean lit a cigarette.

Rocco looked like he was in fight mode. His entire body tensed as he spoke. Whatever he was saying made my brother's face crumple. That face told me this had nothing to do with me. He went from serious to horrified, devastated, and disbelieving as he shook his head. He got in Rocco's face, pointing at his chest as he said something. Dean tossed his cigarette and stood between the two like a referee at a boxing match. My stomach coiled tightly. Dominic turned and walked away, kicking the pebbles and screaming so hard that the veins in his neck bulged. He looked like a fighting bull waiting for a red flag. As if it would calm them down or let me hear, I pressed my hand against the glass and leaned forward. While my brother lost it, kicking, screaming, and pacing, Rocco and Dean just stood there with matching expressions. I'd thought it was blank, but I realized they were angry—that quiet anger I was terrified of. Now I had three men to stay away from while they brewed. I sighed and went back to the kitchen to finish washing the dishes.

CHAPTER TWENTY-FIVE

Lenora

WE WERE IN THE DARK AGAIN. THAT IS, UNDERGROUND WITHOUT sunlight. I'd been upstairs when the three of them finally walked back inside, and it was like listening to a bunch of teenagers who had been sent to their rooms. Downstairs, a door slammed. Upstairs, two slammed. Boom. Boom. I wondered if they'd fought after all. Lunch came and went. I made four sandwiches and took my time eating mine, hoping one of them would come out of their rooms. They didn't. By dinner time, I was no longer hungry, but I was also tired of waiting, so I went to what I assumed was my brother's room and knocked. No answer. I knocked again. No answer. I didn't hear running water, which meant he wasn't showering. A light was on from one of the nightstands, which meant he wasn't sleeping.

I tested the doorknob and found it unlocked, so I peeked inside, hoping he was dressed and not doing anything. I'd have to bleach my eyes for later. I found him sitting in a leather chair in the opposite corner of the room. I shut the door and walked over, my hands getting clammier with each step I took. He remained completely unmoved. I couldn't even tell if he was breathing, which scared the hell out of me. One of Dad's men was found dead in his apartment; by all accounts, he looked like he was just sitting there watching television. If Dominic were dead, I wouldn't be able to cope. When I finally reached him, I confirmed that he was breathing, but he looked completely checked out. If it were Gabe, I would wonder if he was on drugs, drunk, or both, but Dominic liked to be in control and wasn't that guy.

"Dom?" I said quietly.

His head snapped up, eyes catching mine. They looked vacant, similar to Rocco's when he kicked me out of his room last night. This situation was different, though. Dom could tell me to leave, but unless he physically pushed me out of his room, I wouldn't budge. I walked closer until I was right in front of him. He took a deep breath and exhaled as I stood there.

"Not now, Nora," he said, his voice hoarse. *Not now, Nora.* Those were the exact words Rocco had said to me last night.

"Are you okay?"

That was the stupidest question of all time, but I wanted him to tell me he wasn't. If he did, maybe I could help him. Not that he'd let me. These men had too much pride for their own good. Whatever this was, it must have been huge for them to act this way. His phone buzzed on the side table; it sounded loud in the deafening silence. I went over and lifted it when I saw Rosie's face on the screen.

Dom shook his head. "Not now."

"But it's Rosie." When the call went to voicemail, I looked at the screen and saw that he had twelve missed calls. I was sure a lot of them were hers. She must have been losing her freaking mind. "Dominic."

He looked at me again, still blank. I felt out of my element. He'd normally never turn down a call from Rosie. My mind jumped to the worst conclusion I could conceive: someone died. Someone important. Someone they loved. The thought made my stomach drop. I didn't know how to handle him when he was like this.

"Can I call Rosie back?"

"I can't talk to her," he said, his voice breaking.

No tears were coming down his face, but it was the closest thing to a sob I'd ever heard from him. It rattled me to the core. Gabe was the more emotional brother. He didn't care if anyone saw him crying, laughing, or yelling. Dominic had always been serious. A jokester, sure, but I'd never seen him like this. I set the phone on the bed and walked behind him. He may very well shrug me off, but I didn't care. The only way I knew how to comfort him was to wrap my arms around him. He brought his hands up and held me tight, as he dropped his head and his body shook. He still didn't make a sound.

"Did someone die?" I asked quietly.

A sound tore through him. He sounded more like a wounded animal than a hurt man. I bit my lip to keep from wobbling, trying so hard not to cry, but it was impossible. With my arms around him, I could feel the weight of his grief. I was going to repeat the question and ask what was wrong, but I waited for him to compose himself. If someone had died, who? My stomach felt like an empty pit while I awaited his answer.

"No," he said, finally. The confirmation should've eased my concern, but it didn't because he was still struggling.

"Can I call Rosie back?" I whispered against his hair, squeezing him a little tighter. "She has to be worried sick."

"I can't talk to her," he chanted hoarsely. "I can't talk to her. I can't talk to her."

It felt like a hand was gripping my throat from the inside. My strong, untouchable older brother was breaking before my eyes, and I didn't know what to do or how to help. I didn't know how to take some of this pain from him, so he didn't have to bear it alone. He'd often done it for me, taking my calls when I was crying over something—hugging me tight when I felt lost or heartbroken. I'd always told myself I'd do the same for him, and here I was, at a loss. The only thing I could do was call Rosie. I kissed his head and unwrapped my arms. When I picked up the phone and lifted it to his face to unlock it, I saw a tear roll down his cheek, and I couldn't bear it. I walked away so I could call Rosie without completely losing my shit. I didn't know what happened and it didn't matter. When he hurt, I hurt. I took a breath and called Rosie.

"Oh my God, Dominic," she said loudly.

"It's me."

"Nora?" She sounded confused, then worried. "What are you— where's Dominic? Is he okay? Are you okay?"

"We're safe," I cleared my throat and walked to the ensuite, shutting the door slightly and sitting on the closed toilet. I lowered my voice. "But Rocco found something on my dad's USB drive that fucked him up, and when he told Dom what it was, he also lost it."

"What was on it?"

"I. . ." I shut my eyes and took a shaky breath. "I don't know. I didn't see it, but it doesn't matter. Dominic is a mess."

"What do you mean a mess?" she asked. "Is he angry?"

"I wish he were angry." My voice came out a broken sob, despite my efforts to hold it back. "He's sitting in his room, fucking crying, Rosie. Dominic crying."

She said nothing.

"Hello?" I sniffed, wiping my nose with the back of my hand. "I need to see him."

"He said he couldn't talk to you," I whispered, hating that relaying that would undoubtedly hurt her.

"I don't care. Where are you?"

"I don't know. In the middle of nowhere, Florida," I said, then panicked. "Is it safe to talk on the phone?"

"Yes," she said. "I don't care if you're on Mars. I need to see him."

"I wouldn't even know how to tell you where to go." I started crying again. "I don't know where we are."

"Can you put him on the phone?"

"He said he couldn't talk to you," I repeated, holding back a sob.

"Listen to me, Nora," she said with an authority that made me fix my posture. "You're going to walk up to him and hand him the phone right now."

"Okay." I stood up, nodding as I wiped my face as if she could see me.

I walked out of the bathroom and found Dom sitting in the same chair. His elbows were on his legs and his face was pressed into his hands. He wiped his face and looked at me. My hands were shaking out of control as I muted the phone.

"She's really worried, Dom," I whispered. "Like really worried. She wants to come over here, but I told her she can't. I don't even know where we are. She needs to talk to you and make sure you're okay."

He took the phone as I handed it to him. For a moment, he just stared at the screen. I held my breath, hoping he wouldn't end the call. He took a breath, unmuted it, and set it against his ear. His defeated expression broke my fucking heart. I couldn't bear it. I turned and headed to the door. Rosie would know what to say. As I was opening it, I heard him apologize to her over and over. I shut the door behind me and leaned against it, catching my breath and sniffling back tears. I wish I had it in me to ask more questions, but how could I, when it was so deeply ingrained in me that I should never question anyone in La Cosa Nostra?

I wasn't even sure what would happen if I did. I'd lost track of how many grown men my father beat for asking a simple question. I loved these guys. They were my family, my home, and all I knew, but I was, but I was well aware that the way they treated me was not how they treated enemies. Whatever this was, it was big, and even though part of me wanted to know what happened, the smarter part of me wouldn't let me ask past "Did someone die?" As I headed to my room, I passed Rocco's and noticed his light was on, but I wouldn't go there. There was no way I'd subject myself to his cold indifference again. I got into bed, brought my covers up to my chin, and crawled into the fetal position, wishing I could call my mom right now. I wasn't sure how long I lay there, staring into the darkness before I fell asleep, but the sound of a door shutting jolted me awake. I turned over and sat up slowly as I watched Rocco emerge from our shared bathroom.

"Did something happen? Do I need to leave?" I asked, my voice hoarse from sleep, from crying.

He shook his head and stopped walking. The bathroom's light cast a sinister glow upon him, which should have terrified me. I didn't move. He wasn't close enough to touch, and I knew he put this distance between us for my benefit. Despite the space between us, I could practically feel him vibrating with something I couldn't understand. It wasn't just lust; something else was here, something darker that he was holding back. On principle, I should have turned him away, but I knew I wouldn't. My heart pounded hard. Fear and desire were so tightly entwined that I could barely distinguish one from the other. I knew bringing him to my bed and giving him the reins to unleash that darkness could be dangerous, but I wanted him. *This*, being with him like this, was the only thing in my life that I could control. Being with him was the only thing that gave me a bit of power and didn't make me feel helpless. With a deep breath, I slowly lowered the covers and got out of bed, walking until our chests were almost touching.

He didn't move, but I could feel how tense he was. His eyes were troubled, despondent. I lifted my hand and softly stroked his face, relishing the feel of his stubble grazing my skin. His body shuddered at my touch, and it took everything in me not to jump on him and wrap my legs around him. I knew he'd let me. I knew he'd do just about anything I asked him to do right now, and the only thing I wanted him to do was to let himself get lost in me. I dropped my hand and took both of his, pulling him toward my bed until he sat on the edge. I took my gaze from his to make sure the door was locked before I began to strip. It wasn't a sensual strip tease. I didn't even know if I was capable of that. I reached behind me and undid the knot of the bandana top, gathering it and tossing it aside. I unbuckled my shorts and let them slide down my legs, kicking them off. With my panties, I hesitated. Once I took them off, I'd be completely naked, and he was still wearing a black t-shirt and dark gray sweats.

His quiet, labored breaths gave me the courage to soldier on. I hooked my thumbs at the top and slid them down my legs. Since he was facing the light now, I could see the smolder in his eyes, the hard set in his jaw. He wasn't my Rocco: the charming, grinning, flirty version of himself who chose happiness. I wasn't sure what category to put him in right now, and as I stepped forward to straddle him, I decided it didn't matter. I wanted all of his versions– his pain, anger, and laughs. I knew I couldn't have him forever, but he was mine until I walked down the aisle. I set my knees on either side of him. His hands instantly moved to my waist as I set my arms on his shoulders and tipped his nose with mine so he'd look me in the eye. The intensity in them took my breath away.

"I want you to do whatever you want with me," I whispered. He screwed his eyes shut, his grip tightening to the point of pain, but I didn't move.

"Don't say that to me right now." His voice was low, hoarse. *From screaming? From crying?* It didn't matter. His agony hit the pit of my stomach just the same.

"I mean it." I rolled my hips on his erection and moaned from that alone. His eyes popped open, the blue blaze that promised to burn.

"Lenora." His voice sounded pained as his hands traveled to my ass. "I can't."

"I want you to use me." I leaned in and licked the tip of his nose as I ground my hips again. "Please. I *need* you to."

"Fuck." It was a harsh curse as he squeezed so hard that my body shot up with a gasp. A carnal need like I'd never seen consumed his eyes. It started a fire that licked at my core. "Do you think you can be quiet when I fuck you?"

I nodded quickly. I wasn't exaggerating when I said I needed him to. Even if I'd been apprehensive, the moment his hands were on my body, I was lost to the feeling that consumed me each time he merely looked at me. Suddenly, I felt like if he didn't get lost in me, in my body, I might die.

"Please." I ground my hips one last time.

That was all it took. We clashed in a bruising kiss, a spar between our tongues, our teeth were knives puncturing each other's lips. He was a ticking time bomb, radiating tension, desire, grief, and anger, and I wanted him to go off inside me. We weren't alone in the house, but I didn't care. Consequences didn't exist in this moment. Just us. As I pulled his shirt off, he lifted and flipped me, so I was on my back and he was hovering over me. He only looked at me for a second before his lips were on my nipples, his teeth biting each one and then the rest of my skin as he made his way down my body. I gasped and writhed. He opened my legs wide. There was no teasing, no drawing it out.

He licked and ate me like a starved man, like it would be the last time he'd ever taste my pussy, and he needed to commit my taste to memory until the end of time. His teeth clamped on my mound as he slid a finger inside me, then another, and another. He drove into me roughly, each thrust of his fingers more and more maddening. I was so wet that I should have been embarrassed by the sounds that filled the room, but he consumed me and I didn't care. It was pain and hunger, and my entire body hummed with pleasure as he brought me to orgasm, my hands covering my mouth to stifle my scream. He stood and wrapped his hand around his cock. He bit his lip and looked at me as he pumped up and down. I got on my elbows to watch him, waiting for him to get inside me. He didn't. He continued the movement, pleasuring himself while winding me up. I brought a hand between my legs and began touching myself. He hissed, letting go of himself and dropping to his knees as he sank between my legs again. I gasped at the slow long lick from crack to clit. He continued until he pulled another orgasm out of me.

When he stood, he pinned me with a stare. "Not a sound."

I covered my mouth with both hands again, my eyes widening as he yanked my legs, brought his hands to my ass, and pulled me up. He thrust into me fully, hard and deep. My body jerked at the rough intrusion, a sound escaping my lips before I could stop it. Rocco's face was ecstasy and anger, a deadly combination. He grabbed a pillow and covered my face with it. A part of me panicked, but then he started to fuck me harder, rougher, while bringing his thumb to my clit, and I lost all thought. My muffled moans hit the pillow as he continued to pierce me deeply. When my lungs began losing oxygen, I began to thrash beneath him, tears spilling from my eyes. Suddenly, the pillow was off my face. I took in a loud gasp and then another, trying to fill my lungs with air. He slowed down and pulled out completely, letting my body down slowly on the bed.

"Flip." He smacked the outside of my thigh. "I want you on all fours."

I was slow to get up, my arms shaky from the ordeal. His hand came down on my thigh, another hard slap. I moved faster, getting on my hands and knees and looking over my shoulder. His smoldering eyes drank me in as he positioned himself between my legs. In a blink, he wrapped a hand around my hair and pulled it as he thrust inside in one go. He was so big and so deep that it felt like he was hitting my organs. He paused, his hand loosening on my hair as he let out a string of curses. He felt incredible despite his roughness, or maybe because of it. It was animalistic, raw, and completely different from how he'd been the other times. I welcomed it, pushing myself toward him and meeting his thrusts. My scalp burned at his tight grip on my hair. With his other hand, he slapped my ass as he began to move faster. With his hold on my hair, he pulled me toward him until my back was almost to his chest and slowed down his stroke.

"See what you signed up for, Principessa?" he asked harshly. "Do you still think this was a good idea?"

"Yes," I whispered hoarsely. "Please don't stop."

A rumbled sound vibrated through him as he let go of my hair. He didn't let me adjust as I fell onto my hands; his hand came around and started rubbing my clit. My knees started to shake, and I was on the brink of another orgasm. He stopped rubbing abruptly, taking his hand away and slapping my ass hard. I screwed my eyes shut, my lower lip wobbling at the loss of contact. I suddenly hated that I couldn't scream for him to put it back where it had been.

"Do not come," he said roughly against my ear. "Don't you dare fucking come before I tell you."

I took a shaky breath and nodded, though I wasn't sure I could keep that promise. I kept my eyes closed to concentrate on holding back when I felt a wet finger brush against my other hole. I stilled, my entire body clenching in refusal as he moved it in circles, pushing it in slowly as he continued to fuck me in slow strokes. I whimpered.

"Relax for me, baby," he coaxed softly in my ear. My body obliged immediately, my muscles letting go of the tension wrapped around them. He groaned as if this pleased him. "Yes. Just like that. Good girl."

I felt myself grow wetter. It was a Pavlovian experiment, and my body was conditioned to react to his words. With his other hand, he rubbed my clit, then stopped and, on a harsh breath, instructed me to do it. A shot of pleasure coursed through me. It was too much. Every part of me was full, alive, and on edge. He moved the finger he had in my hole to the rhythm that he was fucking me as I continued to rub myself. My body began to clench tight, and I knew that no amount of instruction would keep me from exploding. He took his finger out of my ass and leaned forward.

"Keep rubbing your clit while I fuck your pussy," he said, his voice strained. "I'm going to put my finger in your ass again." He touched that hole. I clenched again, unwillingly. "And you're going to fucking come for me without making a sound. Can you do that for me? Can you keep quiet?"

"I d-d-don't know," I said shakily, louder than I should have.

He bit my shoulder. "You can, baby."

I nodded, new tears forming. It was too much. He stuck his finger back in and started to fuck me harder, faster. What he was doing was already too much, creating a path of pleasure that began in my toes and made its way to my spine, my core. I stopped touching myself.

"Are you going to be a good girl and come for me?" he growled in my ear. I whimpered. He changed his position slightly, moving his body lower, and rolled his hips once, twice, applying pressure with his finger, and I was gone.

My body took flight. All I could do was feel. I'd never done drugs, but this must have been what people who did them were chasing, this high that took away all thoughts. I was unsure how long I'd been floating outside my body. When I opened my heavy eyelids, Rocco was in the bathroom washing his hands, and I was completely clean between my legs. He switched off the faucet, dried his hands, and grabbed a bottle from under the sink. I fell back onto the mattress, closing my eyes again. He moved me and got in bed next to me, propping himself up on one elbow while his hand traveled between my legs. I closed them tight in protest.

"Open your legs for me, Nora." It was a soft request that made my eyes shoot open.

I studied him for a moment. The shadows on his face seemed to have vanished, even temporarily, and I felt comfort that I'd been able to help. I opened my legs for him and felt him apply something cold and wet. It felt marvelous against my battered flesh. I sagged down with a relieved exhale as he soothed me. He was still looking at me, studying every breath and every expression my face made as he applied more. When he was finished, he wiped his hand on his leg and brought it to my face. He didn't say anything as he leaned in and kissed me. It was slow and tender, and it broke my heart more than anything he'd done to me previously. When he pulled away, he searched my eyes one last time before turning me so my back was facing his chest. He wrapped his arms around me and rained kisses on my neck, across my shoulder, behind my ear, and on top of my head. Then he buried his face in the crook of my neck and exhaled.

"If you could go anywhere, where would you go?" I whispered.

"I've never really thought about it," he said.

"Really?" I frowned, twisting my face to look at him.

"I've been to many different places and always go back to New York."

"That's home for you," I said. It made sense.

"My home was stolen years ago. My family's in New York, so that's where I go."

"You mean my brother and them," I said.

"And my brother." He kissed the tip of my nose. "Where would you go?"

"Colorado."

He laughed lightly as he frowned. "Colorado? Why? To get pot? You know it's legal in New York, right?"

"Not for pot." I turned over so I was on my back and could see his face better. "It just looks so beautiful. The mountains, the snow. All of it. Like a postcard."

"I guess."

"Have you ever been?"

"Nope."

"Really?" I felt my eyes widen.

"Why would I go to Colorado?" he laughed lightly, and even though it was at my expense, I relished the sound, content to have lifted some of his darkness, at least for a moment.

"I just told you why."

"I'll make a note of it." His eyes danced.

"What about The Netherlands?" I asked.

"You sure this isn't about pot?"

I laughed, pushing his chest. "Rocco."

His mouth hitched. "I've been to the Netherlands."

"And?"

"And I liked it. I would go back."

"What about Greece?" I asked, suddenly wanting to know if he'd checked every single place on my bucket list.

"Never been."

"I'm dying to go there." I ran the tip of my finger down the defined line between his pecs. "What about California?"

"California's huge." He opened his mouth and lightly bit the tip of my finger when I ran it from his chest to his lips.

"L.A.," I said first.

"Not my scene."

"San Francisco."

"Beautiful, also not my scene, and expensive as fuck."

That made me smile for some reason. "Japan?"

"Love Japan."

"Wow." I smiled until I thought about my situation, and the daydream vanished. "All those places are on my bucket list, and I probably won't visit them."

"You will." He said it with such conviction that I almost believed him. I turned in his arms, pressing my back to his chest again. "My perfect little Nora. I'd go anywhere with you," he murmured against me.

For a moment, I let myself imagine that this was my life, wrapped in Rocco's strong arms, planning trips together. I let myself imagine us in Paris, Japan, and Colorado. I pictured the scowl on his face when I did something he didn't like and the smile he rewarded me with when I did something he enjoyed. I was smiling as I shut my eyes and drifted to sleep.

CHAPTER TWENTY-SIX

Rocco

M Y HEART FELT HEAVY AS I WATCHED LENORA SLEEP. SHE WAS SO
fucking sweet. Too sweet. When I pieced together what
her father had done, the only thing on my mind was
vengeance and what better way to get back at him than through
his daughter? It was what had been brewing inside me the last
few days. I'd come up with ten ways to use her as bait. I'd done
a lot of shit in my life, but never to a woman. It was what made
me walk away from that high-paying government job. They sat
a woman on the interrogation chair in front of me and expected
me to do my worst, and I couldn't. I'd already done my worst
to grown men, to young men—some of whom had been guilty,
others who I'd been told were guilty, but deep down, I knew
weren't. I'd done what I had to do anyway. I drew the line at
women. There was no fucking way I was going to waterboard a
woman. With Lenora, things were different. It should have been
a no-brainer. I went to her room first to see if I could look her in
the eye and still go through with what I had planned.

I should have known better, though, with the anger and
pain inside me that I wanted to unleash. I shouldn't have walked
in here. She wasn't just some woman I could hurt, fuck, and
walk away from. I pushed her. I wanted her to tell me to leave. I
wanted her to fucking scream. I could have let her. The walls in
her room were soundproof. No one would have heard her, but
I wanted her in pain. I wanted her throat to be sore today from
all the screams she held back, from the sobs she wouldn't let
out. I thought she'd call it off when she realized I wasn't going

to be the kind way I had been with her before. I thought she'd look at me like I was a monster. I wanted her to, so I could leave that wall between us and get her out of my mind once and for all. Instead, she looked right at me, right through me, and welcomed me anyway. I crossed my arms and leaned against the wall, watching the rise and fall of her chest as she slept soundly. She was so innocent, and I was such a fucking asshole.

In his twisted way, Giuseppe didn't want to hurt his daughter. Marrying her off to Adriano meant he'd have control of his land and ports, but it also secured her safety. Here, he was a nobody, but back in Italy, people wouldn't fuck with a Salvati. Using her as bait would be easy, but I knew I'd never do it. Even if I didn't feel this palpable, terrifying connection to her, I couldn't do it without hurting Dominic, Gabe, and Rosie; they were my family. They were the only ones, besides Michael, who understood the pain I'd been carrying all these years, the grief that consumed me. They'd lost their mothers that night, too. And Dominic, fucking Dom, my best friend, my brother. I saw the light go out in his eyes when what I told him sank in. I saw the pain magnify as he sat with the news because his father hadn't only been responsible for his mother's death but also mine and Rosie's.

"*Rosie,*" was all he'd said, his voice shaking.

As angry as I was, I knew it didn't compare to what he felt. All these years, Giuseppe treated me like a son. He'd welcomed us into his house like family. He'd been one of my father's closest friends. And in all that time, he knew what he'd done. He knew what he'd stripped us of. But I wasn't his son. Dominic was, and after his mother died, he'd been taken to Italy to live with his father, the man responsible for all of it. I was livid, but more than anything, my heart ached for all of us. What Giuseppe De Luca had done was unimaginable. Unforgivable. He paid forty thousand dollars to kill our mothers. He paid to kill his ex-wife, the mother of his children, for God's sake. Who the fuck did that?

I banged my head against the wall behind me and turned to leave Lenora's room. I returned to mine and used the bathroom on the other side to shower. Bathrooms connected the rooms. I'd locked both doors that led to Dominic's before I went to his sister's room. The connected bathrooms from room to room were something we'd kept from the original structure. The person who sold it to us was a scientist who'd gone mad by all accounts except his own. When we got it, the square box went up and down like an elevator. We just had someone gut it, so we could make it ours.

We didn't use it often. I'd only stayed here twice. Dean was the one who used it the most, and he'd always blindfolded people when he brought them in and out, so they never knew where they'd been. To them, when the blindfold was off, it was just a house, a nice hideout while Russo figured out their next move. Blindfolds were necessary and something I knew my brother wouldn't like when I brought him over later. Mikey, who didn't fuck with any of this and wanted to stay as far away from crime as possible, took the rest of the week off to help us see this through. Gio and Loren were still staying back, just in case, but Rosie was on her way down with Michael. I tried to talk her out of it, but she persisted, and because I knew Dominic needed her here, I agreed and added it to the list of reasons Dom had to justify killing me.

After I dressed, I went to his room and knocked. When he didn't answer, I saw him sitting in the same chair I'd left him yesterday afternoon. I let go of the door and walked over, sitting in the chair opposite. All of our years together had formed an unbreakable bond that let me feel his pain as he could mine. I rested my elbows on my knees and let my head fall as I waited. It didn't matter if he spoke or didn't. I wanted him to know that I'd still be here, despite his father's actions. I needed him to know that I didn't blame him for anything. How could I when he'd suffered as much as I had?

"All this time," he said, his voice hoarse, barely audible. I sat back and looked at him. "All this time. . ." He shook his head and met my eyes. "When Gabe and I got to Italy, Giuseppe cried. He fell to his knees and cried. I'd never seen my father cry. He mourned her as we did, and now, I just— Was it all fake? Were they fake tears? Fake emotions? Was it guilt and not sadness?" He swallowed hard, eyes filling with unshed tears. "And fucking Rosie. Fuck! And you. And Mikey." He took a deep breath to control his emotions, but I felt them in my chest, pressing down, suffocating. "He took them from you. My dad."

I'd come in here to tell him I'd be gone but would be back in an hour. I'd come in here to tell him to shower and change for Rosie's arrival, but I was still keeping that from him. I thought I could shoulder his pain and do those things, but I couldn't trust myself to speak those words. I could barely swallow past the ever-growing knot in my throat. Somehow, I managed to stand up and walk over to him.

"You're my brother, Dom." I set my hand on his shoulder and squeezed it. "What he did was unforgivable, but you're not him." I dropped my arm and stepped back to look him in the eye. "You're not him. This isn't your cross to bear. There's nothing to forgive you for, and I know Rosie feels the same."

At the mention of her name, he tensed and swallowed hard. Fuck. I needed to go pick her up. As angry as I was, as heartbroken as I felt, I didn't want Dominic to torture himself.

"Shower. Change. Go downstairs. I have something I need to do. I'll be back soon." I crouched in front of him and made him meet my eyes again. "You're my family, my brother. You always have been, and you always will be."

CHAPTER TWENTY-SEVEN

Lenora

RELIEF WASHED OVER ME AS I STEPPED INTO THE KITCHEN, WHERE my brother spoke to Dean. Their tones were low and hushed. Not a whisper, but close to it. When they saw me, they paused their conversation to say hi before they continued. I gave them space as I put an everything bagel in the toaster and made myself a coffee. I heard my father's name a few times during the conversation but couldn't make out what they were saying. My only thought was that maybe the somber mood had been about him, but after playing out scenarios, it didn't make sense. The only possible reason I could think of was that dad was sick and dying, and they didn't want to tell me about it yet.

My heart stopped at the thought of that. Dom's voice started getting louder behind me as I spread cream cheese on my bagel. Three things happened at once. I heard Dominic's anguished voice say, "My father killed them, Russo. He killed my mom, Rocco's mom, and Rosie's mom. He did this.". The alarm started going off as he said this, and my knees gave out. Above me, I heard sounds and voices that seemed so far away that I couldn't make out what they said. My father killed his mother. That's what he'd said. My father killed Rosie's and Rocco's mothers. A sob formed in my chest, but I couldn't let it out. I heard a louder voice than the rest and felt someone lift me as I started to blink. Rocco's face was hazy, but I was in his arms.

"I'm so sorry," was all I could get out, a choked sob. . .

He held me tighter. When I stopped crying, I moved so he could set me down. He steadied me, and I put both hands up to let them know I was okay.

"It was just the shock," I said, taking the Coke can Dean offered. When I looked at Dominic, Rocco, and Rosie, my lip started wobbling, and my eyes filled with tears again. "I'm so sorry."

"It had nothing to do with you, Nora," Rosie said, pulling me into a hug.

"I shouldn't have said that in front of you," Dom said, pulling me against him once Rosie let me go.

"You think you should have hidden the fact that our dad is. . . ." I took a step back and looked at his face, his eyes sad and swollen. "He's a fucking monster."

There was nothing to say about that, so Dom nodded.

"I got her, Dom. Go," Rocco said.

My brother turned to Rosie, and she was instantly in his arms. He walked them out of the room and headed upstairs. From where I stood, I could see them shaking as they held each other, and my tears started again. My father did this. How could he? My father, the man who had given me life, the one who smiled and reminded me how similar I was to him. The one who set me on a path I didn't want to go down and promised it was for my own good, promised he'd always do right by me. I heard something akin to a pig being slaughtered and realized it was coming from me. Rocco lifted me in his arms again and took me to the den. That was when I fully came to, and it dawned on me that I was in his arms, crying over the man responsible for his mother's murder. I pushed against his chest to sit up and tried to get off his lap.

"Where are you going?" He held me tighter.

"I'm so sorry," I whispered as new tears formed. I couldn't even look him in the eye. "I shouldn't be here. You shouldn't comfort me after what my father did to you."

I tried to get up again, but he was too strong. He tipped my chin up. His eyes softened when I looked at him. "I want you with me."

I'd never wanted to kiss him as badly as I did then. My eyes fell to his lips, and his fell to mine, but instead of kissing me, he pulled my head into his chest again and whispered that it would be okay. My mind raced to my mother, and the pain in my chest returned. What would happen to her if he found out she helped me? Would he kill her, as well? I set the thought aside and sat up again. This time, I looked around. We were in the den, where there were two couches, a television, and the armchair we were on.

Dean and a man I'd never met occupied the sofa in front of us. He was older, very handsome, and had Rocco's blue eyes, so I figured it was Michael.

"I'm sorry," I said to him, swallowing past the lump in my chest.

"You have nothing to be sorry for." Michael smiled kindly. He didn't seem surprised to see me on his brother's lap, which made me wonder if he'd told him about us.

Dean's expression was amused and confused, like he couldn't wrap his mind around Rocco and me. I could practically see his brain working to figure out when and how it started. I sat back against Rocco's chest and felt the sobs building again as I thought about Dominic and Gabriel. My poor brothers. They didn't deserve this. My lip quivered again, and Rocco pulled away slightly to look at my face. He softly pressed his finger against my lips to keep them from moving. When he was sure I wouldn't cry again, he moved his hand to my cheek and his thumb softly against it. His deep blue eyes held mine, and beneath the turmoil and pain, I saw a flash of something else. It filled me with enough comfort to calm down. I took more deep, shaky breaths as he held my gaze. Only then did he look away, but even as he did it, he pulled me against him. I wasn't sure if he knew he was doing it, but his mouth was pressed against my hair as he spoke to his brother and Dean. What would Dominic think if he walked down here and caught us like this? I wanted to get out of his lap just in case, but Rocco didn't seem worried, so I pressed my face to his hard chest and closed my eyes as I breathed him in.

CHAPTER TWENTY-EIGHT

Rocco

I WAS STILL HOLDING LENORA IN MY ARMS WHEN I HEARD DOMINIC and Rosie's footsteps coming down the stairs. Dean and Michael shot me a look, warning me to set her on the other couch. I didn't. I couldn't. I couldn't let go right now. Not when she'd discovered how much of a monster her father was. Not when she felt completely alone and was taking comfort in my touch. I was a bastard for it and certainly didn't deserve it, but having her in my arms was the only thing keeping me from losing my mind. Even if I hadn't felt Dominic's presence behind me, the pointed way Russo looked at me would have notified me. He was holding Rosie's hand and pulled her to the empty couch. She brought her feet up and folded herself to his side. She saw us first. Her brows pinched, her eyes widened, and then she just settled for a deer-in-the-headlights look, because she knew as well as I did what this meant.

Dominic got comfortable before his eyes snapped in my direction. He looked at his sister in my arms and met my eyes again. I saw the confusion, the question, and the anger unfold in his eyes all at once. I felt it. Rosie must have also moved from underneath his protective arm and set her hand over his. His jaw tensed as his eyes narrowed on mine, but he said nothing. I knew I had Rosie to thank for this. I also knew that in a few minutes, I was going to be a dead man.

Dean cleared his throat. "So far, four men that match the description of Giuseppe's crew have been going from hotel to hotel with a picture of Lenora."

At the sound of her name, her head snapped up. She sat up a little, letting her legs hang crossways over mine, and looked around. As soon as her breath hitched, I knew her eyes had met Dominic's, and she tried to scramble. I put a hand on her leg and held it. If I was going to die anyway, I might as well enjoy this moment a little longer. This was the problem with doing shit behind your oldest best friend's back. You could only hide for so long before you were caught. I knew it was only a matter of time before Dom exploded. I was shocked he'd lasted this long. I could feel his eyes on my hands, my face, and Lenora. He was still giving me the benefit of the doubt, or maybe trying to figure out when this could have started. He knew as well as I did that I didn't just let women sit on my lap. Even if I did, Lenora looked too comfortable in my arms for it not to be obvious. Dominic's glare turned feral.

Before he stood, Dean said, "This isn't the time, Dom."

But he was already on the move.

"Dominic, what the hell?" Rosie said, but Dom was already in my face.

"What. The. Fuck. . .is this, Marchetti?" he seethed. "Get up, Lenora."

"No." She threw her arms around my neck and turned to her brother.

The glare he directed at me reminded me of the way he looked before we killed the man who'd been abusing Rosie. The way he looked when we ransacked and burned down buildings that belonged to people who had wronged us. I'd never been on the receiving end of this look, just like he'd never been on the receiving end of mine, and I had to admit, I understood why people were scared shitless when we showed up anywhere together.

"Get up, Lenora. I won't ask again." His jaw tensed.

"Dominic," Rosie started.

"No." His shout was so loud that my brother and Russo shot up from the couch and walked over.

"It's okay. Get up," I whispered in Lenora's ear. Her eyes snapped to mine, big and hesitant. She shook her head.

"No. I'll only get up if you promise not to hurt him," she said, her voice fierce as she looked up at her brother, who was looming over us, waiting to attack me the second she stood up.

"You don't have a say in the matter," he said, his voice low, quiet, the way he spoke right before he tore into someone.

His eyes didn't waver from mine, and mine only did when I addressed his sister, still on my lap. I needed her to get off me before he yanked her off, because if he bruised her with his force, I'd have to fight him back and I knew I didn't deserve to. I knew I needed to let him take his anger out on me, even if that meant some broken bones. I deserved it. Shit, he probably thought we just hooked up for the first time in this safe house, so I probably deserved worse.

"Go sit by Rosie," I said, my voice low as I brushed her hair out of her face.

This made Dominic angrier. He clenched his fists at his sides. I knew it was taking everything in him to hold back. When Lenora didn't get up, I stood up, carrying her with me and setting her feet down slowly. She stood in front of me, facing her brother, spreading her arms like a shield.

"Do not hurt him, Dominic. Whatever you're going to do, do it to me, blame me," she yelled, her voice catching. "This was all me."

Dominic tore his gaze from mine and looked at his sister. "If I have to tell you to get away from him again, you're not going to like what happens."

"Go." I tapped her waist gently. She shook her head and turned to me, tears gathering in her beautiful eyes.

"Tell him it was me. Tell him," she cried, her sobs starting up again.

Last night, I'd wanted her tears. Today, they were clawing at my chest. I stopped looking at her brother and wiped her tears with my thumb. I grabbed the back of her head and pressed her face against my chest one last time. The alarm sounded, the whirling started, and the house started moving. Russo was a smart man and knew we had to take this outside. When we were bathed in sunlight, I pulled back and grabbed Lenora's chin, tilting her face up.

"Marchetti, I swear to fucking God," Dominic roared.

"Go sit by Rosie while I talk to your brother," I said. "It's going to be okay."

"Outside," Dean shouted. "Right fucking now, Dominic. Rocco."

I gave a nod. Dominic shouldered the shit out of me as he walked past me; I knew this would hurt. Lenora still looked like she didn't want me to leave.

"Come here, Nora," Rosie said. "This is between them."

I stepped back and turned to the door, my brother at my heels, as I heard Lenora tell Rosie that this was all her fault.

"Dude, what the motherfucking fuck were you thinking?" Mikey said as we reached the door. He slapped it before I could open it, holding my gaze. "She's marrying Salvati."

That sentence made my blood boil. "Over my dead fucking body."

I opened the door while Michael cursed behind me. Russo and Dom were already outside. Dom was pacing, probably winding up his arm to deliver a right hook to my chin. As soon as he turned around and saw me walking over, he charged at me, punching me square in the face. My head turned with the force and my cheek instantly burned. Fuck. It had been a while since I'd taken a punch. I'd forgotten how much it hurt. Still, I clasped my hands in front of me and looked him in the eyes as I straightened and waited for the next one. His eyes were wild as he bounced from foot to foot like he was standing in front of a punching bag. In a sense, he was.

"What the fuck, Roc?" He stopped moving and shoved

me hard. I staggered back a few steps. "My sister? My fucking SISTER?"

I said nothing. He shoved me again. Russo and my brother jogged over but didn't separate us yet.

"My little sister?" Dom seethed. "How could you do this?" He brought his fist up and hit me on the side of my face. I tasted iron and spit blood out. "Fight me, motherfucker. Fight me. You want to fuck around with my sister? Then, you better fight me."

"I'm not going to fight you, Dom." My tongue ran over my bloody bottom gums. I moved my face and spit again. Goddamn. Fucker got me good.

"Fight me, asshole." He shoved me again, but his words were weaker. The pain in his eyes hurt me more than any punch. He paced away from me and put his hands up. "FUCK!"

I remained still, focusing on my heart and my breathing, but I didn't take my mind to a faraway place the way I would have in any other situation. I needed to be present. I wanted this pain. I deserved it. I waited for him to come at me again. Russo and Mikey were so still and quiet, I wondered if they'd stopped breathing. Dominic paced back toward me. I braced for impact. He stopped right in front of me but didn't touch me.

"Why?" His words were calm. The anger in his eyes was replaced by pain. "Why her?"

I exhaled and glanced toward the house as I tried to think of how to answer that. Lenora and Rosie were both standing by the glass, looking horrified. When my eyes met Lenora's, the love in her eyes made me shatter. Fuck. I looked at the ground, spit again, and looked at Dominic, who was waiting for a response.

"It wasn't supposed to happen," I said like an idiot because, no shit, it wasn't supposed to happen.

"NO SHIT. This is my sister, asshole." Dom growled, running his hands through his hair.

I couldn't even stand here and tell him that it had been a mistake or that I regretted it. I didn't. I never would. She wasn't just some piece of ass to me. I would've never put myself in this predicament if I thought that was all she would be. He had to know that. He knew how I operated. I didn't just go around fucking anyone with a pulse. I wasn't a teenager. The last woman I fucked before Nora was Crystal, over six months ago. I didn't have to sleep with Lenora, but I wanted her, and I knew without a doubt that this time next year, I still would. I shut my eyes for a moment, enjoying the sound of the birds nearby and the pebbles each time Dominic moved.

"I know I don't deserve her," I started. "I fucking know she's too good for me."

"If you know that, why did you do it?" he asked, stepping forward and pointing a finger at me. "Because I know, *I know* you're sleeping with her, and you don't do anything without thinking it through a hundred and one times, so please tell me why my best friend, the person I trust most in the entire fucking world, would hook up with my sister. She's going to have her heart broken, and you, what do you gain from this?"

That was a loaded question. I had thought this through a hundred and one times before I decided to go through with it. I tried to talk myself out of it, but every time I looked at her, I was consumed with something I hadn't felt before. It was addictive. And once I tasted her and had my cock inside her, I was a goner. I never played that bullshit game of "Where do you picture yourself in ten years?" because I knew I could drop dead at any moment, so that had never been a concern of mine. With Lenora, though, when I thought about next year, she was there—cooking dinner with me, mixing drinks at Scarab *on occasion*, and smiling, just fucking smiling. When I was with her, I felt a warmth I hadn't felt since my mother died. This was unprecedented for me, but if that wasn't love, I didn't know what was. I didn't say all of these things aloud because I wasn't about to sound like a pussy in front of these three assholes. Besides, the only one who deserved to hear those words was Lenora herself. Dominic continued to stare at me like I was some alien species. Finally, I spit out the statement I should've probably led with, one I never pictured myself feeling, let alone saying aloud.

"I'd die for her," I said instead simply.

Dom staggered back a step. "What?"

The two bozos on the sideline said a string of things under their breaths.

"I'd die for her." I spit out more blood and chuckled, because, leave it to me to fall for the one woman I'm not supposed to have. "I don't know how else to describe this, Dom."

"You're in love with *my sister*? Jesus Christ, Rocco. You're. . .and she's. . ." He held the bridge of his nose and muttered things under his breath; then he looked at me. "What the fuck, man? You know she's supposed to marry Salvati."

"She's not getting married," I said. His eyes widened. "I don't care if he's a king or a fucking god. She's not marrying anyone."

Except for me, I wanted to say but held my tongue because that would've been overkill.

"You're in love with my sister," he said. A statement, not a question, as if trying to make sure he understood me correctly.

His words didn't warrant a response, so I spat more blood and remained silent. My face was starting to hurt like a bitch. When he moved toward me again, my stomach clenched, my body instantly preparing for the next onslaught. I kept my hands down, though, even as he brought both hands up. I kept mine down and focused on not flinching. He set a hand on each of my shoulders. It was so shocking that I almost moved away.

"Fuck," he breathed, letting his head hang between us for a moment. He lifted his eyes as he dropped his hands. "I just thought. . .I just figured. . ." He searched my eyes, swallowing hard. "I know you'll do right by her. I do. It's just. . ."

"She's your little sister," I said, finishing the sentence for him. "I know, Dom. Trust me. This wasn't planned. I didn't fucking want to fall in love." I scoffed. "Look at you and G and Lor. A bunch of fucking pansies."

His eyes narrowed and he shook his head again. "Fuck, man."

"I don't regret it," I said. "I'll take any punishment that comes my way, but I will never regret your sister."

He looked at me for the longest time. I knew he wouldn't hit me again, but I wasn't sure what he was thinking, which was a first. Suddenly, he stepped forward and threw his arms around me. He gave me an actual full-on hug. I was so shocked by it that I couldn't return it even if I'd wanted to.

"You fucking better be willing to die for her." He stepped away, his brows tugging. "Shit, you actually might."

No truer words had been spoken. The way things were looking, I probably would.

CHAPTER TWENTY-NINE

Lenora

ROCCO WENT STRAIGHT TO HIS ROOM WHEN THEY CAME BACK INSIDE, and I stayed downstairs with Rosie, Dom, Dean, and Michael, brooding, waiting for the acceptable moment to excuse myself and go after him. We were all just standing around anyway. Dominic hadn't said a word to me. He shot me a pointed look and walked over to Rosie to whisper in her ear like a middle schooler. Dean and Michael grabbed a bottle of whiskey and sat in the den. I had no idea what the outcome of their fight had been. I couldn't read my brother's mood. Was he finally blaming me for it? I'd take the blame a hundred times. I didn't care. It was better than seeing Rocco just stand there while Dominic beat him up. I couldn't take it anymore. I either had to ask him or go upstairs, but I couldn't just sit here as if nothing happened.

"What happened outside?" I asked. Dominic's face snapped up. Of course, he just fucking stood there looking at me. "What did you say to him?"

"What'd you think would happen, Lenora?"

"I don't know." I threw my hands up and paced the tiny space. "This is my fault, you know? I was the one who kept pushing him. I didn't want. . ." I swallowed, this was going to be TMI for my brother, but I was past caring. "I didn't want Adriano to be my first."

"I didn't want to hear that, but I understand," Dom said after a moment.

"The point is, if you're going to be mad, be mad at me."

"You know what they say, Nora. It takes two to tango." He turned and opened the fridge.

"I know, and I'm telling you that I was the one who started the dance."

He turned around, looking amused at my response, and for the first time in my adult life, I wanted to hit my brother. I would have if I thought it would hurt him. Instead, my heart sank as I went over this mess. We were already in the middle of an important disaster that my father created, which just added to it. Would Rocco leave? Was that why he was taking so long upstairs? Because he was packing? Had I been the cause of breaking up a lifelong friendship? Damn it. Of course that had crossed my mind initially, but I didn't think it would actually happen this way. I don't know what I thought. I guess I thought we'd take this secret to our graves along with my heart, which only seemed to beat for him.

"Is he leaving?" I asked. "Is that why he's upstairs? He's leaving?"

It was hard not to wither underneath my brother's stare. "Why don't you go upstairs and find out, and while you're at it, tell him to get his ass down here."

I went, but my steps faltered and I turned around again. "Are you going to hit him again?"

He raised an eyebrow. "Do you want me to?"

"No, I don't want you to." I threw my hands up. "I didn't want you to in the first place."

"He's a big boy, Lenora. He can take a few punches. He's had worse." He looked away momentarily. "Tell him we're waiting for him."

I rushed upstairs. Dean had lowered the house when everyone came inside, so it was dark again. God, it had been torture watching them outside, and it was even worse now that I didn't know the extent of the damage I'd caused. I stood in front of Rocco's door and stared at it. Would he be mad at me and kick me out of his room? It was his right to do that, but I wasn't sure my heart could take it. I opened the door. He peeked out of the bathroom as I walked inside and shut the door behind me. He was shirtless, and while normally his body would have beckoned all of my attention, his battered face had it now. I pressed a hand over my heart, breathing shakily as I walked over. When I reached him, I lifted the tips of my fingers to the dark bruise forming around his left eye. He watched me as I did it and didn't flinch when I brought my other hand to his jaw and ran my fingertips right next to his split lip.

"I'm so sorry," I whispered, searching his eyes, my fingertips still on his face.

"Don't apologize." He turned his face and kissed the spot where my pulse beat, cupping my face softly as if I was the one who was all bruised up. He lowered his forehead to mine and shut his eyes.

"He shouldn't have hit you."

"Yes, he should've." His eyes crinkled when he pulled back to look at me. "I got off easy. If the tables were turned, I would have probably murdered him."

"No, you wouldn't have," I said softly. "I feel so awful. First, my dad, and now, I feel like I ruined your friendship."

"What are you talking about?" He pulled away again. "You didn't ruin anything."

"I did." I lowered my head.

"All you've done is make me happy. How could you have ruined anything?"

I swallowed. "But Dominic. . ."

"Is fine. He'll have to get over it and get used to seeing us together."

My head snapped up. "What do you mean?"

"I plan to be by your side until you get sick of me." His thumb made soft circles on my cheek.

"But. . ." I frowned. He had to know that was impossible, right? I blinked back tears.

"I'm in love with you, Lenora."

I inhaled sharply. "What?"

"I'm in love with you," he repeated.

"Oh, my God." I set a hand on my stomach because the butterflies wouldn't quit.

"I'm not telling you this because I expect anything from you." He kissed my forehead. "I'm just telling you because when I was out there getting my ass kicked, the only thing I could think about was how I felt about you."

"Rocco." My words were whispered. The tears I'd been holding back began trickling down my cheeks. Rocco Marchetti was in love with *me*. I swallowed past the knot in my throat. "I'm supposed to marry Adriano. My father will. . .well, look at what he's capable of."

"Fuck them."

"You can't just shrug them off. My father is a monster." I wiped my tears. "And Adriano's family is very rich."

"And?"

"What do you mean 'and?'" I pushed his chest lightly. "He's a billionaire. He'll kill you just to prove a point."

His dark chuckle curled inside my belly as he pinned me with a serious gaze. "'A billionaire,'" he said, air quoting the words like I'd made it up. "You think there's a chance in hell that a 'billionaire' could take me out? Come on, Lenora."

I rocked back on my heels. The Salvati Family had money that opened up doors meant to be bolted shut, but Rocco was probably right. My father had described Rocco as someone who didn't need a weapon because he was already a deadly weapon. He'd said it so proudly that thinking about it now, knowing what he'd done, filled me with anger.

"You don't have to worry about me." He brought my hand up and kissed it.

"Okay."

I dropped the topic because I believed him and would rather have spent however long we had together actually being together. I sat up on the counter, flinching every time he hissed as he tended his lip. I couldn't stop staring at him. I wanted to lick every single square of his abdomen. His face, even beat up, was perfection. He'd said he was in love with me. My heart skipped a beat. I replayed it and bit my lip to keep from laughing out of pure joy.

His eyes shifted to me. "What's so funny?"

"Nothing, it's just. . .I'm in love with you too."

He dropped the ointment in his hands and turned to me, eyes flaring as he stood between my legs and gripped my thighs. He let go of my left thigh and brought his hand to the nape of my neck, threading his fingers in my hair and tugging it to tilt my face.

"Tell me again," he growled, his words rumbling through my entire body.

"I'm in love with you."

I couldn't stop the smile that formed on my face. He exhaled heavily, wrapped an arm around me, and lifted me. I hooked my legs around him and threaded my hands behind his neck. He sank his face into my neck and breathed, shivers ran through me.

"I love you, Rocco Marchetti," I whispered.

"Fuck." He pulled back and placed a soft kiss against my lips.

I would have died with a smile if the safe house exploded at that moment. I didn't know how we'd stay together, but I knew I had to do everything possible to try.

CHAPTER THIRTY

Rocco

"**Y**OUR CAMERA IS OUT OF FOCUS," DOMINIC TOLD LORENZO FOR the third time.

"Are we sure this is safe?" Russo asked. "Not bugged?"

"Positive," Loren said, as he fidgeted with the camera.

"This is what happens when old men try to use technology," I said.

"I'm not old," Loren growled. "Thirties are not old."

"Here, let me do it," Gio said, doing something to the screen and refocusing it. He looked into the camera and hissed. "Damn. What the fuck happened to your face, Marchetti?"

I shot him a look. "Are we going to talk about the issue at hand, or do you wanna gossip for the next ten minutes?"

Gio pressed his lips together as he stared at me. If no one else were here, he'd go the gossip route. The world could be ending in the middle of an alien invasion or some shit, and Gio would still be asking questions about things that were none of his business. When this conversation was over, he would start blowing up my phone to ask what happened. Nosey motherfucker. This meeting was bullshit, anyway. I was itching to get the fuck out of this safe house and go after Giuseppe. Just thinking about him made my blood boil.

Loren cleared his throat and folded his hands on the desk like a fucking math teacher. "Giuseppe sent Rifle down there."

I sank back in my chair. "Fuuuuuck."

"Aren't you cool with him?" Dom turned to me.

"Cool enough, but he's a hired gun." I drummed my fingers on the arm of the chair.

Rifle, short for Rifleman, was a sharpshooter. It was something we'd bonded over at the shooting range. We both took our rifles there from time to time and had a little fun with the targets. We'd try to make it harder for each other and make bets. I usually won. We learned that we knew some of the same people. So yeah, I was cool with Rifle out there, but I didn't trust people who made a living off killing. None of us did.

"Who'd Giuseppe put a hit on?" I asked.

"Whoever's helping Nora, so basically, all you motherfuckers," Gio said.

"Does he know we have her?" Dom asked.

"Don't think so. They think she ran away on her own and is using the USB drive for blackmail. They've only said that they want her alive and well enough to walk down the aisle."

I stilled. Worst-case scenario, all of us die, and she ends up marrying that son of a bitch. In the best-case scenario, Adriano and Giuseppe would be six feet under before she even tried on the wedding dress.

"Giuseppe means to start a war," Gio said. "My dad was at his house last night and said he could practically see the smoke coming out of his ears."

I leaned back in my chair. "What does Joe say about all of it?"

"He didn't have much to say." Gio shrugged. "What is there to say? When Giuseppe wants something, he gets it."

"He claims that if the USB drive and ledger are given back, and Lenora shows up for the wedding, he'll put all of this behind him," Loren said.

"And you believe him?" I shot him a look.

"I do," he said. "What he's gaining with the Salvati's is much bigger than a USB drive and a ledger only he understands. Besides, it's his daughter. You think he'd hurt her?"

None of us said a word, but I was sure Lorenzo could hear our resounding "yes" anyway.

"He's responsible for the murders," I said.

"You're gonna have to be more specific," Gio said.

"Our mothers," Michael said behind me.

"What the fuck is he doing there?" Loren sat straighter in his seat. "You took him to the safe house?"

"He's my brother."

"He's a cop," Loren spat.

"I'm not a cop. I'm a detective," Michael said. "There's a difference."

Loren glowered.

"We have bigger things to worry about," I snapped.

"My father was responsible for the massacre in Providence," Dom said loudly to end Loren and Michael's beef. Once again, silence filled both sides of the screen.

"He couldn't." Loren shook his head, brows pulled lightly. "He wouldn't."

His reaction was warranted. Anyone who had been around Giuseppe back then would tell you how distraught he was after his ex-wife died. Looking back now, maybe it was the guilt he felt. Or maybe he was a psychopath who happened to be a good actor. I couldn't be sure which was true. He'd always treated us like we were family. He was a monster to many but never to us. *Or so we thought.*

"He did," Dominic said.

"How do you know? You have proof?" Gio asked, eyes wide on each of us.

"It was on the USB drive," I said. "That and a whole bunch of other shit that we haven't even gone back to look at."

"I just. . ." Gio sat back in his chair. Loren was still in disbelief.

"Do you think Angelo knew?" I asked.

"Fuck." Loren let out a breath. "I don't think so. I'd like to think he would have done right by you guys and ended Giuseppe if he knew. I mean, there's a code—women and children are untouchable."

"I agree. It would be out of character for your father to sit back," Dean said to Loren.

"And murdering my mother is perfectly in character for my dad?" Dom spat.

"It is." Dean leaned back in his seat. "I hate to say it, but it is."

"Now what?" Loren asked, after another bout of silence.

"I have men on the ground waiting for me to tell them where to go," Michael said. "In case you decide to attack first."

"Cops?" Loren asked, as if the word left a bad taste in his mouth.

"No," Mikey said firmly.

Loren opened his mouth to respond.

I slammed my fist on the table. "Your bickering will get us nowhere. They could be cops, robbers, farmers, astronauts, or circus clowns, for all I care. They're risking their lives for us just the same."

Loren grunted at that and let it go.

"What's the status on our soldiers, Marchetti?" Gio asked. "Do we send them there? Keep them here?"

"We need Nico, Marco, and Matti to stay put over there," I said. "Jamaican Mike is taking care of the situation at the ports with Big Mike's help." I took a breath, running my fingers through my hair. "I'm at a loss with what to do with the young soldiers. Some of them have been arrested for petty crimes. I don't think they can handle this shit. Giuseppe will wipe them out."

Gio nodded in agreement.

"Has anyone put tracking devices on Giuseppe's cars?"

"Benny and Ray-Ray tagged two of them. One of my hackers is tracking them, so we'll know where they are soon," Dean said, raising his palms. "The hackers aren't cops, Lorenzo, since you're so interested in what people do for a living."

"Jesus Christ," Loren muttered, running a hand through his hair.

"You started this shit," Gio said to him, then turned back to us. "Emile was able to take over the cameras around Giuseppe's apartment and get surveillance on him and his inner circle. So far, he's still going in and out of his building. Adriano's also been there a few times."

"We also sent backup security for Sofia, in case he decides to use her to get to Lenora," Loren said, "She's out of the country burying her mother, but you never know."

I slumped in my chair, realizing I had taken away Lenora's only way to contact her mother. I should have at least told her she could borrow my phone. I felt like such an asshole. She had every right to push me away after how I'd acted; instead, she welcomed me. Accepted me. I straightened my posture and set my hands on the table.

"My concern is that Giuseppe may know about the location of this safe house," I said.

"How would he know?" Dom's head snapped in my direction.

"Open any file on there." I pointed at the computer where the USB drive was plugged in, and the files were ready to be opened. He picked the one I knew his mother would be in. I should have warned him against those years. He hesitated when he saw his mother's name but clicked it anyway.

"What the fuck?" he breathed as he clicked through the pictures of his mom grocery shopping at the nail salon, drinking wine in her kitchen, and dancing with his stepfather.

He clicked out and hovered the cursor over Rosie's mom's name but skipped over it and clicked the folder with his and his brother's name. Dozens of pictures appeared on the screen. Dom playing football with me. Gabe holding Rosie's hand. Dom looking into the window of the ice cream shop Rosie used to work at. He opened and closed countless folders, finding every single

one of us including Joe, Angelo, Charles, and Adriano. The list
went on and on. The ones with the most folders were his children, his current wife, and his ex-wife. He must have spent a for-
tune to watch that many people simultaneously. When he got
tired of looking, Dom pushed the computer away.

"He's sick," Gio said. "Watching someone because you think
they're in danger and want to protect them is one thing, but this
is sick."

"How could we not have noticed?" Loren asked quietly, in
disbelief.

It was the question I'd been asking myself since I opened
the USB drive. How could we not have noticed someone following us with a camera? How could I not have noticed? I'm more
aware of my surroundings than most people. They must have
used a long-scope lens the entire time. With my sniper rifle, I
could watch people 1,200 meters away, and I was sure there were
camera lenses that went the same distance. I glanced at the bag
in the corner that I'd asked Dean to bring with him. My weapons of choice were my body or my Matriarch knife, but I'd use
whatever I could get my hands on to defend Lenora. There was
a knock on the wall behind us, and we turned to see Lenora and
Rosie standing there.

"Can we join you?" Rosie asked, looking at Dominic.

He raised his arm, welcoming her, and she smiled as she
ducked under his arm and settled against him like he was her favorite reading chair. As she said hi to Gio and Loren, Lenora sat
in the empty chair beside me. She looked up at me and smiled
but didn't move to touch me or sit on my lap, which should
have been fine—because when the fuck had I let a fully-clothed
woman sit on my lap anyway? When I was fifteen, maybe. But
Lenora made me want that. I wanted to be able to open my arms
and know she'd instantly be in them. I wanted to touch her, smell
her, and feel her on me as often as possible.

She turned her smile to greet the guys on screen and I

couldn't take it anymore. I reached for her hand and tugged. Her brows pulled, but she stood up without hesitation. When I guided her to my lap, with her legs crossways over mine, she looked at her brother to gauge his reaction. He watched us closely, but he didn't look angry, just curious and so confused that I almost laughed. I tucked her head under my chin and breathed her in as I wrapped my arms around her, eyes on the screen. Lorenzo and Gio both had their mouths hanging open.

"Oh. Shit." That was Loren.

"Well, now we know what happened to your face." Gio's eyes danced.

I raised my middle finger to him but felt myself smile, and instantly flinched at the pain in my lip.

"It was worth it," I said, kissing the top of Lenora's head.

Dominic rolled his eyes. Lorenzo, Gio, and Michael laughed. Rosie smiled. Dean exhaled heavily as he sat back in his seat. Lenora pulled back and looked up at me. When her gaze met mine, she smiled wide, her eyes sparkling with joy, and my chest squeezed again. I hadn't prayed since my mom died, but at that moment, I silently prayed that I'd live to see this smile for years to come.

"How are you coping, Rosie?" Loren asked.

"I feel betrayed and so fucking sad. I can't believe he has the nerve to call me his daughter. All the while knowing he killed my mother." Her words caught. Dom shut his eyes like he was in pain. "I don't think I'll tell my dad or Santi."

Dominic tightened his arms around her and set his jaw on her head.

"If they've made peace with her being gone, maybe it's for the best," Loren said. "I'm sorry."

Rosie offered a small smile.

"What are we going to do about Giuseppe?" Gio asked, looking at me.

Everyone knew I'd hunted down the men who pulled the

trigger, and I was just waiting to find whoever set it in motion so they could meet the same fate. I'd been at this for over ten years. My feelings for Lenora didn't change this. Nothing could. Giuseppe would die by my hands. I just hoped I had a chance to torture him before I killed him.

"I'm going to kill him," I said simply.

Lenora tensed in my lap. She pulled back to look at me, a horrified expression on her face. She turned to Dominic, who was already watching her, and shook her head. Dom looked sad as fuck but said nothing. I felt for them, I did, but their father needed to pay for this. Lenora got up and ran out of the room. I sighed heavily.

"Welcome to paradise, fucker," Gio said.

"You're an idiot," I muttered, looking at the hallway Lenora had gone down.

I wanted to go upstairs and comfort her, but I couldn't. We still needed to figure out how we were going to kill her father.

CHAPTER THIRTY-ONE

Rocco

"I'M GOING TO SUGGEST SOMETHING, AND I NEED YOU TO HEAR ME out before you say anything," Mikey said, pointing at Dominic and me.

"I already don't like where this is going." I crossed my arms and leaned back in the chair.

"What if we make a copy of the USB drive and let Lenora go home with it. . ." he started. I sat up in my seat. Mikey leveled me with a stern look. "Everyone pretends that things are fine. She dresses up and goes to the church for the wedding."

"What the. . ." Dominic said.

"No." I shot out of my seat. "What the fuck?"

"Sit down, Rocco." My brother continued looking at me with the same face he made when I did something stupid. I didn't sit down but crossed my arms and stood next to my chair. "Everyone will be at this wedding. Her dad, Adriano, and their guards. Everyone."

I sat down, set my elbows on my knees, and buried my face in my hands. God damn it. Gio and Dom started asking questions, but I was still going over my brother's idea. IF Lenora weren't part of it, it would be a brilliant plan. I knew if she heard it, she'd agree instantly, but I didn't want that. I didn't want her to leave my sight, and I didn't want her around her father or Adriano. I took a breath and joined the conversation.

"We could have her wired, so if Giuseppe does anything crazy, we could go in there," Gio suggested.

"Or Dominic can go with her, say he found her, and stay with them until it's time to go to the church," I said.

"That would be suspicious as hell, Roc," Rosie said from the kitchen.

"Why, because he doesn't go anywhere without you?" Loren asked.

"Yeah." She shrugged as she turned to the stove and got distracted while studying the kitchen. "I can't believe there's a vent here."

"Pretend you're drunk and have to stay there," Gio said to Dominic.

"I guess I could drive myself there." Dom tilted his head as he considered it.

"Wouldn't he just have one of his men drive you home?" Loren asked.

I was barely listening to their suggestions. I could only think about a scared Lenora facing her father alone. "If she goes to the apartment, I can't sneak in."

"That's what you're worried about?" Dom shot me a droll look.

I shot him one back. "I'm worried about her safety, dumbass."

"You can't climb buildings? In the commercials, they climb buildings," Dean said.

"You're an idiot." I shook my head. "It's the Marines, not Spider-Man training."

"I can call Sofia and have her go," Dom said. "I think she's back in town, and if she's not, once she gets word about what's happening, she'll want to be there."

"That's not a bad idea," I said quietly, because I didn't want to agree.

"There will be innocent people at the wedding," Gio said. "We wouldn't have time to warn them."

"You realize, we have to kill all of them," I said. "If we go through with this, it's not only Giuseppe and Adriano we need to take out. It would be them and their crews."

Dom remained silent. I needed to ask him how he felt about this. If taking out his dad was going to be an issue, he needed to sit this out.

"We can't just go on a shooting spree," Loren said. "Our wives will be there, our parents, Nadia's kids, people who have nothing to do with this. If we miss even one shot. . ."

"Rocco never misses a shot," my brother said. "He can be high up, where the organ is."

"I may not miss, but I can't take out all their men from up there without drawing a lot of attention." I drummed my fingers as I tried to think of who else was a good shot. I couldn't involve anyone in private security. Gio was out of the question. I couldn't be sure that he'd do it without missing. He was more of an in-your-face kind of guy. I looked at Gio. "I may need Petra."

"You know this is her kind of party," Gio said, yawning. "I'll text her now."

"You can count on me," Mikey said.

"No. Fuck no." My eyes snapped to his. "And while we're at this, Dominic, I think you need to sit this one out."

"Fuck no." He made fists with his hands.

"You can't kill your father," I said. "And any little hesitation will throw us off."

"I won't hesitate."

"Dom." I sighed. "Just think about it. If I were in your shoes, I'd hesitate."

"I agree about Dom sitting out, but I'm not." My brother crossed his arms. "I'm just as good a shot as you."

"I didn't say you weren't, Michael. You could lose your job over this."

"I'm more worried about losing my little brother." He

raised an eyebrow. "I'm doing it whether you want me to or not."

"Fuuuuuck." I ran my hands down my face.

"Dom, you should think about sitting out. Marchetti has a point." Gio yawned again. "Let's sleep on it and meet tomorrow morning."

We ended the call and sat in silence.

"I don't want you there." I kept my eyes on my brother. "I invited you here because it's Florida, and you had the right to know what happened to Mom, but I won't risk your life or your job."

"I'm not asking for your approval, Rocco."

"I don't even agree with this fucking plan." I ran my hands down my face again as if it would change the fucked up reality I was living.

"You know this is the only way," Dean said. "The smartest way."

"If anything happens to her. . ." The words caught.

God, if anything happened to her, I'd fucking lose it. I stood up and walked out. I needed to do something. Hit something. Or someone. I didn't trust myself to say anything else to them, and I sure as hell didn't trust myself with Lenora right now, so I went to the small room we'd designated as our gym. The punching bag would do for now.

Lenora frowned. "Did you go for a run?"

"Punching bag." I walked to the bathroom and switched on the shower. She followed and stood outside with her arms crossed, watching every move as I washed.

"What happened in the meeting?"

"There's a plan but I don't like it. I'm trying to think of

another way." I let my head hang for another moment before switching off the showerhead.

"What's the plan?" She handed me the towel and took a step back. She looked like she'd been crying again.

I finished drying myself, got dressed, and pulled her to the bed with me.

"Rocco, you're scaring me," she whispered, setting her chin on my chest. "What's the plan?"

"The plan is to take you back to your father with the USB drive and have you act normal for a few days, so basically, be a brat," I smiled at her, and she pinched my nipple over my shirt. "Fuck, Nora."

She grinned. "Continue."

"You go to the church and walk down the aisle so we can take them all out," I said with a breath.

"Oh." She sat up and folded her legs, looking at her hands as she thought about it. She looked unsure when she looked twice. "When you say *take them all out*. . ."

"Someone will take the bystanders somewhere safe."

"But. . ." She looked down again, folding and unfolding her hands. "You'll kill Adriano and his men?"

"Yes."

"What about my mom?"

"She'll be safe," I said.

If we ransacked them, they wouldn't have time to react. By the time they realized what was happening, it would be over. At least, that was how it played out in my head. Even after settling on the plan, I couldn't shake the uneasiness in my gut. Lenora lay back down, setting her head on my chest. I turned the lights off, closed my eyes, kissed the top of her head, and squeezed her tight, wishing I could cocoon her inside me so she would never get hurt.

"Roc," she whispered.

"Hm."

"What about my dad?"

My eyes popped open. I stared at the dark.

"Rocco."

"What are you asking me, Lenora?"

She sat up. I did, as well. Even though we were in the dark, we were close enough to see each other. "Are you going to. . ." She took a breath. "Are you going to hurt him?"

"Yes."

"Will you kill him?" she whispered.

"Yes."

She let out a strangled sob that made my heart sink. I reached for her and she let me. She let me wrap her in my arms and hold her as she cried. When she was finished, she took a few gasping breaths and wiped her face.

"Please don't kill him."

I tensed. "You can't ask that of me. I'll give you the world, anything you fucking want, but you can't ask that of me."

"Rocco," she shouted, crying again. "I know he's a monster. I know he deserves to pay for what he's done. But there are other ways. There has to be another way to get payback."

"This is the only way I know."

"No." Her tortured voice was a knife to my heart. "Please."

"What would you have me do, Lenora? What's the alternative?"

"He could go to jail. He'll serve life. He'll rot there, but at least he'll still be. . .alive," she whispered.

I shook my head. "This is how it has to be."

"It doesn't." She pulled away and got out of bed. "Who made the rules? Why does death have to be the price everyone pays?"

"Come back to bed." I reached out for her, but she took another step back. "Not until you promise." She gasped another sob. "Not until you promise you'll try another way."

I put my hands over my face and sighed deeply. I couldn't do that. I was a lot of things, including a liar, but I wouldn't lie to her. This would be our downfall, the thing that would eventually tear us apart. She stormed out of the room, slamming the door shut as she left. The room felt cold, dreadful in her absence. I wondered if I should make peace with it, and whether this would be the beginning of the end.

CHAPTER THIRTY-TWO

Lenora

I WAS GETTING DIZZY FROM GOING OVER THE PLAN SO MANY TIMES, but I agreed that it was a good one. As long as I kept up the ruse, it should work. I was sure I could do it. After all, I'd coasted through life pretending. Thinking back on it now, I had been so trusting of my parents, my father specifically. He'd even pitched my arranged marriage as some sort of favor to me because I needed a strong man, a wealthy man, to take care of me when he was gone. He'd continuously said that, and I bought into it for many years. I'd even bragged about it once or twice in college when my few friends were obsessing over finding their soulmates. I'd said, "Thank God I don't have to worry about that." But then, Papà chose Adriano Salvati, and my acceptance of it faltered.

It wasn't just that he was too old for me and I wasn't attracted to him. Adriano was very popular amongst the ladies back in Italy. I took comfort in that. I had no qualms about turning a blind eye to his indiscretions if it meant he'd spent less time trying to touch me, until he expected me to start popping out kids. I shivered at the thought. I'd been wanting an out so badly that I hadn't even stopped considering what it meant for my father. And that was before we found out that he had their mothers murdered. I went through the plan again and shut my eyes, willing the pain in my chest away.

If I went through with this, I'd be sealing my father's fate. My actions would set the plan in motion, and if Rocco made good on his promise, I'd never see my father again. I understood that what he'd done demanded some sort of punishment. If I tried, I could understand why they wanted to kill him. I wasn't an idiot. I knew my father was horrible, but he was still my father. He was still the man who untangled my hair when I was little and taught me how to ride a bicycle. He was still the one who gifted Aanya to me when he saw how lonely I was during his visit, the summer of my junior year at boarding school. We didn't always get along. He made decisions for me that drove me crazy, but he was still my father. I couldn't explain this to anyone except maybe Dominic, and I was sure he wouldn't understand since our dad murdered his mother. Rocco was out for blood. I was scared about what would happen if he made good on his promise. Would I see him the way I did now, or would he become a monster like everyone said my father was? I swallowed back my sob. I was sick of crying.

"Hey." Dominic walked over and sat opposite me on the Greyhound we were traveling back to New York in. Another ruse.

"Hey." I pushed my back against the wall behind me and stretched my legs on the empty seat beside me.

"I noticed you're keeping your distance," he said, "from Rocco."

I nodded, not trusting myself to speak without the words sounding tortured.

"Are you. . .over?" He frowned.

"I don't know."

He stared at me. "It's because of Dad."

"How am I supposed to accept that he's going to murder my father?" I whisper-shouted. "How can you be okay with this?"

"You don't think I'm struggling?" He leaned forward, taking over the aisle as he rested his elbows on his knees. "It's fucking tearing me apart, but it's what has to be done."

"Why?" I swallowed hard. "Why can't he just go to jail? Why do all of you always have to take matters into your own hands and not abide by the same laws as everyone else?"

He looked away briefly. "It's all we know."

"He's your father," I said, then lowered my voice. "He's our father. What will Gabriel say?"

"I think Gabe would agree with the plan."

I crossed my arms and shook my head, turning my attention to the back of the seat in front of me. Gabe had grown close to Dad. There was no way he'd agree with the plan.

"He killed our mother, Nora," Dom said. I looked at him again. "He killed three innocent women just because he fucking could. And then he hid it from us for almost fifteen years."

"I know." I bit the inside of my mouth. "I get it. He's a monster. You deserve justice, I know. I'm just saying there are other ways."

"Why did you take the USB drive?"

"You know why."

"You wanted to blackmail him with it. What was your end game?"

"I was hoping he'd just call off the entire thing."

"Lenora." Dom shot me a look like I was naive. Maybe I was. "You can strip him of everything, and he'd still force you to walk down the aisle."

"Not if I threaten to go to the cops."

"Oh, Nora." He laughed, shaking his head. "I have so many ideas of what Dad would do to you, but I'll just stick to what I know for certain, which is that we own the fucking cops. We either have dirt on them or pay them. You think it'll be different for Dad?"

"He's not from here. He doesn't know the cops in Providence or New York."

"He doesn't have to." His words were louder now. "He can make anyone flip. Do you know why?"

"Why?" I whispered.

"Because he's not above going after their families. He goes

after whatever they love most, and that's how he makes them bend to his will. That's the kind of man he is."

"He wouldn't." I looked at him with watery eyes.

"He killed my mother, Nora," he said, his voice lower now, tired. "Without a second thought, he killed the woman he claimed was the love of his life. You don't think he'd do the same to yours?"

His words sent a chill down my spine. I wanted to argue with him, to tell him he would never do that, but he was right.

CHAPTER THIRTY-THREE

Lenora

I DIDN'T SAY GOODBYE TO ROCCO. I DIDN'T SAY GOODBYE TO HIM inside the Greyhound, because I was too caught up in my feelings about him killing Dad. Outside, I couldn't risk saying goodbye just in case people were watching. I felt his eyes on my back the entire way inside the building. I tried hard to stay strong on my way to Dad's penthouse. Thankfully, Rosie and Dominic were with me. The story was that I'd called Rosie when I got back, and Dominic was so worried that he rushed over to bring me. We'd gone as far as calling mom to assure her I was fine from a new phone we'd picked up on the way. When I stepped foot in New York, I had to assume I was being monitored. By my dad. By Adriano. Tomorrow, I was supposed to have a day at the spa for my bachelorette, and even there, I had to continue the ruse that I didn't want to marry Adriano but was trying to make peace with it. It wasn't too far off from the truth.

My stomach flopped when the elevator doors opened up in his penthouse. The guard by the elevator, Ronny or something, gave me a stern look, but that was the norm. At least, that was what I told myself. Rosie must have noticed my hesitation, because she held my hand in hers and squeezed. I was shocked that she wanted to come along. When I voiced that, she said, "I'm going to treat him the exact way he treated me all this time," she said.. We were almost in the kitchen when my father popped his head out, smiling as he met us in the hall. He said hello to Dominic and Rosie before turning to me.

"Welcome home, Lenora," he said. "You gave us quite a fright."

"I'm sorry about that." I looked at the floor. His smile looked more like a grimace when I looked at him again.

"Dominic, Rosalyn, thank you for bringing her home," he said, still looking at me. "Lenora and I have important things to discuss."

"Dad," Dominic started, walking around him so he'd look at him. "Can I have a word?"

Dad exhaled and walked back to the kitchen with Dom. "Sure."

I covered my face with shaky hands and hoped Dom could convince him to let them stay over. Their voices rose as they argued, but I couldn't hear much with my pulse roaring in my ears. Whatever was said didn't work. Dom walked out of the kitchen with a hard look and grabbed Rosie's hand. She turned to say goodbye to Dad, who smiled at her like nothing was wrong. Dom ignored him and walked over to me.

"If you need anything, call me," he said, setting a hand on my shoulder and squeezing. He looked like he wanted to say more but couldn't.

Rosie hugged me. "Stay strong for us, okay?"

I nodded and watched them walk into the elevator, leaving me alone with my father. I'd never been afraid of my father. I'd never had reason to be. The person here right now was not the father I knew. With that in mind, I put up my shield and turned to face him.

"I'm sorry I scared you," I said quietly. "I was always coming back. I just needed time."

"You said that but you're not sorry you left," he said. I shook my head. "And you're not sorry you stole from me."

"I thought I could make you change the wedding." Tears covered my vision.

Before I could think, he was on me, his hand gripping my

hair tightly as he pushed me into the wall behind me, his green eyes cold as he got in my face. I whimpered, tears streaming down my face. Dad squeezed harder. My skull felt like it was on fire.

"You thought you could steal from me and get away with it because you're my daughter?" he seethed. "You thought you'd be able to get away with this?"

"I-I-I just wanted time," I said through tears.

"I've given you time," he roared, pushing my head against the wall with a thump before letting go of my hair and pacing away. My hands went to my head as if that would alleviate the pain. "I've given you everything you've ever wanted. I ask for one thing and you can't do it."

"I'm sorry." My lip wobbled. "I'm sorry."

"You are not sorry." He walked back over.

Before he even got to me, I squeezed my eyes shut and braced myself. He slapped me so hard, my head turned to the completely opposite side. I gasped loudly as I opened my eyes, holding my burning cheek. He'd never hit me before, even when I used to get on his nerves when I was a kid. A sob bubbled in my chest as I held my face with my right hand and set my left over my chest. He grabbed my hair again, squeezing. I tried to take a deep breath between sobs, but his hold never eased.

"How do you think this has made me look?" He pushed my head back and roared, "How do you think you made me look in front of all of the families?"

"I said I was sorry," I managed to gasp out. "I can't take it back."

He let me go and stepped away, eyes narrowed. "Did you show anyone what you stole?"

"No!" I shouted, desperate to get out of this. "I didn't even see what was on it!"

"Are you lying, Lenora?" He stared harder.

"I swear. I swear on everything. I hooked it up to the

computer and took it right back out because I. . ." I tried to get myself out of control, but my words came out as a wail. "I was scared I'd see you as the monster everyone said you were."

My entire body shook as I cried into my hands. "I'm sorry. I mean it. I'm sorry."

"Are you going to continue causing trouble for me?" he asked, his tone much softer, more like the dad I knew.

I shook my head, hands still on my face. "No, I promise. I'll do as you ask."

"Good." He walked over to me, set his hand on my head, and gave me a little massage. "I'm sorry for that, Nora. Sometimes my anger gets the best of me."

I wiped my face and lowered my hands, unable to look him in the eye.

"Give me the things and come to the kitchen so you can get something to eat," he said.

I picked up my bag from the floor and handed him the ledger and USB drive.

"Good." He gave a nod. "Let's go."

I followed. If he brought Adriano and a priest here, I'd marry him on the spot. That was how shaken up I felt. He pointed for me to sit, and I sat down on my usual barstool as he opened the fridge, brought out a container of leftover Pasta alla Norma, my favorite, and set out some fruit, water, and juice. I wasn't hungry, but I was afraid to turn it down once he'd heated the pasta, so I started to take small bites.

"There are many things about me that you wouldn't understand." My father stood across from me and set his elbows on the counter, plucking a green grape and popping it into his mouth. "I've done a lot of things that I wish I could take back. I may go about things the wrong way, but I only do what's best for you, Nora."

"I know," I whispered, eyes on the pasta again.

"I didn't even tell your mother, you know," he said. "With her mother dying and all, I didn't want to worry her."

I bit my lip and looked at him, tears in my eyes again. "Please don't tell her."

"Maybe I will. Maybe I won't." He ate another grape. "We'll see."

I wiped my face and started playing with my food. I couldn't eat anymore. I glanced away from him and saw a folder within reach of me. On top of it, there were pictures of Aanya.

"What is that?" I jutted my chin out at the pictures.

"Oh." He walked over and picked up the papers. "We got some beautiful pictures of her." He laid them out in front of me. I felt myself smile. "It's too bad we had to get rid of her."

"What?" I dropped my fork, looking from the photos to my father. My stomach clenched so hard I had to cover my mouth in case I vomited. Still covering my mouth, I asked, "You killed her?"

"Killed her?" He laughed, throwing his head back. "Of course not. I know how much you love that horse. I would never kill her." He looked at me like I was crazy. I hadn't even fully relaxed when he said, "I sold her."

"T-t-to who?"

"Some stable that needed another horse. She'll be fine there." He picked up the fruit and turned around to put it away.

I looked at the pictures of Aanya again until tears covered my vision. He'd sold my Aanya, my comfort. I'd been closer to her than I was to him. Aanya knew all of my secrets. She'd witnessed all my laughter and tears. I set my hand over her face like I always did, and a sob raked through me before I could stop it.

"Why?" I wailed. "Why?"

"Because, Lenora, you need to be taught a lesson." He crossed his arms.

I wiped my tears, but a new wave of them came. "I said I was sorry."

"You did, and I believe you. I also believe that you didn't

snoop through my USB drive, and I appreciate you being honest about it," he said. "You can't take Aanya with you to Italy. She's happy in her new home. You should be happy too."

I felt like I couldn't breathe, but I made myself go through the motions anyway—I stood up, threw away what was left on my plate, cleaned the plate and fork, and grabbed the water.

"I'm going to sleep," I said, keeping my back to him. My voice was hoarse, and I wasn't sure he could hear me, but I didn't care. "I'll see you tomorrow."

"Goodnight, Principessa."

I flinched. He had no right to call me that anymore, but I couldn't tell him that, so I pulled my bag into my room, set it down, and locked the door behind me. I cried until I fell asleep.

CHAPTER THIRTY-FOUR

Rocco

I FIDDLED WITH THE PEN ON MY DESK BEFORE I THREW IT AGAINST THE wall with a scream. It hadn't even been twenty-four hours, and I was already losing it. I'd gotten word that she was at the spa today, and Rosie had been texting me updates. I didn't respond but I kept reading them, wondering why I'd asked her to torture me like this.

> **Rosie: it looks like she got no sleep**
>
> **Rosie: she doesn't want to eat anything**
>
> **Rosie: she keeps crying randomly and won't tell us why**
>
> **Rosie: idk what that motherfucker did but she's not well**

I gripped my phone and contemplated throwing it next. I set it down carefully instead. The spa they were in wasn't far from Scarab. I could probably get there in ten minutes, tops. I hadn't figured out how to do that without Giuseppe's guards seeing me. I needed more time to think about it, but I had none. They'd be there until five o'clock, and it was already one. I searched for the spa and looked at the businesses on either side: a ballet studio to the right and a yoga studio to the left. I called Rosie.

"Who's driving you today?" I asked.

"Marco and Nico, but Giuseppe's men are all over them," she whispered. "They can't help."

"Fuck." I let out a breath. "Do you know anyone in Madame Rose's Ballet?"

"Hmm. . .shit, I'd have to think about it," she said. "Let me ask Cat." She asked and responded, "Yeah, we know someone."

"I need to see Lenora, and this would be the only way."

"Oookay, what way is that exactly?"

"Just. . .don't worry about the plan. I need whoever your contact is to meet me a few blocks away."

"My contact?" Rosie laughed. "Aye, aye, sir."

I rolled my eyes. "You're such a pain in the ass. Can you do this or not?"

"Yep. We're already on it," she said. "See? Aren't you glad we're on your team?"

I hung up on her.

Rosie: Lexington and East 42 in 30min

Me: thanks

Their contact was a tall, redheaded gay man named Jack. During our three-block walk, he "schooled me" on the Swiftie thing and told me I was "missing out" for not knowing who Olivia Rodrigo was. He was entertaining. I'd give him that. When we were near the spa, I put a ballcap on.

"Oh, is this a covert mission?" he asked.

"It is, actually."

"Should I have worn a costume?"

He was wearing what looked to me like a Popeye the Sailor Man costume. I laughed. "I can't tell if you're joking or not."

He grinned. "I just finished a performance for a field trip. This was kind of a rush job."

"Well, I appreciate you helping me out," I said as we crossed the street. "You wouldn't happen to share a door with the spa?"

"Not a door, per se, but we both have a second story. It's not big enough to do anything with it, so we use it for storage. There's a door that connects, but it's like really small." He gave me a once-over when we got to the opposite corner. "There's no way you'd fit. It's fit for a second grader, that small."

"Why have a door at all?" I shook my head. Some things in this city made no fucking sense.

He shrugged. "We both have doors that face an alley out back."

"That might be complicated. I don't know how much Rosie told you. . ."

"She told me nothing, so I asked nothing, just in case the phones were being monitored."

My brows rose. "This isn't your first covert mission, then."

"Nope."

"Well, there should be security out back. It wouldn't be good if they see me."

"Ah." He nodded. We stopped walking a few steps away from the businesses. "I could distract him."

"With your little getup?"

"Hey, I'll have you know that my brother is a scary motherfucker, and he taught me well."

"If you say so."

"Trust me, we got this. You just listen for me to say, 'Oh my God, thank you' before you come out."

I could not fucking believe this was my life right now. I'd defended my country, I'd done horrible things in the process. I'd lost count of how many people I'd killed and tortured, and now I was supposed to put my trust in a man wearing fucking tights and a costume in the middle of the day. Hopefully, with his help, I wouldn't have to kill Giuseppe's guards, because that would put a serious dent in our plans.

Me: cameras off on Lennox?

Dean: off

I took a breath. "Lead the way."

❦

I walked down the hall, looking for Rosie. She told me they were down the hall to the left. I'd already seen four women wearing nothing but towels. If I'd known this was how people walked around here, I would've joined years ago. Rosie walked out of a room wearing a white bathrobe.

"Oh my God, you made it," she whispered. "I already told management a guy on my security team was coming here to bring something."

"Where's Lenora?" I looked over her head into the room, but it was empty.

"She's in there." She pointed at the room next door. "This is our alone time."

"So you're all sitting here getting yourselves off while the rest of us are risking our lives?"

"Rocco." She slapped a hand over my mouth, eyes wide. "We're getting massages."

"Oh." I shrugged. "You said alone time. What the fuck am I supposed to think?"

"Men are so fucking. . ." She shook her head and groaned like she was annoyed but recovered quickly, because there was an evil sparkle in her eye when she asked, "Speaking of men, how was Jack?"

"He was wearing tights and a sailor costume," I said. "But he's pretty badass."

"She's in there." Rosie grinned, grabbed my arms, and tried to turn me around. I turned sideways and looked at the door.

"With a masseuse?"

"No, she's just there. She turned down the massage. She

got her nails done and drank the champagne, but she's just. . ." Rosie's eyes watered. "Sad."

"Thanks for this." I pulled her head against me and kissed the top of it. "I mean it."

I opened the door, shut it, and locked it behind me. The room was dark, smelled good, and had the soothing sound of waves playing. There was a massage chair, but further in, there was a white couch, where I found Lenora lying down on her stomach. I didn't know what her reaction to seeing me would be. She might scream or push me away. She might kiss me and welcome me. I couldn't tell, but we hadn't even said goodbye and I wasn't going to let tomorrow arrive without seeing her first. I kneeled next to her, taking my cap off and setting it on the ground as I ran my fingers through her soft hair. She sniffled.

"Nora," I said quietly. She turned around, eyes puffy and wide as she looked at me in disbelief.

"How?"

"I have my ways."

She launched herself at me. I wrapped my arms around her and stood, sitting down on the couch and setting her on my lap. She shifted on my lap to straddle me. My hands slid underneath her bathrobe, up her smooth thighs. She rocked against me when my hands went higher. I leaned in for another kiss. This time, when she pulled away from the kiss, I saw tears streaming down her face and took my hands out of the bathrobe.

"Hey." I cupped her face with both hands and wiped her tears away with my thumb. "It's going to be okay."

She shook her head, her lip quivering like she was about to lose it. I put my thumb on it, as if that would somehow remove the pain. I knew she'd be like this right before the wedding. It was one of the reasons I had to come here today. I wanted to assure her that it would be okay, that she would be fine, that we never had to talk about what happened to her father after tomorrow, and that even though the thought of it ripped me in half, I'd love her even if she chose to walk away from me.

"Tell me what's wrong, baby."

"H-h-h-he got rid of Aanya." Her voice broke as she said the name.

My body went rigid. "Your horse?"

She nodded.

I waited until I trusted myself to speak again without blowing up. "He killed her?"

"He sold her." She shook her head. More tears sprang from her eyes. "He sold her to hurt me."

"Fuck." I held her tighter and rocked her slowly. He was such a fucking asshole. I needed to make sure I found out exactly where her mother was, because I knew that would be his next move. "We'll get her back. I promise."

"We don't even know who he sold her to, and now I have to marry Adria—" She hiccupped. "Now I have to marry Adriano and I won't have you or Aanya, or anything I love that brings me comfort."

I squeezed her tighter. "You're not marrying him. It's going to be okay."

"He's a monster," she whispered once her tears subsided. She wiped her face and pulled back. "He's a monster, Rocco."

"I know, baby." I wiped more tears away.

"I hate him."

I sighed heavily. She was speaking out of anger so I wouldn't bother to tell her that I hated him too. What he did was fucked up, but it could have been worse. He could have had Aanya killed and shown Lenora pictures of the slaughter. It was what I would expect of him. A man who could kill a child was capable of anything, and Giuseppe had done that twice—that I knew of. I pressed my lips to Lenora's forehead and promised that everything would be okay.

"He hit me," she said, her voice so quiet I almost missed it. A heat wave ran through my body.

"What did you say?"

"H-he hit me."

I pulled back to examine her. "Where did he hit you?"

"He slapped me." She pointed at her right cheek. "And he grabbed my hair really hard like he wanted to rip it off my head. . ." she paused when her lip started wobbling again. "And then he pushed the back of my head against the wall."

My fists clenched on her lap. I closed my eyes and focused on breathing. I thought I'd felt rage before—when people owed me money, when I found out a husband was beating his wife, when I found out about the dad raping his daughter. I'd taken care of all of them, not out of rage but out of principle. The rage I felt right now was blinding.

"Rocco," she whispered, snapping me out of my haze.

My jaw ticked as I ran my thumb over her cheek. "If I thought for a second he would get violent with you, I would never have sent you back there."

"I'm sorry," she said quietly.

"You're sorry?" I asked. "For what?"

"For upsetting you. You already hate him so much, and now. . ."

"Lenora." I wanted to grab her by the shoulders and shake her. Instead, I stared. "I love you. Yes, I hate him, but *I love you*. I'm upset because knowing you're in pain hurts me."

"I love you too." She brought a hand up to touch my face softly. "So much."

I felt some of my anger dissipate. Not all, but some, as I leaned in and kissed her. It was a slow kiss, a deep one that I never wanted to end, but it had to. I kept my forehead on hers as I stood up and set her down slowly.

"Don't leave me," she whispered, grabbing my shirt. Her broken plea was almost too much to bear.

"I will never leave you. I have to do some things before tomorrow." I kissed her again. And again. And again. "Everything is going to be okay. I love you. You're strong and brave, and mine. Remember that."

"I'm yours," she said quietly. "Will I see you tomorrow? You'll be there for me?"

"Always, Principessa." I kissed her one last time. "Always."

She nodded, the sad expression never clearing. I wished I could throw her over my shoulder and take her away. Instead, I picked up my Mets cap and took two steps back.

CHAPTER THIRTY-FIVE

Rocco

I ENTERED AN EMPTY ROOM AND LOCKED MYSELF INSIDE AS I THOUGHT about my next move. What I wanted to do was kill Giuseppe's guards right now, but that would cause alarm, and we couldn't have anything fuck up tomorrow's plan. As it was, we kept the plan close to our chest and only told the people involved. It wasn't that we didn't trust our people, but one slip-up was all it would take for the entire thing to come crumbling down. Since Giuseppe was smart and had his men hanging out with ours so they could *"become friends and network,"* we couldn't risk it. I didn't even want to snipe. I wanted to be in the church to protect Lenora, but we didn't have enough men to do that, and I knew my place was behind that rifle. Petra would be sitting in the third row, where Lenora would stop momentarily. She'd be the one to take Lenora away. If all went according to plan, they'd have no issue getting out of the church and to safety. Nico, Marco, Mattia, and Tony knew the plan. Dean, Gio, and Loren would walk through the main doors and start taking down Giuseppe's men. He'd brought thirty with him, that we knew of. That was what scared me. Giuseppe was a slimy motherfucker. I needed to split his men up. We needed a plan B. For now, I just needed to get out of there. I pulled out my phone and called Jack. He'd agreed to help me in and out of here. He answered quickly.

"Is it time for our covert mission?"

"In a minute," I said. "Who did you say your brother was?"

"I didn't." I could hear the smile in his voice. I hated when people dragged shit out.

"Are you going to tell me?"

"Harry O'Conner."

I blinked once, twice, letting it register. "No shit."

"I told you he was a badass."

"I'll call you back in a second."

As I hung up, I laughed despite myself. Badass was one way to put it. Harry O'Conner had recently become the head of the O'Conner organized crime family. He'd taken the Russians out of Irish territory the first week he got there, which was impressive. He was also an acquaintance of ours. Not a friend, not an enemy. Someone you wanted in your corner, though. As I thought this through, Jack remained silent on the other end of the line. The idea popped into my head like a light bulb in a cartoon. I could ask Harry for help, but I'd owe him a favor if I did, and I hated owing people favors. I leaned my head against the wall and exhaled, as I looked up at the ceiling and thought about what I could offer Harry. My services, for one, but he had enough manpower and didn't need me.

I could give up Joe Masseria, who had the drug ring on lock, which I knew Harry wanted. I wasn't sure I wanted to go that route, since Joe was Gio's dad and he'd stayed true to his word. He'd left the U.S. to us as long as we gave him room to sell drugs. He'd always been against drugs, but when you take over your Colombian wife's cocaine empire, things change. Right now, I'd give Harry just about anything. I pinched the bridge of my nose, aware that I was in a spa surrounded by amazing smells while plotting murder. It was a smart plan, though. As things stood, we'd lose some of our people if O'Conner helped. . .so, I texted the group chat:

Me: EM

Loren: NOW?

Gio: omw

Dean: omw

Dom: right now?

Me: NOW NOW

Loren: omw

Dom: omw

I left the room and called Jack back. "Stay on the phone and let me know if he's still out there."

"Got it." I heard rustling, then more rustling. The door opened. "Oof, taking out the trash is exhausting," he said. I waited. "Hold on." I waited some more. "Okay, the coast is clear."

I got out of there, thanked Jack, and drove to The Place as I brewed my new plan. I needed to fill my brother in, but as much as I trusted him, I couldn't invite him to our meet-up spot. The safe house was one thing, since it was virtually untraceable, but if anyone thought to follow him here, we'd be fucked.

"No. FUCK NO," Dominic said when I told him the plan.

"Our plan is fine the way it is," Gio said.

"Do you think we need backup?" Dean asked. "And is it worth the price?"

"I'll pay whatever price and deal with Harry personally," I said. "This is the best shot at all of us making it out of there alive."

"He's not wrong about that," Gio said. "We're trying to ambush them with what, ten, fifteen people? They have thirty."

"That we know of," I said.

"I get that," Loren started, "but what if the Irish turn on us during our own ambush?"

"They won't," Dean said. "That's not how they operate."

He was very familiar with the Chicago Irish family. While his dad was Italian, his mother's partner—who had treated him like a son—was their second in command until he was killed. Dean was still close to the current boss.

"They're a lot like us, right?" Gio asked. "Women and children are off-limits to them?"

"Yeah, they abided by that even before we had that meeting to clarify," Dean said.

"Why?" Dom asked. "Why are you changing the plan?"

"We may not have enough people," I said, taking a breath as I looked at him. "Giuseppe hit Lenora."

His chair screeched as he stood. "What?"

"He hit her. Slapped her around, pulled her hair, banged her head against the fucking wall, sold her fucking horse out of spite," I said, my voice growing louder with each point.

Dom looked horrified and angry as he plummeted back into his chair. "Are you serious?"

"Dead serious."

"And now you want us to team up with the Irish to take down La Cosa Nostra," Loren stated, trying to make sure he understood.

For a long time, I'd had it in my head that we weren't Cosa Nostra. Our fathers were legit Sicilian immigrants who were heavily involved in organized crime, and therefore, La Cosa Nostra. That wasn't us. Not really. Being born and raised in the U.S. gave us different experiences with different cultures and races. Even our food was different. We did share the same core standards: We were loyal to the oath of Omertà, we didn't sell drugs, and women and children were off-limits. Their rule about women and children only pertained to their own men. Ours meant all women and children. Dealing drugs was tempting since it was profitable and we owned businesses where drugs were being passed around anyway, but we tried not to fuck with it. There was a hierarchy we all followed.

Once Giuseppe was out, his underboss would take his place. Since his underboss would no longer be alive if our plan worked out, Lorenzo's father, the consigliere, could technically step up. I doubted he would, but it was something he'd help with.

"The plan is to take down Giuseppe and the men he brought with him. If you want to spare their lives and let them decide where their loyalties lie, then by all means. . ." I shrugged. "I just want him."

"I can't believe he hit her," Dom said quietly. "And Aanya? Fuck, Nora must be distraught."

"She is."

Dom's eyes snapped up. "You saw her?"

"I just came from the spa," I said. "And distraught is the perfect word to describe her right now."

"I'm worried about the people attending the wedding who aren't part of this," Loren said. "Will they be in the line of fire?"

"No. I think we should keep what happens inside the church the same. O'Conner's people can take down the guys outside, while we work inside."

"It would serve as a good distraction," Gio said. "And Giuseppe would never see it coming since his war with them ended."

"Their war," I said. "Our fathers wanted them gone too."

"Right," Loren said. "Which is the reason I worry they'll turn on us."

"They won't," Dean said.

"And if they do, you fucking shoot them," I said, irritated. "Do we know where Sofia is?"

"I thought about her as soon as you told me about Aanya. If my dad wants to hit Lenora where it hurts, he'll strike there," Dom said. "As far as I know, she's safe. If we can get some of O'Conner's people, we can have Mattia watch her."

"Send Tony. Mattia's still a little green," I said. "He's still learning."

Gio took a deep breath. "Fuck it. I vote yes on the Irish invasion."

"I vote yes," Dean said.

Lorenzo looked at the two of them and shook his head. "Fine. If shit goes sideways, though. . ."

"We'll kill them all." I smiled as I looked through my contact list until I found his number.

"Marchetti," Harry said as he answered. "Are you calling to offer me a free year in your new lounge?"

"If that's what it takes."

"Uh-oh." He chuckled. "I heard my little brother helped you out today."

"He's a good kid," I said. "Brave. That's rare these days."

"Tell me about it." He sighed. "So, what can I do for you?"

"I'm going to put you on speakerphone," I said.

"Ah, the whole gang is there, then?" He asked. "Must be important if you're calling me."

I put him on speaker phone, shot Lorenzo a look that I hoped he understood as "SHUT THE FUCK UP AND DON'T INTERRUPT," and told Harry the plan. He listened quietly, only interrupting to ask what church, how many people, and what we would do about the women, children, and innocent bystanders. When I finished talking, I took a deep breath and waited.

"God damn," he breathed. "Giuseppe fucking De Luca."

"Yep."

"Dominic," he said, "Is Dominic there?"

"Yeah, I'm here."

"You gonna be okay popping your dad?"

"Well, Harry, I just found out he had my mother murdered, so I think the world will make do without him."

"Fuck." Harry was quiet for a moment. "We'll need to meet beforehand to coordinate. We can't go in there blind."

"I agree."

"Russo, how do you feel about it?" Harry asked.

"I think it's solid."

"The important question is, what do you think?" I asked, staring at the screen.

"I think I want to be on the right side of history," he said. "Let's take the fucker down."

CHAPTER THIRTY-SIX

Lenora

"**W**HERE'S MOM?" I ASKED MY FATHER AS HE WALKED INTO THE suite.

There were five glam people here doing hair and makeup and one seamstress doing last-minute things to the dress. I was standing in front of the mirror, hair and makeup done, thinking about how wonderful it would be if I were getting ready for my wedding with Rocco. For that to happen, my father would have had to be a different man, flawed as he was. Before the other night, he'd never treated me poorly. Now, all I could do was replay every memory. I tried to picture his face in them, looking for a sign that he was just trying to gain my trust, so that when it came time to break it, I'd roll over and accept it.

"Your mother will be late," he said, eyeing me in the mirror once before turning around.

"Late where? Here or to the church?" I stared at his back and watched him stop walking and cock his head.

"She'll meet us at the reception afterward."

"She's not going to watch me get married?" I turned around so quickly that the seamstress fell on her ass.

"She's busy right now." He turned to look at me.

I glared at him. "That's bullshit. Mom would never miss this. Where is she? What have you done?" With each question, my heart grew heavier.

"Why would you ask such a thing?" he frowned as if my words hurt him. He walked up to me until he was right in my face. The seamstress scrambled to her feet. "Do you think I would hurt your mother?"

"I didn't think you'd sell my horse," I said, pulling strength from deep inside me. "I didn't think you'd hit me."

He smiled, bringing his hand up to squeeze my face once before lowering it. "I would never hurt your mother. I just thought it would be best if she stayed away, considering she was the one who helped you escape the other day."

My heart dropped. "What?"

"You think I don't know that she helped you?" he asked. "I know everything that happens, Lenora. I suggest you remember that for the future."

"Where is she?" I whispered, tears springing from my eyes.

"She's safe. I've decided to pick my battles and not punish her for what she did. She said she only gave you a few days to decompress, not helping you run for good, and I believe her."

I didn't answer. I couldn't without confirming or denying what he was saying, and I no longer trusted him. For all I knew, he was putting ideas in my head to see how I'd react to them.

"Okay," I said quietly, turning back to the mirror slowly. "I'll see her afterward, then."

"Good." He smiled again and left the room. "Let's hurry this up. Your groom awaits."

CHAPTER THIRTY-SEVEN

Rocco

I

T WASN'T EVEN HOT OUT AND I WAS SWEATING. SO FAR, SILVATI'S
family had arrived with four security personnel in tow. Adriano
himself was stepping out of the back of a black town car as I
adjusted my scope and wiped it. Through it, I looked at his face
up close. He was smiling like he had the winning numbers to
the fucking Power Ball, which in a sense, he did. What better
prize than Lenora? I kept him in my line of vision as he walked
through the church. I was on the roof two buildings away. I
wanted to be inside where the organ was, but this gave me a
clearer view of everything and a better shot. Dominic, Gabe,
Loren, Dean, and Gio were already inside. Gabe's only job was to
stay out of the way and get people to safety. When he discovered
what their father had done, he said he wanted to kill him with
his bare hands. I'd invited him to the after-party, but I wasn't
sure he'd show up. If the tables were turned, I wasn't sure I'd be
able to show up and watch my friend torture and kill my father
either. For Lenora, I was going to try to go easy on him, and if
Dominic went, I'd do the same. They were more important to
me than vengeance.

I stepped away from the rifle and looked around. Giuseppe's
men couldn't see them and didn't know how to look out for
them, but O'Conner's men surrounded them. The cue for them
was the beginning of the bridal song. The cue for me was the
fourth pew from the altar. At the third, Lenora would bend over
to fix her dress, and I'd shoot Giuseppe's kneecaps, then Adriano
in the head. Once Giuseppe went down, Petra would shoot the

men on the church's farther side, and O'Conner would take care of the other side. Inside, Gio, Loren, and Dean would open fire and get the rest. This had to fucking work. It had to fucking work.

I looked at the street again when I saw a black Rolls Royce pulling up. Adrenaline started coursing through me. I held my breath when it parked in front of the church. I watched as Giuseppe's head of security opened the door for them.

Giuseppe stepped out first, followed by Lenora. My heart stopped. I didn't know why I thought seeing her in a wedding dress would be easy. I'd told myself it was just a piece of clothing. I'd reminded myself that she hadn't even picked it out and that this wedding wasn't going to happen, but fuck, seeing her in that dress twisted the knife already implanted in my chest. She looked virginal, but I knew better; I had already defiled every hole in her body. I would have laughed if I could find it in me to be amused. Even if I were, the amusement would've died when I saw her face. Her dark eyes, bloodshot and pained, seared into me, despite their inability to meet mine. She wouldn't know where to look even if she wanted to. Her father looked around, though. Of course, he did; his paranoia had been heightened.

"Have you seen her mom?" I asked in the mics we were all connected to.

"She's not here," Dean said. "I'm having some of O'Conner's guys and ours check all of Giuseppe's spots."

Fuck. I breathed in and out. I hoped he hadn't killed her.

"Do we take out Adriano's cousin?" Gio asked quietly. "He's in the front row."

"Leave him," I said. "He's not a threat and he's in love with Adriano's girlfriend."

Petra snorted. "Maybe they'll live happily ever after."

"Like a fairytale," O'Conner said.

"They're almost inside," I said.

"In position," Petra said.

"Copy. In position," I said.

"In position," O'Conner said.

"Ready," Nico said.

"Ready," Tony said.

"Ready," Mikey said.

We got four more "Ready" responses from O'Conner's guys.

The bridal song began to play in our ears, and everyone inside stood in unison. From the corner of my eye, I saw O'Conner's men move in on Giuseppe's security outside. I glanced at my watch and checked the time. Two minutes. We had a two-minute window to get this done. I looked for the others one last time—Petra standing outside on the roof and Michael wandering down the block, waiting for his cue to get any innocent bystanders out; Gil and Lorenzo pacing their marks in the pews; Rosalyn and Emma observing from the altar. . .across from two Salvati men. Dominic was sitting in the first pew. When I looked at the aisle again, my heart stopped beating.

She started walking down the aisle and I closed my eyes for a split second, habitually asking God for forgiveness in silent prayer. I was one of those people. The ones who avoided church and talking about God but were willing to get on my knees when my life was falling apart. He was always my last resort. She made it to the third pew and stopped walking. For a brief moment, she let go of her father and fixed the bottom of her gown, and her heel stuck at the edge. I could practically feel my mother's ghost judging me for what I was about to do. I tapped the side of my weapon once, twice—a habit. I took a breath, then another, and held it as I pulled the trigger.

CHAPTER THIRTY-EIGHT

Lenora

MY HEARING WAS GONE. MY HEART FELT LIKE IT WOULD BEAT OUT of my chest. I was horrified by the amount of carnage I'd just witnessed, but most of all, I was in disbelief at my current situation. I'd done everything my father had asked of me, believing he'd always keep me safe. But when the bullets started flying, he grabbed me and used me as a human shield. He went down hard and dragged me to the floor with him. I couldn't stop screaming as I heard bullets whizzing by, the cries drowning out the popping sounds of guns. I thrashed against my father, begging him to let go, but his grip only tightened. My eyes darted around wildly in panic and fear, looking for my brothers, Rosie, and Emma—all of them had been close by moments ago. When I didn't see them, fear gripped my chest. I silently prayed they wouldn't get a good shot at my father's head. I couldn't let him die. He was the only one who knew where my mother was. A sob caught in my throat at the thought of her, but I refused to let it out. His arms felt like chains around my body, cutting me each time I tried harder to get out of them. I cried out in desperation.

To my left, Adriano and his two groomsmen were dead. I stopped my screaming to assess the carnage. Judging from his absence and the lack of blood in the altar, I assumed the priest was unharmed. I couldn't see the damage to the rest of the church from this position, but I could only imagine. I did the sign of the cross and prayed the guests were able to get out. I wasn't sure how long I'd been lying on top of my father, with his arms squeezing me, but I started to scream again. I screamed until my throat hurt, until my voice was hoarse.

"Shut up," he kept repeating. "Shut up. Shut up. Shut up."

I was sure he would have slapped me with each word out of his mouth if he weren't holding my arms.

"I hate you," I screamed, my voice breaking—not from tears of sadness, but anger. "I fucking hate you, and I hope you die!"

"You don't mean that," he said quietly. If I believed he had a heart, I would have thought he may have been heartbroken, but I knew better.

"I do. I mean it." I tried once again to get out of his arms.

I'd glanced around to check on the others, but hadn't stopped to think why my father was still on the ground with me. By now, he could have gotten up and run off with me. For the first time since he'd pulled me, I looked down and started to scream. My white gown was covered in a pool of blood. The church was eerily silent. My screams were the only sound—why hadn't anyone come for me? Where was Dominic? Where was Rocco? Oh my God. Had they been killed? Dad had increased security for this event. Rocco and the others had to have been outnumbered. Fear overwhelmed my anger and I screamed again, the panic setting in.

"Where's Mom?" I asked.

"If we get out of here, I'll take you to her."

"Where is she?" I yelled as loudly as I could.

At the sound of a door creaking open and slamming shut, I stopped screaming. I stopped moving completely, trying to make myself invisible. Maybe they'd think I was dead. I knew it was useless, but if it was one of his men, I was doomed. They'd take me away with him and use me as an object for bargaining. That was all I was to him. I'd finally realized that. The footsteps stopped and I held my breath when I felt someone looming over me.

"Principessa." At the sound of Rocco's voice, my eyes popped open.

"Oh, my God." I started to cry, as relief washed over me.

He looked like he was about to enter combat, dressed all in black with a bulletproof vest. With the glare of the sunlight shining down from above through the stained glass windows, I couldn't see his face.

"Let her go, Giuseppe," Rocco demanded.

"Why would I do that?" My father took his arms off me and squeezed my neck until I gasped. He loosened his grip a little, just enough for me to breathe. "As soon as I let her go, you'll kill me."

"So you've figured it out then," Rocco said, his voice low and calm, as if my father wasn't about to choke me to death.

Or worse, what if he snapped my neck? A shiver ran through me at the thought. I continued to look up at Rocco, a dark angel standing above me.

"That you would turn on me?" my father asked. "I had a feeling."

"Do you know why?" Rocco asked.

I whimpered. He was having a fucking conversation like we were at fucking brunch.

"Why don't you enlighten me?"

"Don't worry, I will." I heard the smile in Rocco's voice and saw the bottom of his boot come up in front of my face. I shut my eyes tight and braced myself. I knew he wouldn't hurt me, but I wasn't sure what my father's next move would be. The hands around my neck tightened so much that I felt myself in a daze, drifting away, and then I heard a crack.

CHAPTER THIRTY-NINE

Rocco

I CARRIED LENORA IN MY ARMS AND LEFT GIUSEPPE BEHIND ME. Usually, I'd never turn my back on a man, especially one like him, but I knew Gio and Lorenzo would be walking through the side door any moment now. When I heard it open, I looked over my shoulder to make sure it was them and continued toward the front doors. If I closed my eyes, I could almost picture this as our wedding day. Lenora in a bridal gown, me carrying her away to consummate our marriage in the back of the limo on our way to the reception. It would be beautiful. The way she held onto me, as if her life depended on it, gave me hope that she might still want me even after all of this. Maybe it was false hope, but I let myself pretend a little longer. When we got outside, I walked to the SUV that awaited and set her down in the backseat as my brother stood by the passenger door. Lenora's grip tightened on my neck as I tried to let her go.

"Don't leave. Please don't leave," she said, her voice hoarse from screaming.

I pulled her arms away from me and looked at her. Even with the makeup streaking down her face, her hair a mess, and all the blood, she looked beautiful. I kissed her lips softly and let myself pretend a little longer. When I pulled away, there were unshed tears in her eyes.

"Are you going to kill him?" she asked, her voice hitching at the question.

Gabe, who was in the passenger seat, looked back. He was also in shock. They'd both known the plan before the wedding, but it didn't surprise me that they were still in shock. Bloodshed wasn't something you could prepare someone for.

"Yes," I answered.

"You can't." She grabbed my vest. I sighed heavily. Even after he used her as a shield, she was against it. I wouldn't say that, though. I understood how difficult this must have been for her.

"Nora."

I could see the terror in her eyes. "If you do that, we won't find out where my mom is. He's the only one who knows."

"That's what you're worried about?" I pushed the veil from her eyes and brushed my lips against hers, tasting the tears trickling down her cheeks.

"He deserves to die," she whispered against me.

I pressed my lips against hers, kissed her forehead, and helped her get the train of her dress inside. I shut the door as Mikey got into the driver's seat. We'd had to call in a lot of fucking favors for this to go off as seamlessly as it had and would have a lot of people breathing down our necks soon. She lowered the window and looked at me. I could tell she wanted to say something, but I didn't want to hear it. Not right now.

"You'll be safe, Principessa." I smiled. "Go."

CHAPTER FORTY

Lenora

THE SECOND WE DROVE AWAY, THE GRAVITY OF WHAT HAD JUST happened kicked in, and I started to sob. We arrived at our destination, and Michael walked me upstairs and handed me clothes that I could use for the time being. None of us had uttered a single word. I was still in such a state of shock that I couldn't tell you what the bathroom looked like or what products I used. When I came out of the bathroom, I walked downstairs and sat beside Gabriel. His arm wrapped around me and pulled me into an embrace, sharing a warm blanket that was draped over him. His body trembled as I nestled against him. My teeth chattered as we sat there. Michael placed two mugs in front of us and sat down with his own on the couch opposite.

"Tea," he said.

"Thank you." I tried to say, but my voice was gone.

Gabriel nodded but didn't speak. He was still shaking. I took a sip of my tea, flinching as I swallowed, and looked around. It had a similar layout to Dom's and I wondered if the same person had designed it or whether they lived close to each other. It was spacious and modern with beige walls, except for the wall behind the television, which was painted a charcoal color. Overall, it felt cozy.

"I like your house," I said, my voice barely audible.

"It's Rocco's," he replied.

I glanced around again with this new information in mind and liked it even more. I wondered where we were—my only experience of New York had been from a car window, going from location to location without ever exploring. The only things I could point out for sure were famous landmarks like Central Park, the Empire State Building, and the Statue of Liberty, none of which I'd visited. My sight landed back on Michael, who was on his phone now, texting.

"Do you know if my mom is safe?"

His eyes snapped to mine. "She is. She had no idea the wedding was moved up, so she's still out of the country. She'll be back tomorrow morning."

My gaze fell on the large coffee table that spanned the middle of the two couches. My throat was so raw that I flinched each time I took a sip of tea. I couldn't stop thinking about the way my father had lied to me. It shouldn't have been a surprise, but it hurt that he'd tried to use my mother against me. He had used Aanya and then my mother against me, but he never tried to use Rocco, which meant he wasn't aware of us. I set my hand on Gabe's moving knee and our eyes locked. His were red and watery, reflecting the profound sadness that I felt.

"I'm sorry," I whispered.

His lip trembled as he looked at me, and he brought a hand over his mouth as he began to cry again. I pulled away when he set his elbows on his knees and dropped his head. It was incredible how much damage one person could do. I rubbed my brother's back as he cried, which made him cry harder.

"Gabe, you should shower," Michael said. My brother shook his head. "It'll help."

"Gabe, go." I stood up and pulled his arm.

He wiped his face and stood. Michael stood and walked him to a room downstairs. I folded my legs under me and wrapped myself in the blanket, closing it tightly around me. Michael walked over and sat in the same place he'd been.

"Do you think he's dead already?" I asked.

Michael sighed heavily. "I don't know."

"I hope he is." I blinked away the new wave of tears that threatened. "I really hope he is."

He remained silent. Just like Rocco, he wouldn't say a word if I talked badly about my father. They were good men. There was no doubt in my mind that if the situation had been reversed, my father would have attacked their characters without a second thought.

"Are Rosie and Emma safe?" I asked. "Cat?"

"Everyone is safe." He offered a comforting smile.

I held the blanket tighter. He looked so much like his brother right now. Maybe because they were both dressed in all black.

"Do you want to speak to your mom?" he asked after a moment.

"Can I?"

"Of course." He pulled out his phone and scrolled, pushing a button and putting it up to his ear. "Ro. Hey, no, we're fine. Lenora wants to speak to Sofia. Okay." He handed the phone over to me. I held my wrist with my other hand to keep it from shaking as I set it to my ear.

"Nora." My mother's voice broke into a sob and I could no longer control my own.

"He made me think he'd kidnapped you because you helped me run away," I managed between loud sobs. "He made me think I'd never see you again."

She sniffled. "Is he. . ."

"I don't know." I wiped under my nose with the back of my hand. "I think so. If not, he will be."

She remained silent.

"I'm so sorry, Mami."

"Sorry for what? I should have been there."

"You couldn't have been here." I took a shaky breath. "He killed Gabe and Dominic's mom." A pained sob left her mouth and hit my heart directly. "He killed Rosie's mom too. And Rocco and Michael's."

She cried louder. I swallowed back my own tears and my throat hurt twice as much.

"At the church," I continued, "he used me as a human shield so he wouldn't get shot."

She wailed against the phone. "I should have been there."

"You couldn't have known."

"I should have never left."

"You were burying your mother."

"I didn't know," she said quietly. "I'd always heard, but I didn't know. I. . ."

"None of us knew," I said. "We couldn't have."

"God." Mom took a shaky breath. "My mother warned me. Over and over and over, she told me I shouldn't be with him."

"You couldn't have known."

"Not about that, but I knew he was doing awful things. People talked about it all the time, bragged about it when they sat with him smoking cigars. I just. . .I guess I assumed he was doing those things to people who deserved to pay. I don't know."

"We all did that." I sighed.

"Are you with your brothers?"

"With Michael and Gabe. We're safe."

"Stay there. Don't wander off alone, not even to pick up the newspaper."

"Okay." I took one last long breath. "I love you."

"I love you so much. I'm so sorry." She was crying again. "I'll see you tomorrow."

We hung up and I wiped my tears off Michael's screen and onto the blanket before I handed it back.

"You okay?"

"I think I am."

"Is she okay?"

I shook my head. "She didn't know. About your mom." I blinked away tears again. They just wouldn't stop coming. "She didn't know."

"I investigate murders for a living," he said. "I've had copies of the case files for years. I've gone through them countless times. Rocco has as well. It would have been impossible to link him to the crime without the proof on the USB."

"I just feel like, if someone is that much of a monster. . .I don't know."

"Monsters hide in plain sight," he said. "That's one thing my job has taught me."

"How do you do it?" I asked. "How do you go to crime scenes and remain unaffected?"

His brows shot up. "I don't. Most of the time, I can justify it if it's a criminal. It's awful to say that, but they would have died anyway. But when it's a child? A mother? A father?" He shook his head. "No one, not even the person who claims to be the biggest badass with no feelings, would leave unaffected."

I brought my knees up and rested my chin on them. "Do you think Rocco would leave unaffected?"

His mouth tipped up slightly. "I don't."

"Really?"

"My brother is. . .he's seen a lot of shit. He's done a lot of shit. He's never been unaffected by it; he just justifies it. He's good at separating the man you see from the man he can be." He shrugged. "He only ever kills criminals, so I guess it's easier for him to excuse his actions."

"He's a criminal though." I frowned. "A criminal killing a criminal."

"Yeah. I guess you're right." Michael chuckled. "Killing someone can never be justified, but the men Rocco has killed have raped their daughters, beaten their wives within an inch of their lives. They didn't deserve to live."

I nodded slowly as I thought about it. I'd always seen it in black and white. If you kill, you're going to hell and you're a terrible person. We're not gods; we don't get to choose who lives and dies, but I understood the logic behind Rocco doing what he did.

CHAPTER FORTY-ONE

Rocco

"**O**UT OF RESPECT TO YOUR CHILDREN, I'M NOT GOING TO MAKE this hurt as much as it should," I said to Giuseppe, who was chained in the warehouse.

Before walking into the church, I'd taken a moment to thank O'Conner and his crew. It was a weird moment, one we knew changed the course of our histories going forward. I was sure both our fathers would have been confused, since their relationships had been turbulent, to say the least. We shared a mutual respect and maybe the beginnings of a real friendship. What I knew for certain was that, without them, none of it would have gone down as flawlessly as it had. No one was injured besides those we were targeting.

I'd made Rosie take Dominic home. He'd said he wanted to be here for this, but I knew him. I knew that he'd be okay with it tonight but have nightmares about it for the rest of his life. I'd sent Nico and Mattia to make sure he'd go home and stay there. Nico was dying to raid Dom's fridge and Matti was still traumatized over the penis thing. So my audience was Dean, who was smoking a cigarette; Gio, who was staring at Giuseppe without saying a word; and Lorenzo, who was drinking a beer. A tough crowd. Giuseppe tried to laugh, but his age and the state he was in wouldn't let him move much. He looked around, though.

"I have to say, I'm impressed," he wheezed, and he actually looked and sounded it.

It was something he'd said to me so often in the past, every time he heard what I was up to, that it took everything in me to keep my head in the game. I had to remember that all the times he'd praised me or congratulated us, he was hiding the fact that he'd killed our mothers.

"You are so fucked up." I walked toward my table of instruments.

I wasn't lying when I said I'd make it quick, but that didn't mean I couldn't make it painful. I could do many things but I wanted to stay true to Lenora, and that meant if she asked me whether or not I'd tortured him, I'd have to be able to truthfully say I hadn't. Our relationship had started off rocky enough. From here on out, I wanted it to be smooth sailing—if she'd have me. I grabbed my Matriarch and stared at it. I'd never given much thought to its name until this moment. It was fitting. I turned to Giuseppe. His head was lolling, eyes barely blinking, no doubt from the loss of blood. I could just leave him here to die. They'd tied off his knees to keep the wounds from bleeding out, but that was a very temporary fix. If I decided to give him mercy and let him live, which I wouldn't, he'd most likely need both legs amputated. I looked at the guys, who were still in their seats, waiting in silence. Even Gio was uncharacteristically quiet. Maybe he was in shock. Loren had finished his beer and now had his arms crossed and his legs stretched out in front of him. Same as Dean. I walked to the lever and pulled it just for a second, a gush of water coming down on Giuseppe. He yelped in surprise, then shook from the cold.

"What will you do, Marchetti?" Giuseppe asked, teeth chattering. "Will you torture me like you do the others?"

"Not exactly." I walked over. "I already told you, out of respect for your children, I'm not going to torture you."

"This is all for a crime committed over a decade ago," he said. "A mistake."

"A mistake." I pressed my lips together and nodded, pretending to think it over. "What I don't understand is, why did you kill my mom or Rosie's? I can see how in your sick, twisted mind you'd want to get rid of Carmela, but why them?"

"You're a smart man. I bet you can figure it out." He raised his head, the water from his hair running down his face.

"That's what I figured," I said.

If he'd only killed Dom's mom, he would have been the number one suspect. Even if he denied it, people would point fingers at him and eventually find out. It was a lot easier to prove something true or false when you had a starting point. Since all of the women had been gunned down, it seemed like a rival family's doing. In many ways, he'd gotten away with the perfect murder. If not for Lenora's blackmail idea, none of us would have found out until after he died and the furniture in his office was moved or searched.

"You and I are a lot alike," he said. I held back my glare. "I started just like you. Torturing. Not for the government, of course, but it was still torturing."

"I bet that made your dick hard."

"Perhaps." His teeth clattered. He shut his mouth to contain it.

"We are nothing alike," I said, stepping forward to slash my knife from his left shoulder to his right hip. He hissed. "I don't kill women. I don't get off on fucking up people's lives for the fuck of it."

"Not yet," he grunted. "You will. This will not be enough soon."

"Well, then, it's a good thing you're my last kill." I smiled.

He laughed, or tried to anyway. "You'll see. You enjoy this. Like me."

"I used to. I don't anymore," I admitted, cutting from his right shoulder to his left hip. He screamed. "This, though, having you here, this I'm enjoying."

He closed his mouth, his jaw tense as he tried to bite back

his pain. I had to give it to him. Even old, even in this situation, Giuseppe wanted to keep his composure.

"Dominic hates you," I said. "Gabriel hates you." I took a step back and tilted my head. "Lenora really fucking hates you."

His eyes narrowed. "They're my kids. They're just upset."

"Maybe." I nodded, pacing in front of him. "Maybe."

He looked over my shoulder. "Costello, your father would be ashamed."

"Because I'm not joining in on the fun?" Loren said behind me. "Nah, my father has never been about this. You know that."

"Your father—"

"May just take your place now," Loren said. "Everyone else is dead."

Giuseppe's eyes widened on him, then me.

I nodded. "It's true. You're the only one left alive."

"My. . ." His chest heaved.

"Your what? Your legacy? Your empire? Your plans to expand?" I asked. "You should have probably thought about that before you killed your sons' mother, sold Lenora's horse, and used her mother as a bargaining chip."

"No." His eyes widened like he was just now realizing that his death wasn't just about his physical self being extinguished.

"Yes," I said. "Of course, we won't know what the future brings. Maybe Lenora will want to keep your estate in the old country. Maybe we'll take our kids there one day."

His eyes, already wide, seemed to double in size. Tears swam in them. He didn't speak, so I continued on. Emotional warfare was the worst kind of torture. To Giuseppe, that meant using his possessions against him.

"That's right. Someday, maybe someday soon, I'm going to marry your daughter," I said. "We'll have little blue-eyed or brown-eyed babies running around, and you'll never get a chance to meet them. How sad for you."

He opened his mouth, his lip wobbling. "She'll hate you. After tonight, when you go to her, she'll turn you away."

"Maybe, maybe not. Maybe I won't give her a choice." I got in his face again. Now I was just talking shit, but he didn't know that. If he thought I was a monster, if he thought we were similar, I'd use that. "Maybe I'll force her to marry me. She already gave me her virginity, after all, it won't be so difficult."

He spit in my face and started swearing in Italian. I had no fucking idea what he was saying. I caught one or two *stronzos* in there, but that was about it. I wiped my face with the back of my arm and smiled at him.

"You're lying."

"Am I?" I laughed. "Do you want me to call your precious Principessa? Do you want to ask her how many times I fucked her?"

He shook violently against the chains, a wet squeal coming from his throat.

"It's okay, Giuseppe," I said. "I'm not a monster like you, and because of that, I'll give you this one thing before I kill you: Your sons will be fine. Rosie will be fine. And I don't care what it takes, but I'll make sure that your daughter will be fine, because I love her. I mean that."

I paused for a moment. His gaze grew clearer and his rage began to fade away. With the blade in my hand, I struck him on the right side of his chest, pushing the knife in until I knew it had reached his liver. Withdrawing the blade, I jabbed it into his leg, piercing the femoral artery. I took a few steps backward and watched as the red liquid seeped from his body. No amount of blood he shed would ever make up for all of the pain he'd caused. I let the knife fall from my hand as I walked away, still watching the life drain out of him. The chains rattled as he shook uncontrollably. When his head fell forward and the shaking stopped, I pulled the lever, watching as the water and blood flowed down the drains underneath him. I switched it off, walked over, picked up my newly cleaned knife, and tossed it into the bucket of disinfectant. While I washed my hands and arms, Dean set the phone to his ear and said a few words before putting it away. Calling the cleaners, no doubt. They'd take Giuseppe's body to the crematorium and clean up this mess.

"Why do you do that?" Gio asked, the first words that had come out of any of them since Loren responded to Giuseppe earlier.

"Do what?" I threw my gloves and the paper towel I'd dried my hands with in the trash—more things that would be burned tonight.

"Disinfect the knife every time." He nodded at the bucket. "You're killing them anyway. What's the point?"

"I don't know, Giovanni, maybe because I'm not a dirty fuck." I picked up my jacket and walked over to where they stood.

"Well I, for one, give this performance an eight out of ten," Loren said.

"Seven out of ten," Dean said.

"Nine out of ten, Gio said. "And half a point for the disinfectant."

I shook my head but couldn't fight my smile. They were fucking morons, but I loved them. Outside, we rolled down the door and Dean took out his pack of cigarettes. I took one from him. I never smoked cigarettes. It was either cigars or joints for me, but tonight called for a cigarette. Gio and Loren also took one. The four of us leaned against the wall as we smoked. Mikey took Gabe and Lenora to my house, but I wasn't sure if they were still there. For all I knew, they'd be at Dom's house by now.

"What are you going to do about Nora?" Loren asked, as if reading my thoughts.

"Nothing." I inhaled and exhaled. "The question is, what is she going to do about me?"

That was the truth. I'd give her some time to grieve before going to her. If she told me she never wanted to see me again, I'd respect her decision. It would kill me slowly, but I loved her too much to force something she didn't want. After her father calling me a monster and telling me I was just like him, maybe walking away would be the smartest choice.

CHAPTER FORTY-TWO

Lenora

OPENED MY EYES IN A DARK ROOM BUT DIDN'T MOVE. I KEPT MY NOSE buried in Rocco's pillow, wishing it was him instead. He'd been gone a long time. I didn't want to dwell too much on what he was doing. Was he torturing Dad? Had he already killed him? Did it even fucking matter? I kept replaying what happened at the church and at his penthouse. I'd been so angry about it, but now I was just sad. I felt so stupid for ever thinking of my father as anything other than a monster. At the sound of movement, I sat up slowly. Rocco was sitting in the chair in the corner of his room. It was dark so I couldn't really see him, but I knew it was him. I felt him. He didn't move after I sat up, and I wondered if he'd fallen asleep in that chair, then wondered why he hadn't come to bed with me.

"Hey," I said, but my voice was a whisper, still gone from all the screaming.

"Hey."

"What time is it?"

"4:40."

I blinked. "Did you just get home?"

"No, I've been here a while."

His words were flat. I hated not being able to see his face.

"Do you want me to leave?" I asked, biting the inside of my cheek to brace myself for the answer.

"Of course not." He sighed. "I thought you might have when Gabe left."

"I wanted to stay." I swallowed. "I hope that's okay."

He let out an unamused laugh. Sadness instantly consumed me, but I kept going. I'd walked through life with my head down and my words held back. I'd never done that with him, though. Because he never judged me or treated me like I was made of porcelain.

"Do you not want to come to bed with me?" I asked. "It's okay if you don't."

Again I was met with silence, but then he spoke. "I don't think that's a good idea."

"Oh." I bit my lip and wiped the tears from my face. "Okay."

How many tears could one person shed? How much heartbreak could one person endure? Neither of us said anything. I pretended to go back to sleep but was wide awake when he left the room, finally, after what felt like an eternity. When Nico came to pick us up earlier and I told him I wasn't going, he provided me with a brand new phone that I assumed my brother sent. He'd already set it up and added some contacts in it for me. It was six in the morning when I finally decided I could no longer stay in his bed. I had another shower and changed again. Rosie had sent me clothes, so I wore the bottoms, but I borrowed a hoodie from Rocco's closet. It was huge on me, but I wanted to have something of his.

He'd said so little to me last night, but I read his silence. It was over between us. I swallowed back tears. The rest of the time I'd stayed in bed, I'd been crying quietly. When he left, I just let myself cry. In the shower, I'd cried again. And now, thinking about it, I wanted to cry some more. I'd try not to. One look in the mirror told me I shouldn't. My entire face was swollen. My arms had imprints from where my father had held me down. Bruises covered my neck from when he tried to choke me. As all of the images accompanying each bruise hit me, I began to cry again.

By the time I made it downstairs and to the kitchen, I was finally all cried out. Michael looked freshly showered and dressed.

He was leaning against the counter, reading a newspaper. When he felt my presence, he looked up and his eyes—so much like his brother's—held a look of compassion as he took me in.

"Is he. . ."

"He's not here."

I bit the inside of my mouth and looked away. Fuck. I couldn't keep crying.

"I'll take you to your parents' penthouse. Your mother should be there by the time we get there."

I nodded, biting my cheek, unable to look at him. "I'm ready to go when you are."

He pushed off the counter. "You sure you don't want coffee? Tea?"

I shook my head and continued to stare at the front door. He sighed heavily as he walked around the counter and grabbed his keys. I looked around one last time as I followed him out. He locked the door and pulled out his phone to text someone. I wondered if it was to tell his brother that he was safe to come home since I'd be gone. I hated how much that hurt me. I hated how much I'd gone through this past month, but what I hated most of all was the realization that, in my case, freedom and happiness were mutually exclusive. With Dad gone, I had my freedom, but would I ever find happiness without Rocco? Considering that I didn't even want to think that was a possibility, I doubted I could.

"Why doesn't he want me?" I asked in the car.

"What makes you think that?"

"He didn't say much when he was in the room, and what he said made it pretty clear that he didn't." I looked out the window, taking in the bodegas as they were opening up for the day.

Michael exhaled. "My brother isn't used to someone like you."

"What does that mean?" I turned and looked at the side of his face.

"Someone good. Genuinely good," he said. "He probably doesn't think he's worthy of you."

"He didn't seem to think that before."

"Yeah." He shrugged. "I think you should give him some time. He's the kind of person who sits there and tears apart every single scenario to see how he could have done it differently, and then does it again, until he's convinced that the way he did it was the only way."

"What does that have to do with me?"

Michael shot me a look. "Come on, Nora."

"He had no choice," I said. "My father had to die. I understand that now."

"Maybe he doesn't." He turned down the street of the penthouse. "Giuseppe was your father, but he was also very important in Rocco's life. In all of our lives, to an extent, but he welcomed Rocco like a son, like he was a triplet to Gabe and Dom." He set the car in park in front of the valet and signaled for him to wait. "He did what needed to be done, yes, but that doesn't mean it sat well with him. You know how I said Rocco wasn't unaffected by all of the things he did? You're witnessing it in real time."

That made sense. "Do you think I can help?"

"Being alive and well is enough." He turned off the car and got out, telling the valet something before opening the door for me.

I took his hand and climbed out of his truck. We were quiet as we headed to the elevator and quiet until we were almost at my parents' floor. I felt like pushing the emergency button and drilling him about his brother, demanding that he tell me everything I needed to know to salvage this. The doors opened and the two of us stepped out. One of Mom's guards stepped forward and smiled at me, then shook Michael's hand.

"This is where my watch ends," Michael said.

"Thank you for everything." The tears that welled in my eyes made it hard to see him. "Everything."

He pulled me into a hug and kissed the top of my head. "Anytime."

"Will he come to me?" I asked when he pulled away. "If I give him time?"

"He'd be an idiot to stay away."

CHAPTER FORTY-THREE

One month later

Lenora

❝I SERIOUSLY CANNOT BELIEVE YOU BOUGHT IT." I LAUGHED, SHAKING my head.

My mother had gone and purchased the little coffee shop she loved so much. She was originally going to give it to me as a wedding gift. She'd started the process even before everything went down. She said the second she saw my face light up when she mentioned buying it, she knew it was the right move. Of course, at the time, she thought this would be for me what her apartment in Naples had been for her. I'd had weeks to wrap my head around all of it, but this was the first time we'd been in here with the keys to the place.

"You said you wanted to stay in New York." She pulled me into a hug. "And you always said you wanted to put your degree to use."

"Yeah." I laughed against her. "I didn't mean you should get me a real business that I could potentially run into the ground."

"Nonsense." She pulled away, smiling wide. "You'll be great. Besides, the entire staff agreed to stay on and Dorothea will continue managing the books and showing you the ropes. You can always call Lorenzo to help with the numbers."

I shot my mother a look that made her laugh. Lorenzo would probably turn this place into a gold mine, but I didn't trust any of my brothers' friends not to try to launder money through here. Their businesses may be legitimate, but I knew all of them had at least one place they used for laundering. Besides, Loren would probably make me fire half the staff to save money. He was stingy like that.

"You can call Rocco," she said with a wink. "He's only a block away."

"Mom." I shot her another warning look that she ignored with a smile.

I strolled around the room. I wasn't going to lie. I did wonder what Rocco would think about me owning my own coffee shop. I could go to Scarab and ask him, but I wouldn't. A month had passed since I'd last heard from him, and even though every day, I woke up hoping he'd come back into my life, I didn't want to make the first move. I'd done that already. I wanted to be with him so badly, but one thing this experience taught me was that I was stronger than I thought I was. He'd said those words to me. He'd made me believe it. It wasn't like I was moping around waiting for him.

For three weeks, Gabriel, Dominic, and I were helping my mother out with the properties she was now the sole owner of. She'd offered them the estate in Palermo, which they both refused. I'd told them to burn it down for all I cared. I didn't mean that, though. I'd always loved that estate. In the meantime, we'd agreed to keep it between the four of us. Mom suggested we could finally put the grape trees to use and make some wine. That was all it took for my brothers to come up with all the different ways a winery could be profitable.

My brothers wanted her to keep the estate in Connecticut. It wasn't like she needed anything that Dad had left in her name. And after everything, she didn't want most of it, but that estate was her baby. She'd been the one to buy the land. She'd met with architects and contractors and had everything made to her liking. The only thing Dad had there were his paintings, which Mom wanted to donate to museums. She'd always hated keeping them there, where "only Dad's mafioso friends, who knew nothing about art, would see." The only things left to sort out were Dad's businesses, and my brothers were handling that as they saw fit.

I chose to stay in New York, which my brothers were thrilled about. Mom would be nearby in Connecticut, and she'd helped me find a rare two-bedroom with a huge private terrace. It was far too big for one person, but I loved it. The guys and their wives had helped me with the furniture and stocking up the kitchen. All of them except Rocco, which stung deeper than I wanted to acknowledge. I pushed that thought aside and tried to maintain my excitement about the coffee shop and the party I was having tonight. Everyone was coming over for a housewarming party. We'd have drinks and charcuterie. I'd already decorated the place and set up the small bar–a gift from Gabe– for the festivities. I looked around the coffee shop again. When Rosie found out about it, her first question was, "Will you have brunch on Sundays?" I'd laughed, but it was a good question.

I turned to Charlie. "Do we serve brunch on Sundays?"

"We do." He laughed and went back to the bread he was making.

Charlie was a little older than me and had worked here since the coffee shop opened. Most of them had, and they'd been excited and welcoming when they found out that Mom bought it for me, which was nice. It made for a smoother transition.

"Good. I have some friends who love brunch."

"You mean, everyone in the world?" Charlie raised an eyebrow.

"Not *everyone* loves brunch." My smile dimmed when I thought about Rocco and the choice words he had to say about it.

"You okay?"

"Yeah." I blinked, shaking my head. "Sorry."

He went back to the bread. Mom walked back over to me and told me to say hi to the camera. I waved and smiled as she spoke Spanish to whoever was on the other end of the call, telling them how amazing the place was and how they had to visit. With Dad gone, she felt comfortable inviting her family and friends from back home. Before, she'd only gone to them or met with them somewhere for vacation, but never had them in our space. It was too risky, she'd said. When she said things like that, it made me stop and wonder how paranoid she must have been during her marriage.

"You ready to go?" she asked, putting her phone away.

"Do you think I can walk?" I asked. "By myself?"

"I think you can do whatever you want." She set a hand on my shoulder and smiled. "Of course, security will still follow you from afar, just to make sure. Only for the next few months. After that, you can drop them."

"Okay." I smiled.

It was still better than having to get in the back seat of a car all the time. I'd fully intended to go home, but my feet went in the other direction, and before I could talk myself out of it, I found myself walking to Scarab. I'd told myself to let him come to me, but I couldn't wait any longer. Rocco was patient. I wasn't. I needed him to answer one question. If it wasn't what I needed to hear, I'd walk away and never look for him again. I was approaching the door when it opened. I stopped dead in my tracks and held my breath. When I saw it was Nico, I let it out, but then a woman walked out, fixing her lipstick, and I felt my heart plummet into my stomach.

I hadn't even considered the possibility that he'd moved on. It had only been one month and I thought he was as in love with me as I was with him, but maybe I'd been wrong. Or maybe this was how he coped, by hooking up with other women. The woman, who looked a little familiar, turned to Nico and laughed at whatever he said, then looked in my direction. We locked eyes and I felt like I was going to throw up. She smiled at me and walked the other way.

"Lenora," Nico said. "I didn't know you were coming."

"I wasn't." I looked at the door, at the woman walking away, and finally, at Nico. "I see that he's busy. Please don't tell him I came by."

Nico's brows pulled and I turned around to walk the opposite way.

"Lenora," he called out, then cursed as he jogged over and grabbed my arm. "Wait."

"What?" I snapped, looking up at him.

"I don't know what you think you saw, but that was Veronica," he said, searching my eyes. "You know, Dom's Veronica, the one married to a woman. . ."

"Oh." I blinked and looked again, but she was long gone.

Of course, I knew Veronica. The last time I saw her, she had her hair in a blunt bob. Now she had it to her elbows and was suddenly blonde. There was no way I would have recognized her. She'd been working for my brother, running Oui for years. I'd heard Rocco say something about her helping with Scarab while we'd been at the safe house, but I hadn't put two and two together. It didn't matter, though. That experience was enough for me to snap out of it and realize I shouldn't have come here. Nico looked over my head and stood straight.

"Lenora?" At the sound of Rocco's voice, my heart stopped.

"Did you tell him?" I whisper-shouted.

"No," Nico said, keeping his lips from moving. "I came after you. How could I have told him?"

I closed my eyes.

"Lenora?"

I took a very deep breath and let it out as I closed my eyes. New clarity broke through my thoughts. I'd been walking around without a purpose for so long that I'd forgotten the most important thing. My newfound freedom didn't just extend to my future in business decisions. Freedom allowed me to choose who I wanted to be. Not that De Luca girl whose life was planned out, not Giuseppe's untouchable virgin daughter, not the woman with the unbreakable arranged marriage. I'd chosen Rocco. Me. I'd done that. Now I had my own business, my own apartment, and was free to make my own choices. I'd chosen to walk down the street today instead of getting in a car. I'd chosen to walk to Scarab. With that in mind, I opened my eyes and reminded myself that I was whoever the fuck I wanted to be. I turned around and wished I'd given myself a little pep talk on how to react to him, because the moment I saw him, my insides began to play tug of war. He looked tired and in need of a haircut, with bags under his eyes and a shadow on his face. If possible, his muscles looked more pronounced, as if he'd been living at the gym. As I walked over, he looked at me like he wasn't sure whether I was real or a mirage.

"How'd you know I was here?" I asked, stopping a couple of steps from him.

His eyes took me in from head to toe and back, his mouth slightly parted like he still wasn't quite sure I was here. "I saw you on the cameras."

I gave a nod and looked away, smiling at a mother walking by with her little girl.

"What are you doing here?" he asked, clearing his throat.

"Oh, I was just in the neighborhood." I shrugged. "Figured it was a nice day for a walk."

His brows pulled as his blue eyes went up and down the block, searching for security detail, no doubt. I hoped the man my mom had following me was well hidden.

"You're here alone?"

"Yep."

He looked like he didn't approve, but he didn't say

anything as his eyes studied every inch of my face. "Were you going to come inside?"

"I thought about it," I said, "Then I realized that if you wanted to see me, you would have reached out by now."

"How?"

"Via phone, like everyone else."

"I don't have your number."

"Dominic said you were the one who bought the phone and put in everyone's numbers."

"That doesn't mean I took the liberty of saving yours in mine," he said.

That hurt but I didn't react. "Why?"

"Because if I had it, I would have called you every single day."

I swallowed. "And you didn't want to?"

"Of course I wanted to." He ran his fingers through his hair and let out an unamused chuckle.

"You're going to have to explain this to me then, because I don't understand what you're saying." I crossed my arms.

"Can you. . ." He looked toward Scarab. "Do you want to come inside?"

I looked at him for a long moment as I thought about it. Even in his state of disarray, he was the most handsome man I'd ever seen. My ideal man. The one I'd loved for as long as I could remember. The one I finally had and lost, and if I was reading this correctly, could have again. I wanted him. I wanted him to pull me into his arms and kiss me, to tell me that he was sorry and he loved me, and to say all the things I'd pictured him telling me every night before I went to bed. I wasn't going to make *that* move, though. Not this time. I reached into my bag and pulled out a card and a pen. My mom had cards made for me with the coffee shop's information. I'd laughed and told her to keep up with the times. We didn't hand out business cards anymore; we added each other on Snap. She was unamused, and right now I was grateful for this. I wrote down my phone number and address and clicked the pen as I put it away.

"I'm having a housewarming party tonight, in case you want to come." I handed him the card. He took it, looked at it, and glanced up at me again. "The party starts at eight. You can come at seven."

His mouth twitched. A simple gesture that warmed me inside. "Will you be there at seven?"

"I will." I smiled at him, turned around, and walked away.

CHAPTER FORTY-FOUR

Rocco

I'D REPLAYED MY INTERACTION WITH LENORA A MILLION TIMES WHEN she left, a million more at the barbershop, and a million more as I showered and got dressed. I'd be lying if I said I'd been completely in the dark. I knew she'd been to Italy and Connecticut. I knew she'd been here for a couple of weeks, but I wasn't expecting that to last very long. It was one of the many reasons I'd stayed away. At first, I stayed away because of what I'd done to her dad, which both Dominic and Gabriel told me was a shit reason to not go after her. Then, because she finally got her freedom. For the first time in her life, she could do whatever she wanted to do, and I didn't want to hinder her options. She could go to India, California, or Japan.

She could finally visit all of the places on her bucket list. She could date whomever she chose. That possibility pained me to think about. After seeing her in my bed, I could only lie in it with the image of her lying there. She'd looked so perfect. Every day when I walked into Scarab and looked at the bar, I imagined her laughing and mixing drinks. I knew time wouldn't help me. I'd never move on from her, and if I was being completely honest, as shitty as it was, I hoped she could never move on from me. I hadn't expected her to come to me. I definitely hadn't expected her to hand me a business card with the name of the coffee shop I'd walked by a few times.

I was switching off the bathroom lights when my phone started buzzing with a call from my brother. I pushed the green button and set it on speaker.

"What's up?"

"Does Lenora like wine? Red or white?"

I frowned. "What the fuck? Why are you asking me that?"

"I'm going to her house tonight, and I want to take something besides flowers."

I shook my head and bit back a smile. He was such an asshole. He didn't know that I knew about the housewarming or that I was about to head to her house.

"You're too old for her, Mikey. Give it up."

"I don't know. I have a feeling she likes older men," he said. "We'll find out tonight."

"Yeah, I'm sure you will." I grabbed the phone, turned off the rest of the lights, and walked downstairs.

"She invited me to her house."

"How romantic." I grabbed my keys. "I'll talk to you later. I have a date in twenty minutes and I don't know what kind of wine Lenora likes, so try calling Dom."

"A date with whom?" he demanded.

"A woman."

"You know what, Rocco, you're a fucking idiot." He hung up on me.

I laughed as I slid my phone into my pocket. I had no argument for that anyway. Maybe I had been a fucking idiot for not going to her before. I looked at the address again. Her place was only four blocks down, so I didn't even bother with a car. I didn't know what the parking situation was over there anyway. Again, I laughed. My Principessa had her own business and her own place. Dom hadn't said a word about either of those. Maybe it was payback for being with her behind his back. Knowing I hadn't helped her with either pushed the knife into my chest a little deeper, but I was too proud of her to let it bother me too much. I stopped in front of her building for a moment, before pushing through the revolving door. It was fancy as fuck. I walked up to the desk and gave the woman my name. After a few clicks, she smiled up at me and told me to go ahead. The elevator smelled like that damn spa they'd gone to the day before the wedding. The Red Wedding, the newspapers were calling it. *So* original. Between Mikey's guys, ours, and O'Conner's, we'd managed to twist the story into a Romeo and Juliet scenario, where a mean mob boss and a duke were at odds. We'd also managed to keep everyone's names out of the papers.

Once I reached her floor, I noticed only two doors. Fancy as fuck. I knocked on hers, wiping my hands on my jeans. I couldn't remember the last time I'd been this nervous. Maybe when I'd called her mother earlier today. We'd been on the phone for over an hour, talking about the future, my plans with her daughter if she'd have me, and her vision for the future now that Giuseppe was gone. It had been an emotional and enlightening conversation. When Lenora finally opened the door, my heart felt like it might pop out of my chest. She was so fucking beautiful. She was wearing a short summer dress and no shoes. Her hair was in waves and her makeup was minimal, her brown eyes twinkling as she opened the door wider and let me walk inside.

"You got a haircut." She took in my hair and face along with the rest of me.

"It was time." I handed her the box I'd been carrying under my left arm. "This is for you."

"You didn't have to get me anything." she said, taking the box and looking at it, then at me. "Did you wrap this yourself?"

"I did." I kept my eyes on her face, even though I was dying to look around to calm my fucking nerves. "It's no big deal."

She glanced up at me, eyes watery. "It is *to me*."

I swallowed, not trusting myself to speak. Thankfully, she moved away and walked further into the apartment. She set her box on the kitchen counter and crossed her hands over her stomach, as she waited for me to say something. I took in the place. It was perfect. Perfect in general, and definitely perfect for her. The kitchen was nice, modern, and much bigger than mine. It

was an open concept, so from the kitchen, you could see everything. She had a small bar, where she'd already set up two pitch-
ers of premixed drinks next to martini glasses. The rest was
simple, with nice couches, and a television that I was sure one
of her brothers picked out for her. Probably Gabe since it looked
just like his. I didn't dare walk into any of the rooms. When I'd
taken it all in, I turned back to her.

"This is really nice."

"Thanks." She smiled, looking around. "I love it. Do you
want me to show you around?"

"If that's what you want."

"Come." She turned and walked to the door on the right,
showing me a guest bedroom. It was already fully furnished. The
bathroom and closet were both a nice size. Then she turned and
opened up a door with a set of stairs. I followed her up. I tried
not to peek under her dress, but even *I* didn't have that kind of
willpower. I couldn't see much, just the tips of her ass cheeks,
which was enough to create a problem in my pants, so I looked
away quickly. We reached a door. She opened it and stepped outside. My jaw dropped when I followed.

"This is huge."

"It's my favorite part." She sighed happily as she looked at
the city.

It was a huge space, similar to the one Gio had back in
Chicago. The feeling it gave was what everyone felt when they
stepped off the airplane and into this city. Like you could conquer
anything. She had two outdoor couches, a table, and some trees.

"It's perfect." I smiled over at her. "I'm really happy for you."

She turned around and escorted me back downstairs into
her bedroom. It smelled like her. I took a moment to inhale the
scent as I walked in behind her. She had a big bed with a white
comforter and white pillows, and a television mounted on the
wall in front of it. The walls, like the ones in the rest of the apartment, were eggshell. It was the same one I'd used at my own

place. The wall that faced the city was all window. She had light beige drapes covering it. She showed me the large walk-in closet. All of her things took up one side of it. The left side remained empty, and for a fraction of a second, I let myself pretend my shit was in there. The bathroom was also nice.

"It's amazing," I said once she was finished, and we were standing in her room just steps from her unmade bed. My fingers itched to make it for her.

"Thanks." She smiled. "Can we talk now?"

"Here?" I looked between her and the bed.

"I'm comfortable here." She laughed lightly. "What, you can't be in a bedroom with me and just talk?"

I blinked hard. Could I be? Yes. Did I want that? No. "Let's get to it, then."

She sat near the pillows. I sat at the foot.

"Do you want a drink?"

"Not right now."

She gave a nod and leaned against the upholstered frame. "Are you here to explain why you left me and didn't want to reach out to me?"

"Yes."

She raised an eyebrow. "I'm listening."

"I thought the best thing I could do for you was leave you alone. . ." I started.

"Best for me or best for you?" she asked.

I let out a laugh. "Did you not see the state I was in yesterday?"

"Yes," she said quietly. "I thought you chose happiness every day."

That made me smile a little. I had told her that, hadn't I? I hadn't been lying about it either. I did wake up and choose happiness, but that was before I knew what happiness could be. She was looking at me like she wanted an answer, and I wasn't sure what I could give her that would be acceptable.

"I tried, but I realized that before you, I didn't really know what happiness felt like."

She inhaled, her eyes watering. She cleared her throat before asking, "Why did you think being without you would be best for me?"

"Because you're free now. Free to go to Japan and San Francisco and Egypt and all the other places on your list," I said, swallowing before I said the next part. "Free to be with whomever you want. I didn't want you to. . ." I paused. "I didn't want you to wake up next to me in fifteen years and regret not exploring your options."

"I don't want to go to any of those places without you, Rocco." She looked at me like she couldn't believe I'd ever said that. "And the options thing. . ." She shook her head. "You don't think I could have explored my options before? Yes, I was being controlled, but I was in boarding school my entire life. I went to college. If I'd really wanted to, I could have rebelled then." Her brows pulled slightly. "I wanted *you*. I've always wanted you."

My heart stopped beating. "Do you still? Want me?"

"Why don't you continue your reasoning for not coming for me sooner, and then I'll speak," she said quietly. My lips tugged at her demand but turned serious quickly.

"What happened with your father. . ."

"He's gone. He deserved what he got," she said. "Don't bring him into this. He doesn't deserve a mention."

"I thought you'd hate me for it. I thought you'd wake up one day and decide you couldn't forgive me."

"Why didn't you want to ask?" she whispered.

"Because I'm not worthy of you, Lenora." I swallowed past the hard lump in my throat. "I'm not worthy of any part of you. Do I want you? Fuck yes. Will I want you this time next year and this time thirty years from now? I know I will, but that doesn't mean I should have you."

She blinked rapidly and wiped the tears trickling down her

face. "You are worthy of me. And I'm still failing to understand how any of that is a problem."

I moved forward. I couldn't take it anymore. I had to touch her. I moved until the only distance between us was her hands, and then I brought a hand up to cup her face. She leaned into my palm and shut her eyes briefly, as if savoring it, which just added to the list of reasons I wanted to beat myself up. I'd spent an entire month telling myself all of these things and I could have been with her.

"If we do this, it's forever," I said. "If you decide tomorrow that you want to walk away, I'd let you, but I'd go after you anyway until I got you back." Her tears fell on my palm. I wiped them with my thumb and got even closer until our breaths were mingling. "I won't spend a night away from you. This space will no longer be just yours."

"I'm okay with that," she whispered, wiping her other cheek.

"I have wanted you every day since the first night I saw you at that event. I couldn't stop thinking about you, and when you put the thought in my head that I could be with you, even just for a night, I knew I'd take it. I didn't give a shit that you were my best friend's sister or that you were going to marry someone else. I would take you any way I could." I took a breath. "I've never felt this way about anyone and I never will again. You're it for me, Nora. You're what I thought I'd never have."

"I love you," she said.

It was the last thing she could say before my lips were on hers. I kissed her for every day I hadn't been able to this past month—to thank her, to ask for her forgiveness, and to let her know that she'd always be number one in my heart, in my life. I pulled away with a harsh breath.

"I want you to tell me all about your coffee shop and everything else that I've missed." I leaned in and bit her bottom lip. "But first, I need you to get on your back so I can taste your pussy before your company gets here."

Her breath hitched, but she scrambled to the center of the bed, the motion making her dress ride up to her hips, exposing her white lace underwear. I smirked, setting my knee on the bed. I grabbed the string on the side and pulled it, letting it slap her skin. She moved her hips, those big brown eyes drowning in lust. I didn't deserve her, but I was going to have her anyway.

"Open your legs." I backed away just enough and groaned at the sight of her perfect pussy. I'd been dreaming about this for an entire month and wanted to savor the moment, but we were running out of time. She shimmied her hips again. My eyes snapped to hers. "Stay still for me. I need to see you."

"I'll try," she said breathlessly.

"Good girl." I smiled as I leaned in, yanked her panties off, and pressed my tongue against her. I groaned against her. My cock had been hard the moment we walked into this room, the moment I looked up her dress when we went upstairs, but as I licked her pussy and she started moaning my name and tugging my hair, I grew even harder. I paused for a moment and looked up at her. She whimpered at the loss of my mouth and looked at me to see why I'd stopped.

"I love you more than anything in the world," I said.

Her smile was blinding. I let myself capture it for a moment before I dipped my head between her legs again.

EPILOGUE

Rocco

I'D BEEN LIVING WITH LENORA FOR TWO MONTHS. WITH HELP FROM the guys, I'd moved half my closet to hers the night of the housewarming party. We must have looked like we'd robbed a dry cleaner with all the clothes in our hands, but I didn't care. I owned the cleaners on that block anyway. I woke up with her in my arms every morning and pinched myself. I was learning to accept the good things the universe was throwing my way without questioning it or bracing myself for something bad to happen right after.

I walked her to the coffee shop every morning, and every afternoon, I met her to walk her home. On the nights she wanted to get behind the bar at Scarab, I returned home to escort her there. She'd laughed the first time I'd returned home to get her and told me she could walk alone. I agreed. She could, but she didn't have to as long as I was alive.

I closed my eyes and took a deep breath. I had to admit. I understood why Sofia kept this house for herself.

"You are such an asshole for making me do this," Matti said as I opened my eyes and laughed.

"Hey, think of it as hazing, of sorts."

"Right, because seeing you cut someone's dick off didn't count?" He shot me a look.

"When are you going to get over that?"

"I don't think I can."

"Yeah, that was not the most welcoming sight," Nico agreed.

"Both of you, shut up and do your jobs," I said, turning away to walk into the house.

"One day, you're going to do this for one of us, Marchetti," Matti called out.

I set my hand on the door and laughed, throwing my head back. "One day in hell, maybe."

Everyone was here awaiting Lenora's arrival. Rosie brought charcuterie. Isabel brought rum. Cat brought pigs in a blanket, the first thing she'd made in the new air fryer she wouldn't shut the fuck up about. All of the ladies—not to mention Gabe and Mikey—got the same fucking thing. My brother said it was the best thing invented since the crock-pot. And he didn't think he was old.

When the door finally opened, everyone turned toward it and yelled, "Surprise! Happy Birthday!" Lenora looked around the room, covering her mouth as she took it all in.

"You guys are sneaky," she said, hugging everyone before she got to me and kissed me. "You're too good at hiding things from me. I'm going to start getting paranoid."

"I only hide good surprises, baby." I kissed her deeply. "Never anything else."

She smiled and turned around. "I can't believe you guys! Especially you, Mom!"

"Hey, it was a good birthday surprise." Sofia laughed as she went around the room to say hello to everyone.

Mattia and Nico walked in from the back of the house and looked around.

"Damn it. We missed the surprise?" Nico asked. "That's my favorite part of surprise parties."

Matti shook his head as he walked over to me. "Everything is set up," he said quietly.

I placed a hand on his shoulder and squeezed it. "Thank you. By the way, I would consider returning the favor."

He laughed as he walked away. Michael lifted his beer from

the other side of the room to toast me. Dominic gave me a look, telling me to hurry. Gabe was pacing. Gio and Dean were sitting down, looking like they were plotting something.

I grabbed Lenora's hand. "Hey, I want to talk to you about something."

She took in my serious expression and frowned but followed me out back.

"I was talking to your mom about maybe getting a house out here," I said. "It doesn't have to be big like this. Just something we could run to when we want a break from the city."

I stopped walking where I needed her to stand. Under the tea lights. Away enough from the door but close enough that they could take pictures. She gasped loudly, covering her mouth with both hands when I got down on one knee.

"Rocco." My name was muffled behind her hands.

"I know I tell you every day, but I'm serious about never spending a moment without you. I'd give up everything for you if you asked me to." I grabbed her left hand when she finally lowered it. "Will you marry me, Principessa?"

"Yes," her response was shaky between tears. Her hand shook as I set the ring on her finger. When she looked at it, she gasped again. "Oh my God, Rocco."

I rose to kiss her, and she leaped into my arms, locking her arms around my neck and legs around my waist. Everyone cheered from their spot by the back door. She laughed as our lips touched.

"I love you so much," she said between kisses.

"I love you more." I set her down slowly and grabbed her hand to kiss the back of it. "Let me show you your birthday present."

"This isn't it?" She asked loudly as I led her away. "This is the best present. . ."

She stopped talking when her horse neighed. She looked at

me, then at the horse, and when her eyes landed on mine again, she burst into tears.

"You got her back," she whispered.

"I told you I would." I opened my arms to catch her as she threw herself at me. When she finished crying, she got to her feet. I wiped her tears and kissed the tip of her nose. "Anything for you, Principessa. Everything for you."

"I love you. I love you. I love you. I love you," she said, kissing me each time. When she stopped, she looked at her horse with so much love and longing that I wished I could kill her father twice.

"Go." I slapped her ass. "She's been waiting for you."

She ran over there, half-crying, half-laughing.

"Aanya," she said against the horse's face. "I have so much to tell you."

I took a deep breath and looked around: at her with her horse and our family, who were now back in the house. I thought about my life —the heartache and challenges I'd gone through before getting to this point—and smiled.

ALSO BY CLAIRE

Read Lorenzo & Catalina's story: BECAUSE YOU'RE MINE
Read Dominic & Rosie's story: BECAUSE I WANT YOU

Want more romantic suspense?

Try my secret society series:
HALF TRUTHS (dark academia)
TWISTED CIRCLES (dark academia)

Want contemporary romance?
THE PLAYER (sports romance)
KALEIDOSCOPE HEARTS (brother's best friend, second
chance romance)
PAPER HEARTS (second chance)
ELASTIC HEARTS (grumpy, sunshine romance)
THE HEARTBREAKER (College, sports romance)
THE RULEBREAKER (college, sports romance, friends-to-lovers)
THE TROUBLEMAKER (college sports romance)
CATCH ME (music industry romance)
THE TROUBLE WITH LOVE (office romance)
THE CONSEQUENCE OF FALLING (enemies-to-lovers)
THEN THERE WAS YOU (enemies-to-lovers, second chance)

Want royal romance?
THE SINFUL KING
THE NAUGHTY PRINCESS
THE WICKED PRINCE

Want something a little different?
FABLES & OTHER LIES (gothic romance)

Want a quickie?
FAKE LOVE

ClaireContrerasbooks.com

Twitter:

@ClariCon

Insta:

ClaireContreras

Facebook:

www.facebook.com/groups/ClaireContrerasBooks

CPSIA information can be obtained
at www.ICGtesting.com
Printed in the USA
BVHW071820260123
657208BV00013B/1105